Wild Rose

The Late Bloomers Series (Book 1)

By Betsy Talbot

http://www.BetsyTalbot.com

Copyright © 2015 by Betsy Talbot

ISBN: 0-9862697-4-3
ISBN-13: 978-0-9862697-4-5

A NOTE FROM Betsy

Have you ever wondered why most of the good love stories happen to women under 30? It's not like we stop loving and living after that age. And we certainly don't stop reading.

That's why writing a series about a group of friends in their 40s who were still loving, adventuring, and traveling the world was so appealing to me. If you don't like the way the world looks, you have to do something to change it! And that's what this series attempts to do: contribute an entertaining, sexy romance series for women over 40 to enjoy.

These characters are a joy to write, and you'll recognize yourself and your friends in the attitudes, quirks, and actions of these five experienced women.

Be sure to read to the end to find the link for all your book extras, like a music playlist, Italian recipes, and more.

In *Wild Rose*, successful landscape designer Rose Quinn is having a very bad summer. First her 19-year-old daughter left home to backpack across Europe instead of going to college. Then a woman she loved like a mother died of a heart attack, making her feel like an orphan all over again. And in just a few weeks her best friend will be moving to New York City. For a single mother who's always had someone else to take care of, Rose is now wondering how to take care of herself.

Handsome Mateo Romero is a transplanted

Spaniard running a restaurant on Lake Como in Italy. A broken heart got him there, but he's made a success of it just like he did his architecture business back in Madrid. One thing he hasn't been successful at is love.

When Mateo hires Rose's daughter for a summer job and gives her a free place to stay, Rose immediately suspects the worst. She won't let her daughter make the same mistake she did at that age, so Rose flies to Italy to confront Mateo. What Rose finds instead is a secret she didn't suspect and a challenge to everything she's ever thought about love and the illusion of control.

Rose's daughter doesn't need saving, but can Rose save herself?

I hope you enjoy Wild Rose's adventure and that you stay in touch to learn more about the other Late Bloomers book releases at BetsyTalbot.com. This is a fun group to write about, and I'm excited to share their journeys with you.

Happy reading,
Betsy Talbot

CHAPTER ONE

DEATH MAKES PEOPLE hungry, Rose thought, as she pulled out another tray of sandwiches from the refrigerator to feed her guests. Just last night she polished off the remnants of the macaroni and cheese, the latest splurge in a month of grief eating and drinking since the news of Miriam's death.

Neighbors, friends, and strangers had streamed through her house for almost four hours this afternoon at the celebration of life service for her friend Vi's mom, a woman who was like a mother to her, too. While the initial burst of grief over Miriam's passing had faded a bit over the last few weeks, having Rose's lifelong friends arrive in town last night brought back a slew of old memories and a fresh round of tears.

The five of them—Rose, Violet, Lily, Daisy, and Ivy —stayed up late reminiscing, getting the real grieving done in private as a family, like the sisters they practically were. Last night was for them; today's service was for everyone else.

Rose looked out the kitchen door at her tall and elegant friend Violet, surrounded by her mother

Miriam's friends and frenemies alike, patiently listening to their stories and small-town gossip. Poor Vi. She looked like Cleopatra with her perfect black bob, straight bangs, and regal face. Vi was a stoic who only shared her feelings with her inner circle, and those people were not in that group. Rose's heart ached for Vi, now an orphan at the age of forty-one.

As Rose unwrapped the plastic film and searched for more napkins, Lily walked into the kitchen. Rose knew she was antsy, uncomfortable with just sitting around and making small talk. Time to put Lily to work.

"Can you start another pot of coffee, Lil? Thanks." Lily nodded her head and started opening cabinets, looking at the options.

"You don't want to use your expensive special roasted stuff for the masses, do you?" Lily frowned, giving the task more concentration than it required.

"Doesn't matter, just pick one." Rose walked over to her friend and gave her a one-armed hug, leaning her head on top of Lily's much shorter one as she balanced the sandwich tray in her left hand. "People will leave soon, and then it will just be the five of us, like old times."

The two friends exchanged a smile and separated, the momentary contact easing the discomfort of the day just a little.

Rose's adobe house on the hill was ideal for the celebration of life service for Vi's mom. The house with the cheery turquoise door was an oasis in the desert, opening to a central courtyard that was overflowing with flowers and comfortable seating. The house was a lot like Rose, warm and cozy, but a little bit off the beaten path. You had to make some effort to get there, but once inside you didn't want to leave.

Guests flowed through the one-level house and courtyard, talking in low tones about Miriam as well as Rose's design choices. She only invited close friends to her home, and as a popular landscape architect in town, people were naturally curious what her own living space and gardens looked like. Rose didn't mind hosting the event—she insisted on it, actually, since Vi's house was already being packed for her move to New York next month. Rose would do what she could to make this crisis easier for her friend, just like she always did. Rose had been a mother figure long before she actually became one, a trait that came naturally to her. She always thought of other people first. It was why Rose was such a good friend and mother—and also why she often neglected her own needs and desires.

Rose was the first person Vi called after her mom died. The painting Miriam had been working on in her studio—a field of sunflowers—had a streak of blue paint down the middle. The sky fell onto her landscape as she suffered a heart attack. Doctors said she died instantly, and Rose hoped that was true. Miriam loved to create, and she'd find a certain kind of karma in leaving the earth while painting it.

They locked up Miriam's house and Vi put the

canvas in her car, and then they both went to the funeral home to arrange the cremation according to the will. The celebration of life service was also one of Miriam's requests, specifically to be held a month after her death so that "people would be over all the crying nonsense" and remember the joy of her life. Rose thought about the joy of her own life: her business, her daughter, her friends. But all that had already happened, and she was just barely forty. What other joys did she have ahead of her? She couldn't even imagine.

Rose snapped back into the present when Ivy walked into the kitchen.

"Are we cleaning out the pantry to feed this horde? God, Vi's mom would be pissed if she knew Jane Alden and her pack of crows were here eating up all your food, Rose. She couldn't stand them." Ivy pulled her long red hair back into a ponytail, then wound it into a messy bun.

"That's small town politics for you, Ivy. You're lucky to have escaped to London. Besides, if I know Miriam, she'll haunt Jane and her cronies just for kicks." Rose set the tray down on the counter and tucked her auburn hair behind her ears. She rubbed the faint vertical crease above her nose and reached into the drawer for an aspirin.

"Lucky? I'd call it damned smart. I think we should all be living in London." Ivy smirked and Lily pulled a towel off the counter and snapped at her with it, eliciting a howl from her victim.

"Smart, maybe, but still not as quick as me." Lily's almond-shaped eyes were sparkling, her jet-black hair hanging straight down to her shoulder blades. Her small frame contained a powerhouse of a body, honed over the years with gymnastics, martial arts training, and yoga. Lily worked as an emergency physician in places where medical care didn't exist: war-torn areas, sites of natural disasters, and locations of epidemics. She spent more time out of the United States than in it, and she said exercise was her therapy for all the horror she saw. As hard as her body was, Lily must see a lot.

"All right, ladies. Let's finish this for Vi and start herding people toward the door. You know she can only take so much of the touchy-feely stuff." Rose was in take-charge mode, a fierce protector of her friends. She remembered what it was like to lose her parents in a rainy car accident twenty years ago and how much she relied on these lifelong friends to see her through her own grief and the surprise pregnancy she discovered a couple of months later. This was a family stronger than blood, and it always had been.

Their mothers were all close friends who had blessed and cursed their firstborn daughters with flower names, a throwback to the peace and free love days of the late sixties and early seventies. The five of them had been collectively called The Bloomers since childhood. In junior high, they hated this nickname and all the jokes it spurred by the Jennifers, Amys, and Melissas who surrounded them. Rose especially hated being called the wallflower of the bunch. As adults, the five friends embraced the name Bloomers as if it were some exclusive club, going so far as to call themselves the Late Bloomers during their ironic hipster phase in their late twenties. No longer ironic but slightly sentimental, they still called themselves the Late Bloomers.

"Daisy is already on it. How someone with such an innocent face can be so shrewd I will never understand. Did you hear her tell them there was supposed to be a violent storm this evening? There's not a cloud in the sky." Ivy said it with a trace of jealousy, knowing her blunt style would never allow such subtle deception. "They're all gathering to leave now, not a doubt in their minds. Daisy should start her own cult."

"She lives in Portland so they think that means she's an expert at rain." Rose's lip curled to one side, admiring her friend's skill at getting people to do what she wanted.

It didn't surprise Rose one bit that Daisy, Lily, and Ivy flew to tiny Hobart, Arizona to support Vi in her time of grief. Rose and Violet were the only ones who remained in their hometown, and soon it would just be Rose when Violet moved to New York.

So much has changed over the years, Rose thought, remembering their various love affairs, career peaks and valleys, and even the birth of her daughter Rachel when she was just twenty. And then she looked at her friends, all working together in their own way to get this makeshift family through the crisis. *And so much remains the same.*

# # #

Daisy ushered the last of the visitors out the door, hugging and thanking them for coming by. Once the door shut, she leaned against it and said, "Can we take out the good wine now?"

For the first time in weeks, Vi laughed. The group was together again, and now the real healing could begin.

"Let's take this morbid party outside for some fresh air. You know my mom loved your courtyard, Rose." Vi stood up with Amazonian grace and walked outside. Rose followed with a box of matches, lighting the dozens of candles she kept in glass cases all around the courtyard. Dusk was approaching, and she knew they'd be out there for hours.

"How are you holding up, babes?" Ivy squeezed Vi's shoulder with one arm, gripping the wine bottle and opener in the other.

"I'm alright, Ivy. Really. I can't tell you how much having you all here helps. And if it's all the same to you guys, I'd love to talk about anything but grief and death and dying tonight. These last few weeks have drained me." Vi always asked for what she wanted, and as the oldest of their group, she usually got it. She sank into her favorite chair as Ivy uncorked the wine and started pouring into the glasses Lily set on the table. "But before we do that, I want to say a big thank you to Rose for organizing this service and helping me with a thousand details and breakdowns during the last few weeks. You always take such good care of all of us, Rose. I couldn't have gotten through this mess without you."

"Cheers to Rose!" Ivy raised her glass and the rest followed. Rose felt the warmth of their love but still blushed from the attention.

"If we're looking for a change in subject, I have an idea. Let's talk about Rose. After all, we're eating and drinking all of her food. No family gathering is complete without nagging and unsolicited advice for the hostess!" Daisy grinned.

"Let's see. My only child left home to travel the world instead of going to college, my best friends are all over the world now, and my love life is totally nonexistent. That about covers it." Rose frowned as Ivy pretended to play a violin at her sad tale.

"Ah, but you forgot about the sexy older man," prompted Vi. The others immediately stopped what they were doing.

"What?" Ivy, Daisy, and Lily spoke in unison, stopping mid-action to look at Rose, who sunk down on the settee and fluffed a pillow as she curled up her legs.

"Don't get too excited. The older man Vi's referring to is one of Rachel's discoveries in Italy. She's decided to squander her European travels to work in a restaurant and get free lodging from some middle-aged Antonio Banderas lookalike who owns the place." Rose took another sip of her wine. "This is not the kind of education I wanted for my nineteen-year-old daughter, but it's not like I can ground her anymore, can I?"

"Maybe you should go over there and straighten him out, Rose. Or I can do it for you." Lily cracked her knuckles and rolled her shoulders like she was getting ready for a street fight.

"I love it that you're a healer by day and a bone crusher by night, Lil. Someone should make a superhero movie about you." Ivy clinked glasses with Lily.

"Funny you should talk about going to Italy. Rachel has invited me to come over for a visit. I'm resisting because I don't think I could stand it if she introduced him as her boyfriend." Rose put her head back on the settee, looking up at the darkening sky. She spotted the first star twinkling and knew it wouldn't be long before her neighbors the coyotes started their nightly howl at the moon. "He's probably the same age as me."

Rose had turned forty a few months prior, and instead of freaking out over it, she felt like she was starting to hit her groove. The faint lines around her hazel eyes gave her face more depth, a seasoning she lacked in her twenties and thirties. Her auburn hair was the thick, glossy mane she'd always wanted after detoxing it from years of over styling. And she had zero desire to wear a pair of skinny jeans, finally learning to love the strong thighs that came from a career spent designing outdoor spaces. On good days

Rose could squint into the mirror and see Sandra Bullock, or at least Sandy's Arizona cousin who didn't have to live up to Hollywood standards of beauty.

But meeting her daughter's potential forty-something boyfriend? That was still a stretch for Rose, something she didn't think she was ready for.

"I think you should go, Rose," Vi said. "I remember when I turned twenty-one and my mom took me to New York for the first time. It was the start of our adult relationship, and I'll never forget it. Sort of a rite of passage, you could call it." Violet stared into space for a moment and then shook her head, clearing the memory. "Why don't you show them the pictures of Rachel's inappropriate maybe-boyfriend?"

"Pictures? Yes, I want to see them!" Daisy was a food writer, and she was very picky about the photos that accompanied her work. She had as much visual talent as she did writing talent.

"This is torture. You know that, right? And this from people who profess to love me." Rose grunted and stood up, setting her wine glass down on the table. In her best Schwarzenegger impression, she said, "I'll be back," as she walked into the house.

When Rose came back with her tablet, she stopped at the door to watch her friends' faces glowing in the candlelight as they talked. It was so good to have them all back together again, to feel their hugs and hear their laughter. Texting and online chats just weren't the same. Rose felt a pang of loneliness just thinking about the day they'd all leave. Then she'd be truly alone for the first time in her life. She wasn't sure what to do with herself.

Rose scanned the entire setting, committing it to memory. The walled courtyard was the real jewel of her house, with a floor made out of rocks, tiles, pebbles, colored glass, and broken pottery. The design was eclectic, haphazard in a way that made visual and textural sense, and Rose loved it even more because she and her daughter Rachel did it together when Rachel was just eight years old. And her best friends were bringing life back into the space now that Rachel was gone.

Rachel. Rose wondered what Rachel was doing in that moment, and she hoped it didn't include a middle-aged Spaniard hiding out in Italy from who knows what. She sighed and walked outside.

"Have at it, ladies." Rose set the tablet on the table and plopped back down on the oversized cushions.

"Yowza. I would definitely eat at his restaurant. Think he's on the menu?" Ivy was the group's manhunter, a woman who knew what she wanted but often changed her mind. She was committed to the single life.

"Look at that hair! How many men in their forties have hair like that? Makes me want to sink my fingers into it and…well, you know." Daisy was suddenly shy, a blush rising to her cheeks.

"C'mon, Daze. Tell us what you're thinking," Lily said. "You know Nico shaved his head during our entire marriage, so I have no idea what kind of activity that hair can inspire. Educate me." Lily dodged the pillow that was thrown at her, laughing despite the painful memory of her recent divorce.

"You guys remember that this guy is possibly dating my daughter, right? The one you all helped raise?" Rose couldn't admit how attractive this man was. It was taboo to think about him as anything other than the enemy as long as he was distracting her daughter from living life with people her own age, going through the normal experiences. Rose remembered her own life at twenty, pregnant with Rachel after a disastrous one-night stand in the crazy days of grief after her parents' accident. Rose would never trade having Rachel for anything, but she didn't want her daughter to go through the pressure of trying to grow up and raise a child at the same time like Rose did.

Ivy picked up the tablet and started scrolling through the photos.

"This guy doesn't look like Rachel's type. When I see her posts, it's all guys in skinny jeans with bohemian angst. I picture her more with a twenty-year-old aspiring musician than a restaurant owner in his forties." Ivy kept looking, her forehead in a frown as she tried to understand Rose's concern.

"Rachel claims that this guy Mateo is not after her, that he just hired her because of her personality and ability to speak both Italian and English, but I don't buy it. He's our age! Remember how dumb we were about men at twenty? There's no way she sees this situation for what it really is." Rose thought about herself at twenty and shook her head.

"You became a mother at twenty and she's traveling the world at the same age, Rose. You can't even compare the two. Besides, she had the Internet growing up." Daisy wiggled her arched eyebrows like a maniacal scientist.

"Darling, I think you need to be a lot more concerned with these young men she's laughing and boozing it up with. If this Lothario has such a hold on her, why is she out dancing the night away with these charming young men?" Ivy tapped a few of the pictures, zooming in on Rachel's apparent full enjoyment of what Italy had to offer. "A selfie is worth a thousand words, wouldn't you say?"

"I guess I didn't really pay attention to the younger guys once I saw Mateo in the picture. I can't stand the thought of some older guy swooping in to steal my daughter away. Rachel is supposed to be with people her own age, discovering things for herself, expanding into adulthood." Rose looked closer at the picture and realized Mateo was only near Rachel in one photo, and that they weren't alone.

"So you want to debut your lovely daughter to the world in front of a parentally screened audience of age-appropriate men? How very progressive of you, Rose. I can't imagine why Rachel isn't more excited about the way her mother is organizing her love life." Violet cocked her head to the side as her point landed.

"I hate it that you all know me so well. But I'm damn glad you're here. Don't make me regret it or I'll take the good wine away and make you drink from the box." Rose tried to steer the conversation away with humor, her go-to strategy when things got difficult. But Violet pressed on.

"Maybe the reason you're so obsessed with her life is because there's nothing new to talk about in yours. When was the last time you went on a date or took a trip? And let's not even think about how long it's been since you had sex, because I'm imagining cobwebs down there right now," Violet said. "You broke up with Steve six months ago!"

"No cobwebs down here, my friend. I do my own housework, don't you know?" Daisy howled with laughter at that one, joined soon after by the coyotes as if on cue, which made everyone else burst into laughter too.

"Listen, I know what you're doing, Rose. It's what you always do: put everyone else first and wait your turn. But guess what? It's your turn now. No one else is ahead of you. Stop taking care of everyone else and start taking care of yourself." Violet emptied her glass. "Today should prove to you that life is short. Mom was only sixty-five, not a sick day in her life. I'm not going to wait to be happy anymore, and you shouldn't either."

"Raise your hand if you think Rose should go to Italy and have an affair with an Italian." Lily commandeered the group to a vote.

"Or a Spaniard," Ivy added.

All hands shot up. Rose looked around the group

and felt the love. More importantly, she felt the pull. For what, she didn't know yet, but she was determined to find out.

"It's unanimous, Rosie. You're going to Italy. And it's not to save Rachel, either. It's to save *you*." Ivy poured a new round of wine for everyone and they toasted, just as thunder cracked the sky and the rain came pelting down.

Rose didn't know if Mother Nature was sending applause or a warning.

CHAPTER TWO

MATEO WIPED DOWN the bar one last time. He looked up as Rachel cashed out the last customers of the night, a tipsy Canadian couple on vacation. She laughed as they chatted, still full of energy after a long shift. She'd probably join the others to go out dancing after he closed up and went home.

Mateo remembered when he had that kind of energy, though just barely. The last few years running the restaurant had taken a toll. There was a bit of gray weaving into the waves of black in his hair, and his business partners in Madrid were always giving him a hard time about it. Alejandro and Ruben were the ones stuck in "Corporate-landia" and Mateo was the one going gray at forty-three while living on a lake in Italy. It didn't seem fair, but he knew the look was working for fellow Lake Como resident George Clooney, so he wasn't going to fret too much about it. Being a handsome single guy in a gorgeous travel destination was not hard on his social life, but the hours he devoted to the restaurant made it difficult to give any woman enough attention to develop a relationship.

Back when he was working as an architect he never worked this hard. Still, the exhaustion was welcome. Designing great culinary experiences was far more satisfying on a daily basis than designing great buildings, which often took months or years to see a final result. And he did enjoy the slow pace of Varenna after a lifetime in bustling Madrid. Mateo was surprised at how well he fit into the restaurant world after twenty years as an architect.

Rachel said goodbye to the Canadian couple, flipping the "chiuso" sign on the door after them to signal the restaurant was closed for the night. Rachel took off her apron and plopped down on the barstool.

"We're all heading out to go dancing in Bellagio. Want to come? The ferry leaves in ten minutes." Rachel touched up her lipstick as she asked, knowing he would say no. She asked him this almost every night, and every time he declined.

"No, you guys go and have fun." Mateo didn't even bother to make excuses anymore. He wasn't interested in the loud thumping music, awkwardly yelled conversations with people half his age, and copious amounts of alcohol required to keep up with the crowd. What he was looking for couldn't be found at a discotheque full of twenty-something partiers.

"When my mom gets here you're going to have to go dancing with us because she doesn't speak Italian." Rachel winked at him and hopped off the barstool, already looking at her phone to find out where her friends were. Mateo waved her off and went back to his closing duties, inhaling the aroma of garlic, bread, and the lingering perfumes of the women who'd been in that evening. He liked this quiet time after closing, the scents of the evening reminding him of who'd been there and what had happened.

"A good night, no?" Chef Aldo walked out from the kitchen, buttoning the cuffs on his fresh shirt as he spoke.

"Yes, a full house. You were smart to buy the extra fish at the market today." Mateo threw his towel over his shoulder and watched as Chef Aldo put on his jacket and groomed his mustache in the mirror behind the bar. He smiled, checking his oversized teeth for stray bits of parsley. Chef Aldo's bald head gleamed even in the dim lighting of the restaurant.

"A smart man learns to anticipate needs, Mateo, a fact my Simona appreciates very much," said Chef Aldo. "And with that, I'm off to continue sating appetites at home." He grinned like a madman, adjusted the newsboy hat on his head, and made his way out the front door.

Chef Aldo's wife Simona was called the happiest woman in Varenna by the locals, a term Mateo used to think was due to her sunny nature. After getting to know Chef Aldo over the past few years, he began wondering if the nickname was a little more sexual in nature, the kind of sly humor older women shared with each other that men didn't always understand. There was a local saying, *"botte piccola fa vino buono,"* which meant that a small cask makes good wine. Mateo thought the short and energetic Chef Aldo might have been the original target of that compliment.

Every time Mateo saw Signora Simona she was smiling, her curly brown hair and pink cheeks the picture of health and happiness.

"No good for a man like you to be alone, Mateo," she often said, patting his cheek.

As he walked through the restaurant on his final check of the night, he reminded himself exactly why it was good for a man like him to be alone. Not every relationship worked like Chef Aldo and Simona's, and he knew of dozens of examples to prove it, including a very painful one of his own. More often than not, love hurt. Mateo was an exceptional architect and a pretty damn fine restaurateur, and even so he hadn't yet figured out how to construct the perfect relationship, to serve up love nutritious and delicious.

As he blew out the last of the candles, he thought about Rachel's mom. Rachel said her mother had never been outside the United States and loved gardening, so he imagined a dumpy, unsophisticated woman with dirty fingernails. Living in a popular tourist day trip destination gave him a daily view of fanny pack-wearing tourists with black socks and white tennis shoes. *No, thanks.* As a Spaniard living in Italy, he took pride in his appearance and couldn't understand the ugly style of dress of people from other countries. Rachel's mom would need far more than a translator to blend in.

But no matter what she looked like, she had to be something to produce a daughter like that. Rachel was vibrant, an adventurous and smart young woman, even if she was a little irresponsible. Who wasn't at that age, though?

The first time Mateo saw Rachel, she was in the middle of a group of people, telling a story in English and Italian. It was rare to see someone so young hold center stage so effectively, and he watched her perform as he poured drinks behind the bar. Her pacing was good, drawing the crowd in slowly to her story like an expert fisherman. Rachel had the group in the palm of her hand before she stopped, looked around with a sly grin, and then said with a flourish:

"And that's how you manage a hangover while riding a camel."

Rachel bowed extravagantly as they all clapped and laughed around her. This was a woman who was not only attractive, but engaging and smart. He needed a woman like that at the restaurant, someone who could speak English and Italian as well as handle the sometimes boisterous customers who were on holiday. When Rachel came up to the bar for a coffee before leaving, Mateo made his move.

"Are you enjoying your time in Varenna?" he asked.

"It's a little too quiet for me, but then again, most places are. I'm beginning to think it might be me," Rachel said as she smiled.

"Your Italian is very good." Mateo probably wasn't

the first person to tell her that.

"Thanks. Everyone in school thought I was crazy to learn Italian, but I always knew I'd come to Italy. Right now I'm just traveling, trying to figure out what I'm going to do next. Lake Como is a great place for thinking." Rachel handed over some euros to pay her bill.

"Have you figured it out yet? Your life, that is. Because I could use a few hints." Mateo smiled at Rachel.

"How boring to have it all figured out! I'm just weighing my options for the next six months, not my entire life. I'll give you the first lesson for free: stop looking at the big picture." She closed her wallet and turned to leave.

"I own a restaurant; I'm always looking at the big picture. Hazards of the job." Mateo liked this spunky girl and thought his customers would, too. "Speaking of jobs, are you interested in some temporary work to fund your travels? I could use a bilingual hostess until the end of the summer. I think your Italian might be better than mine."

She turned back toward the bar, hand on her hip and head tilted. "Hmmm. Practice my Italian, meet fun people, and live in this beautiful place? That's a tough sell." She was flip as she said it, but after a moment of thought she turned a bit more serious. Mateo could see the wheels turning in her mind. "I'm actually waiting on something big to come through later this summer, so it wouldn't hurt to stay in one place for a while and earn some money."

"The summer will be busy, and you'll make some easy cash for the rest of your travels. Plus I think you'll like the staff here. It's very much like family—a dysfunctional and weird family, but still a family," Mateo said.

As if on cue, his head waiter Lorenzo walked out from the kitchen and untied his apron. In Italian, he told Mateo he was going out for a smoke break while Mateo flirted with the American tourist. Before Mateo could respond, Rachel looked Lorenzo in the eye and said in perfect Italian: "*Io non sono un turista. Io sono il vostro nuovo capo.*"

Lorenzo stopped in his tracks. Rachel had just told him she wasn't a tourist, she was his new boss. And she said it like she meant it.

Mateo smiled, thinking of how much Rachel had grown on them all over the last six weeks. Even crusty Chef Aldo loved her, and Mateo knew they'd all be sad when she left. But that was the way of life, was it not? People moved on, whether you wanted them to or not. Mateo found that out the hard way.

CHAPTER THREE

"HELLO, ROSE. I'M Mateo."

Rose sat up straight and leaned into the screen. Her back stiffened and her eyes narrowed, and she looked like she wanted to crawl through the laptop and punch him. Mateo felt himself recoiling a bit, even though she was thousands of miles away.

"Ah, this is a little strange, but Rachel had to leave for a minute and she told me you might be calling, so she left her laptop on the bar and asked me to answer. I'm Mateo, the owner of the restaurant where she works. Rachel said she'd told you about me." He talked fast, hopefully fast enough to calm her down. Mateo didn't have children, but he could understand the kind of freakout a parent could have if they called their kid and a stranger answered.

"Sounds chummy. Do you know when Rachel will be back?" Rose was direct, and he didn't hesitate to answer.

"Rachel went with Lorenzo to the discotheque in Bellagio to look for her phone. She is always losing it." Mateo's instinct for putting people at ease, honed over the past five years of running the restaurant, started to kick in. It was a hard sell, though. Rose was not warming to him, and she was so far from the frumpy, timid gardener he pictured from Rachel's description.

Mateo had always loved redheads, and Rose had a full head of auburn hair. She had a faint sprinkling of freckles on her nose that he found cute, a hint of how much fun she might be if she wasn't suspicious of a certain innocent restaurant owner. Rose had a lean, sculpted look to her face, a more chiseled and refined version of Rachel. Her hazel eyes sparkled, though he knew it was more from irritability than any attraction to him.

"Rachel's been excited about your visit. She tells us that you design beautiful gardens. You're going to love seeing the famous old gardens at the villas in Varenna." Mateo was good at small talk, looking for common points of interest with strangers. Still, he felt like he was standing at the zoo poking the bear, waiting to see what Rose would do, hoping she didn't decide to bite his head off just for fun.

"Do you often talk about parental visits with your, uh, employees? Or just the young pretty ones?" *Mierda! Does she think I'm after her daughter?* No amount of protesting from him was going to change her perception, so he decided to ignore her conclusions as if they were ridiculous, since they were.

"My restaurant is like a family, and my employees are my children. Well, for vanity's sake, let's say they are my nieces and nephews. We all talk about family, friends, books, travel, food, music—all the things that restaurant workers on break talk about around the world. Have you ever worked in a restaurant, Rose?" Mateo asked.

"Yes, I did work in a restaurant when I was younger," Rose replied.

"Then you know exactly what I'm talking about," Mateo said, casually illustrating his relationship with Rachel without getting into a defensive position. His lawyer friend Alejandro would be so proud.

Rose's eyes softened a little, revealing an ounce of credit but still a long way from full trust. She cleared her throat and shook her head, as if to clear her thoughts.

"Rachel decides what she wants and then acts as if it is so, regardless of what anyone else thinks. If you've known her for any time at all, you must have realized this by now," Rose challenged.

"Oh, believe me, she's got Chef Aldo and the rest of the staff doing her bidding. Did she tell you when I offered her the job she told my head waiter she was now in charge? It's not true, but you wouldn't know it by the way they act. If Rachel wasn't just passing through, I'd be worried for my own position." Mateo laughed, a deep and hearty sound.

Rose smiled begrudgingly, and he could tell she enjoyed the story. Mateo was slowly winning her over to baseline stranger status, where he hoped he could start all over again as the guy who was not after her daughter.

"I'm not going to be able to visit Rachel on this part of her trip. I just have too much going on right now," Rose explained. Knowing first-hand just how persuasive Rachel could be, Mateo wasn't convinced this was her final decision, so he kept going as if she'd never said it.

"Rachel told me you were a landscape designer. Do you get a lot of winter work?" Mateo was already matching up points of commonality, and this seemed like the perfect time to drop the fact that he was an architect—at least he was before he started grinding coffee and making pasta for a living.

Rose tilted her head to the side and knitted her brows. "Winter is relative; I live in the desert. Do you know much about landscape design?"

"I'm an architect by trade, so I've done a lot of work with landscape designers in my native Spain. I was under the impression they were all crusty old men. Had I known there were people like you in the business I might not have taken this sabbatical." Mateo gave her his best smile, hoping to charm her.

"That must be one helluva story, how an architect in Spain came to run a restaurant in Italy." Rose didn't directly ask the question, so Mateo decided to bypass it. Rose was going to have to do a little bit of the work, too.

"Everyone's life is a helluva story. That's one thing I've learned from running a restaurant these past five years." Mateo gave a neutral smile, challenging her to keep the conversation going.

"Well mine is about work right now, and I'm pretty sure Rachel will understand. It's not easy running a business on your own." Rose sounded tired, and Mateo understood. Even though he had business partners, the day-to-day running of the restaurant was still entirely up to him.

"It's too bad we won't be able to meet in person. I hate that you'll miss the beauty of Varenna in the early autumn, but even more than that, I'm afraid of what Rachel will be like if she doesn't get her way." He grinned, waiting for Rose to join him. When she did, he felt like he'd just scored a winning goal. "I don't know what your business situation is, but I will tell you that Varenna is beautiful in the fall. It's also when the tourism drops to a manageable level for those of us who live here." He saw her stiffen and wondered what he'd said to cause it.

"I'd have thought you'd love the summer crowds, being a restaurant owner and all." Mateo wondered if she wasn't part detective, the way she was grilling him.

"Oh, the business is great year-round. We could actually still run a profit at off-season levels because we bought the building during the recession. The rent of the flat alone would pay the bills." Mateo didn't know why he was talking about his investments with someone he didn't know, but he felt compelled to keep her on the line. The conversation was drifting in the wrong direction.

"The same apartment you're renting to my daughter for almost nothing? That seems a little counterproductive to me." Rose kept probing.

"Oh, Rachel more than makes up for the rent during the busy season. The fact that she knows English and Italian is great for business, and we make most of our rental income on the flat in the off-season. People come from all over to write and paint here, so the flat is usually rented out for weeks or months at a time. None of those people want to be here during the busy time, so it's perfect for Rachel to use right now." Why did Mateo feel the need to justify his business decisions to this woman?

"So you'll need to free up the apartment soon then? Rachel will have a few more months to travel before returning home for college. I'm sure she told you she's starting school in January." Rose was making an obvious push, but Mateo didn't know where she was going with it. What he did know was that Rachel wasn't returning to college in January, but he didn't want to be the bearer of that news.

"Oh, I'm sure Rachel has a great future ahead of her no matter where she decides to go." Mateo had only known Rachel for six weeks, and in that short time he learned that she did what she wanted to, no matter what anyone else thought. "But yes, she'll be out of the apartment as of October 15 because I have a regular tenant coming, a writer who spends a couple of months here every autumn." He could see the relief on Rose's face at the news. Mateo felt like the big bad wolf and was a little pissed off since he'd done nothing to deserve it.

"Rachel is walking in the door right now." Mateo looked up and waved to Rachel as she and Lorenzo came in, pointing at the laptop to let her know there was a call. "It was nice to meet you, Rose. I hope one day you'll get to see this beautiful part of the world." He turned the laptop around to face Rachel.

"Good news! They still had my phone!" Rachel beamed at him, as if this was the first time she'd lost her phone and it was miraculously recovered. Mateo could recall at least two other instances when she left her phone at a table while she was dancing. Once a handsome man dropped the phone off for her, and once she had to retrieve it like this time. He'd never known someone so careless with her things.

"Your mom is online. I hope you don't mind that we talked about you a bit while we were waiting for you to return." Rachel narrowed her eyes at him as she cautiously stepped behind the bar.

"I think I'll take this to my room. Thanks for keeping her company, Mateo. Just a sec, Mom." Rachel picked up her laptop and walked up the stairs to her apartment for a bit of privacy.

# # #

Rachel howled with laughter.

"I'm still your mother, and I want you to take this seriously!" Rose was fuming. Rachel could practically see the steam coming out of her ears.

"Mom, Mateo is *old*! He's your age, not mine, and there is no way he's into me. And there's no way I'm into him, either. Eww." She couldn't stop laughing as she fell back on her bed.

"You might know that, my dear, but my experience tells me he doesn't. Why on earth would he give you an apartment right above the restaurant just for being a waitress? This man has an agenda, and I want you to be aware of it." Rose pursed her lips to gather her thoughts, a move Rachel knew all too well. The hammer was about to come down.

"Mom, his agenda is to have me work at his restaurant. It's hard to find people who speak English and Italian well enough for locals and visitors, so I help his restaurant run better. That's it." She paused for dramatic effect. "Besides, I'm not a waitress. I'm a hostess."

"I'm just worried about you, honey. I don't want to see you get hurt by a smooth-talking older man. Things happen that can change your life forever." Rose took a softer, maternal approach, which surprised Rachel.

"You think I'm too stupid to know when a guy is into me, Mom? Give me a break. I'm not a child anymore!" Rachel pulled back her shoulders in a huff, saw the look on Rose's face, and realized she'd gone a little bit overboard.

"Rachel, you're old enough now to make your own mistakes. I get that, and I know you'll have your heart broken, be stupid with your money, and probably have a few crappy jobs along the way. It's par for the course in early adulthood, and you can't escape it, so I won't even try to spare you." She took a breath and lowered her voice before continuing. "But when it comes to life-altering decisions, the kind that will narrow your opportunities for the rest of your life? You can damn well bet I'm going to speak up, and I'm going to keep speaking up until you listen."

Rachel's mind whirred. *Oh shit. Does she already know?* Rachel had to think fast, because she didn't want her mom to know, at least not yet. Rose was the joint account holder on Rachel's bank account, a decision Rachel made right before she left on her travels in case she lost her bank card or had any problems abroad. Rose could shut down all of Rachel's future plans with one big withdrawal. Rose may or may not have thought of that option yet, and Rachel didn't want to give her the chance.

"If you're so worried about me, then you should take me up on my offer to visit." Rachel put her hands on her cheeks and said, "Come save me from the clutches of all these older men, Mother Dear!"

Deceiving her mom wasn't difficult—she'd been doing it in small ways for years—but this was the biggest con yet and one she didn't feel good about. There was no way Rose would take out her money while she was in Varenna if she thought Rachel would be left to depend on Mateo. Rachel felt the goosebumps rise all over her body. Her heart pounded in her chest, and she felt a trace of sweat at her hairline. *Time to get off the call before Mom notices.*

"Rachel, are you using birth control?" Rose blurted the question.

Rachel felt like she'd been pushed on the ground. She opened her mouth to respond, but nothing came out. She stared at her mother through the screen. The words came out slowly, "Is that what this is about?" Rachel's voice was a whisper, her earlier secret and guilt completely forgotten.

"Rachel, you are the light of my life and you know that. But I will not pretend it was easy to be a young single mother, or that I didn't have to adjust my entire life plans because of it. And I don't want you to limit your options because you fell for the charms of a man much more experienced in the world than you. You are smart, but you are not yet savvy." Rose had tears welling in her eyes, but she wasn't crying.

"Mom, don't you think you're being a little melodramatic?"

Rose's eyes narrowed and she cocked her head slightly to the side, a look Rachel recognized from watching her negotiate with condescending contractors over the years. "It's time for you to grow up, Rachel. There are unpleasant truths in life, and they don't get delivered in a package with a bow. This is real, and I'm sharing this concern with you because I know what it's like. You don't. And if you were half as smart as you think you are, you'd recognize that."

"I can take care of myself, Mom."

"You're right, Rachel. You have every bit as much

strength as I did, and my mom did, and every other woman who's jumped into something without thinking it through. You could make it through, I have no doubt. Women do it every day all over the world." Rose took a breath before continuing in a softer voice. "But you are my daughter and I love you more than anything. I don't want you to just make it through. I want you to thrive, to have everything in life you ever wanted, and not to be restricted so early in the game."

"Your work here is done, Mom. Message received." Rachel could be just as stubborn as her mother, a fact that she both recognized and loathed.

"Then show me. Stop hiding things. If you're too embarrassed to admit what you're doing, then you probably shouldn't be doing it. Live a life you can be proud of." Rose's eyes softened, pleading for Rachel to meet her halfway.

"I am proud of what I'm doing, Mother. And if you'd come here to visit you'd see it." Rachel had to clench her teeth to keep the next words from flowing out, the ones that would reveal her true secret. But she did not want to deliver the news online. It had to be in person, and since she wasn't going back to the United States, Rose had to come to Italy. And if it had to be under false pretenses, so be it. She'd smooth it over with Mateo later. "Mom, I really need you right now. I want you here. Will you please come?"

With those words, the switch was flipped, though Rachel didn't know how it happened. It was probably some maternal thing she'd never understand. Rose's shoulders went back and her voice got stronger. "Okay, Rachel. I'm coming. I'll be there in a few days, and we'll sort this situation out together."

CHAPTER FOUR

AFTER SEVENTEEN HOURS of travel, Rose landed in Milan. It was morning in Italy, though her body still thought it was the middle of the night. Rose had two more hours to travel to arrive in Varenna, and coffee was a requirement to make it happen.

She thought of Ivy, who traveled around the world for work. Ivy regularly complained about jet lag during their calls, but Rose always thought she was being dramatic, bragging about her exciting lifestyle to little old Rose who was stuck in the desert. Ivy had been a drama queen since they were teenagers so it never occurred to Rose how hard changing time zones could be on a body. Now she knew jet lag was a real thing, and if she didn't have coffee soon she wouldn't be able to make it another hour.

Passport Control was a little intimidating at first, though she was surprised to hear so much American-accented English coming from the people in the lines. In a moment her sleepy brain reminded her that only non-European Union citizens had to go through Passport Control. Everyone else who lived in Europe could travel to Italy as easily as she could fly from one state to the other in the United States. No wonder she didn't hear any Italian, French, or German. After getting stamped through by a no-nonsense officer, she put her passport in her purse and followed the crowd like a fish in a stream.

In the busy Baggage Claim hall, Rose stood at the periphery of the crowd, rereading her email from Mateo with directions. She was still irked that he sent it, as if they were going to be friends or even remotely friendly with each other. Rose was sure Rachel was behind it, trying to encourage the acceptance of the relationship. *Fat chance of that happening,* she thought. Neither of them even admitted they were seeing each other, which made her even madder. Rose wasn't a fool.

The light at the baggage carousel came on and the buzzer sounded, and at that moment the loose gathering of people evolved into a property war, every person standing their ground, legs apart, scanning the conveyer belt for their bags. Rose saw the luggage coming out from the top, so she decided to hang back and wait to enter the scrum until she saw hers.

The giant black bag, the one she had to pay an overweight charge for, finally emerged with its garish orange ID label. Rose tried wedging herself into the crowd to get her bag, but the property warriors held their ground. She walked behind the line of them, watching her bag traverse the route, and looking for an in. No one was budging, and her polite "excuse me" didn't help. Rose watched her bag go back through the tunnel to the start.

"This is ridiculous," she muttered. After years of dealing with crusty contractors and suppliers who wouldn't give her the time of day when her business was small, she knew it was time to take the gloves off. She marched up to the biggest guy she saw, a muscle-bound man in his twenties, and forced her way in just in time to see her bag again.

Rose reached down and tried pulling her giant suitcase from the conveyer belt, but it was wedged tightly between two other bags. Muscle guy was no help. Rose walked alongside the conveyer belt as it moved, pushing people out of the way, yanking and pulling her suitcase until it was free. Two minutes ago, she couldn't find her way in. Now she was disrupting the entire line just to get her suitcase.

The bag's weight shifted faster than she expected, causing her to fall back toward a smartly dressed woman in a cream suit with a flowing chiffon scarf. The woman quickly sidestepped Rose.

"Sorry! I mean, *scusi!*" Rose said as she dropped her suitcase on the floor with a loud thunk. Even though they were on the same flight, the woman looked like she'd just had a full night's sleep in her own bed.

"You shouldn't pack a bag you can't manage," she said in English, before walking over to easily pull her own off the conveyer belt. Rose instantly hated her. *Don't should on me, lady.*

Rose pulled her enormous suitcase behind her, rushing to make the next express train to Milan's Centrale Station, where hopefully she could relax and get a coffee before the last leg of the journey to Varenna. Just as she walked up, the sliding doors closed, and Rose watched her train leave the station. The digital sign indicated the next train was leaving in thirty minutes. So far Italy had not given her a big welcome.

One good thing about a giant suitcase, however, was that it made a great temporary chair. Rose parked it against the wall and sat, contemplating her situation. She had time to brush her teeth and hair and primp a little in the bathroom, and then she'd get a coffee before the next train. Fortified by a plan, even a small one, Rose perked up.

She walked up to a sleek rounded bar in the middle of the hallway in the terminal. People crowded around the bar, drinking coffee from tiny ceramic cups. Rose didn't see any of the familiar lidded cardboard cups from back home, and no one seemed to be walking away with their coffee. She had a feeling her normal venti latte order was not going to work here.

"Per favore." Rose hesitated, her knowledge of Italian almost completely played out with a single phrase. "An espresso?" she asked, holding up one finger and hoping the word was almost the same in the two languages.

The man immediately turned to the machine

behind him to start her coffee. No matter what she got, Rose knew she'd drink it without complaint. When he put the tiny steaming cup in front of her, she downed it in three sips, leaving her three euros on the silver tray with her receipt. By the time the next train arrived, Rose felt almost human again.

The Malpensa Express took her from the airport to Milan's busy Centrale Station. The hustle and bustle in the station was a little overwhelming, especially because she was tired, and Rose was glad to have detailed instructions in English from Mateo's email. Rose had never been on a train before today, and frankly she didn't realize so many people still used them. But in Milan, the train station was larger than the small airport in Hobart, with twenty or more platforms and thousands of people traveling through. The noise echoed in the cavernous station, announcements battling with whistles and the roar of the crowd. Some of the trains looked like long bullets, while others were more creaky-looking regional trains that had obviously been in service for a long time. Rose bought her ticket at the kiosk instead of the ticket counter as Mateo's email instructed. Then she stood back against the wall to watch the commotion around her. The rush of people, the smell of coffee, and the echo of it all was exciting, and Rose realized there were probably more people in the station right now than lived in her hometown. Rose couldn't imagine arriving here with no idea where to go or what to do next. She begrudgingly gave Mateo a mental high five for his help.

Rose looked up at the large leaderboard overhead, waiting for her train number to show up. With just fifteen minutes to spare before departure, she spotted her train and walked over to the platform, a little disappointed that she was getting on a regional train and not one of those sleek bullets. Rose walked up to the green and white machine and validated her ticket, a step she likely would have missed had Mateo not warned her beforehand. She wasn't ready to argue with a train conductor in Italian over the validity of her ticket.

Rose wasn't sure how to open the door of the train or if she was supposed to wait for it to open on its own, so she stood there for a moment waiting for someone else to board first. A couple with weekend bags hit the button on the side of the door and it slid open while the step lowered. Rose followed them on board and found an empty seat right next to the vertical luggage rack, pushing her giant suitcase in the lowest level. She sunk down in her seat with relief at starting the final stage of the journey.

Rose had one hour to gather herself together before seeing Rachel. She'd brushed her teeth and hair at the airport, and all she could really do now was swipe on some lipstick. Rose felt a little pretentious doing it, but she also pulled out a scarf she bought at the airport and wound it around her neck. In Italy all the women wore scarves, and she needed all the help she could get not to feel like some country bumpkin from the desert in this cosmopolitan place. As was her habit, she checked her fingernails for dirt, surprising herself again at the sophisticated pale polish from her manicure two days before. She thought of the new matching bra and panties she had on at the moment.

Violet took her shopping in Hobart three days ago, and instead of a new jacket and luggage, which was Rose's goal, their first stop was the lingerie store.

"You can't go to battle without your base layer of armor," Violet said.

Rose cracked up at the idea of these lacy things keeping anyone safe, but she understood what Violet meant. Before they left the mall, Rose had a new wardrobe, more clothes than she'd bought in years.

Thoreau's quote popped to mind at that moment, "Beware of all enterprises that require new clothes." Rose let out a small snort, and in doing so she caught the attention of her fellow passengers. The openly appreciative stares of the men around her made her look down at her instructions from Mateo as her face turned bright red. She had only been in Italy for just over an hour and she was already proving herself to be less than worldly, even with the new clothes and manicure. This was going to take some practice.

She reached up and touched the necklace at her neck. Vi had surprised her with the gift when she dropped Rose off at the airport.

The gray velvet box had Violet's silver VS logo embossed on the top. A purple silk ribbon was wrapped around the box and tied with a perfect bow.

Rose drew in her breath, knowing this was from Violet's gorgeous line of jewelry. She looked over at Violet, who smiled as she looked straight ahead.

"Well, I can't have you going to a stylish place like Italy without something beautiful to wear, now can I?" Violet played off the generous gift like it was nothing.

The purple ribbon fell away when she tugged on it. Rose opened the gray box to see a silver pendant shining in the dark gray silk lining of the box. The necklace was in the shape of a wild rose. The center was filled with gold raised dots, and the combination together was both elegant and modern. It was the most stunning piece of jewelry Rose had ever seen, and her eyes filled with tears knowing her friend made it especially for her.

"Violet, this is gorgeous. Is this part of your new collection?" Rose couldn't help but stare at the smooth silver petals and the striking contrast with the gold raised center.

"Yes, it's part of the new Secret Garden line. But this one is special because I added the gold to it. No other necklace like it exists. A special gift for a special friend." Violet blinked fast to keep the tears from coming.

"Thank you, Vi. This is beautiful." Rose pulled it out of the box and put it on.

"It's a wild rose. And I expect it to earn that name by the time you come back, Rose. No more of this taking care of everyone else and putting yourself last. It's time to think about yourself, about the kind of life you want to live now that your business is set and your girl is grown." Violet hugged Rose tightly as the other cars in the departure queue honked at them to move on. "I hope this necklace reminds you of that every day, no matter where you are in the world."

Rose closed her eyes at the memory from just yesterday, feeling like it was a lifetime ago. She was in Italy now, and the entire world looked different. Lake Como glistened in the sunlight outside her window, and the green, tree-covered hills were a welcome change from the near-desert landscape where she lived. The train cut through dark tunnels in the mountains, and Rose thought of the light at the end of the tunnel. This was the first time she'd ever experienced it in person. A premonition of things to come? She hoped so.

The train pulled into the Varenna-Esino station, and as Rose tugged on her suitcase, the man across the aisle came over and pulled it out for her, smiling and touching her hands as he gave her the bag. He was dressed casually for an Italian, which still meant nice shoes, pressed pants, and a soft cashmere pullover. Rose wanted to pet him and at the same time ask him where he got his hair products. Men shouldn't be allowed to be this beautiful.

"*Godetevi il vostro tempo in Italia, signora.*" He smiled at her with an open appreciation of her looks and then sat back down in his seat, seemingly content to have exchanged pleasantries with her. Why did it feel so sexual? Rose was not used to this kind of attention from men, mainly because all the men she ever saw she'd known for years. Maybe this was a further taste of things to come? She shivered a bit at the thought. Rose thanked him and stepped off the train onto the platform, looking for Rachel.

"Mom, over here!" Rachel waved her arms wildly. The train station was small, probably no bigger than the ladies room at the Milan Centrale Station, and Rose only had to take about fifteen steps to finally reach her daughter. They hugged as if they hadn't seen each other in years, rather than months. Rachel's hair smelled different, like honey, and Rose realized the odd fact that they no longer shared the same bottle of shampoo. She wanted a bottle of honey-scented shampoo for herself, if only to match her daughter again.

Rose continued inhaling the unfamiliar scent of her daughter's hair, rubbing her back and feeling her warm and safe and in her arms. She knew after this greeting Rachel wouldn't be as warm and snuggly, so Rose took all the physical touch she could get.

When they finally broke apart, Rachel grabbed her suitcase with one hand and Rose's hand with the other and walked through the small train station to the road on the other side.

"You must be dying for a coffee," Rachel said as she steered them toward a lakeside cafe with tables outside. Rose would have to get a picture of herself drinking an actual coffee in Italy to send to the Late Bloomers, preferably with a handsome waiter serving it.

"Oh Rachel, you have no idea how good that sounds to me. But I'll let you do the ordering."

# # #

Far from the hustle and bustle of the Milan station she just left, this little area of the country seemed almost untouched by tourism or modern life. The streets were small and narrow, only a few big enough for cars. There were steep stairs on some streets, making Rose wonder how a car would drive there anyway. Then it dawned on her that these streets were built long before cars were invented. This town existed before the United States was a country, before Italy was a country, even.

The villas dotting the hillside above the town were surrounded by terraced gardens, some of which were probably hundreds of years old. Rose knew there was a wild rose bush at a cathedral in Germany thought to be almost 1000 years old, so why not something similar in this historic place? Once she straightened Rachel out, Rose planned to spend a few days exploring them.

The landscape designer in her wondered how differently she would go about her work knowing her designs would be the basis of centuries of enjoyment. In a way it was like having a child, knowing a part of you would live on. But with a garden, the designer could map out the experience, guide the visitor through wild bursts of color, quiet nooks for contemplation, and perfume the warm summer evening strolls. Yes, with a garden you could create a path to follow, and even dictate the way it would be enjoyed.

With a child, you lost control very quickly, never to regain it again. Rose sighed, coming back to the situation with Rachel. How many mothers from Varenna had rushed to save their daughters from bad love affairs through the centuries? And how many had succeeded? Rose tried to feel something profound in the air, a solidarity with the mothers who had gone before her, but she still felt very alone in this.

Rose looked again at her daughter, her mini-me, and felt a surge of pride. Rachel was a smart, headstrong, and adventurous young woman. Rose remembered the first and last time she ever called Rachel her mini-me out loud and the reaction it provoked.

"I'm 100 percent me, even if I look a little bit like you!"

Now the mini-me reference was entirely internal, nothing she ever said out loud but often felt. But today as Rose watched her daughter wheeling the big suitcase along the cobblestone street, she saw more of the differences between them than the similarities. Rachel was definitely her own woman, still a messy in-progress one, but wasn't that true even for Rose at the age of forty?

What am I doing here? I don't belong, and I don't

have any wisdom to offer. My life is nothing like what I planned, so why am I trying to plan hers?

Rachel was talking about the baker, pointing out his shop and naming her favorite treats, when Rose snapped back to attention.

"Are you okay, mom?" Rachel probably thought it was jet lag, and Rose wasn't going to correct her.

"Yes, just ready for a bite to eat and to sleep for a week. Are we getting close?" Rose smiled to show everything was okay. No reason to admit to Rachel how much she was waffling on the inside. Being a single parent all these years taught her to hide indecision and uncertainty, lest there be a mutiny in the house.

"Mom, only 800 people live here full-time. Everything is close!" Rachel laughed and stopped in the street to hug Rose. "I'm really glad you're here." Rose held her tight, feeling the warmth of their physical connection. Rachel had barely grown out of the teenage "I can't stand to be seen with you" phase, so this spontaneous hugging was a rare gift.

They soon arrived at a restaurant with two outdoor tables under umbrellas. Rachel stopped and closed the handle on Rose's suitcase as she motioned for her to sit down. Orange bougainvillea streamed from the second floor window box, and the scent of warm bread wafted out the window. A chalkboard sign on the sidewalk nearby listed the day's specials, only a few of which she could interpret. With a start she realized they were at Tre Amici, Mateo's restaurant.

Rachel was easing her into this situation, starting with a coffee on the sidewalk. Rose wondered if this was on purpose or simply because of the nice weather. Still, the front door beckoned like a referee at the coin toss. Behind it was the enemy, and Rose wanted to size him up in person. Rose had a strong belief in her ability to judge character. She was a first impression kind of woman, which is why this situation with Mateo had been vexing her so much. She had suspicions, she had photos, and she had Rachel's few comments. She even had the one video chat. But she didn't have a face-to-face meeting to finalize her assessment. Today, Rose would finally know what kind of person he was.

Turning back to Rachel, Rose clasped her hands on the table and took a good look at her. Rachel's face was getting leaner, less like a child and more like an adult, and her hair had grown. Her eyes were positively sparkling with excitement.

A young man with curly hair arrived to take their order. Rose did a double take. How could she know him? Then she realized this was the young man in the photograph with Rachel and Mateo. She looked across the table at Rachel's coy smile.

"Mom, this is the restaurant where I work, and this is my friend Lorenzo," Rachel said.

"*Piacere di conoscerti*," Rose said, surprising both Rachel and Lorenzo. "What can I say? I had some time to practice my Italian on the train," Rose shrugged. She didn't tell them it was the only phrase she knew besides please and thank you. Rose took another look at this young man who was obviously uncomfortable under her gaze.

"I hope you will enjoy your stay in Italy, Ms. Quinn." Lorenzo was nothing if not polite with his stiff English, though he quickly turned his attention back to Rachel and spoke in Italian.

"Lorenzo, will you bring us two coffees? *Grazie*." Rachel grinned as he blushed, made a slight bow, and walked away. Rachel leaned back in her chair with the confidence of a woman who belonged anywhere she wanted to be. Rose remembered herself at nineteen and how everything seemed possible then. She wondered when she stopped feeling that way and hoped Rachel never would.

"I think he likes you." Rose teased as if they were grade school friends.

"Lorenzo? No way. More like a brother, for sure. Better watch it or you'll get an Italian son before you leave."

Better than a Spanish son-in-law who is old enough to be my brother. Rose vowed not to go negative while they were enjoying this reunion, so she kept that thought to herself.

"I think I'll go to the bathroom and splash some water on my face before our coffee comes." Rose stood and walked toward the door before turning around to say, "Don't worry, I'll ask my new son Lorenzo to show me the way." Rose let out a little laugh and then smacked into the chest of a man coming out of the restaurant. He held a tray with drinks, which he raised high in the air to avoid her.

"Oh, sorry!" Rose froze in place, hands held in front of her, worried he'd spill hot coffee all over both of them. The man was a pro, holding the tray high like a statue and waiting for her next move.

"And you must be the famous Rose." Warm brown eyes looked down at her under a mop of wavy dark hair sprinkled with gray. He was about six feet tall and had the lean but muscled look of an active man. And unlike almost every man she knew, he had a flat waist. This was a guy who took care of himself. But then again, you would have to do that if you were dating women half your age.

Rose stepped left while Mateo stepped right, awkwardly mirroring each other. After repeating this move on the other side he asked, "Which way would you like me to go?" A playful smile curled on his lips.

Out of my daughter's life, if you don't mind.

"If that's coffee you can follow me back to the table." Rose regained her footing and returned to her chair.

"I hope you don't mind me putting Lorenzo to work inside so I could come out and welcome you to Italy." Mateo grinned and Rose saw for the first time the 3D version of his eyes crinkling at the corners, pulling his whole face into the smile. Small white cups of espresso on saucers with packets of sugar were placed on the table, along with a small basket of biscotti and two small glasses of golden liquid.

"*Piacere di conoscerti.*" Rose repeated her well-practiced "nice to meet you" phrase.

"Ah, you've been studying. Well, I have to admit my Italian is not as good as my English, but I do okay here. There are a lot of similarities to my native Spanish, so that gives me a head start."

"Well, I don't know how far a few phrases will get me, but with Rachel to translate I shouldn't get myself into too much trouble." Rose decided to shut him down at every opportunity until she had a chance to talk to Rachel about him.

"What do you plan to do during your stay in Italy? There are some beautiful old villas on the hillside, and watching the sunset from this side of the lake is nice. And it is still warm enough to enjoy a famous gelato. But I would imagine your favorite site in all of Italy is your lovely daughter." Mateo laid the charm on thick, but Rose wasn't having any of it. "Please let me know if I can help you plan an itinerary or answer any questions."

"I have a guidebook and a daughter who's been working here all summer as a waitress instead of traveling like she set out to do, so I think I have access to all the information I need." How long before he got the hint and left them alone? Rose was tired and hungry, and her patience was wearing thin.

Rachel's eyes volleyed back and forth between them like she was watching a tennis match. She still hadn't said a word. Was she reevaluating Mateo now that her mom was here to cast him in a truer light?

Rose could only hope. Mateo motioned to the drinks and biscotti on the table.

"Many visitors to Italy dip their biscotti in the coffee, but I won't let you make that mistake. Chef Aldo would have a heart attack. Your biscotti should always be dipped in Vin Santo, a delicious dessert wine that pairs well with the almond in the biscotti. After you enjoy this dessert, then it is time for coffee. No Italian eats anything with coffee, as it is considered the final part of the meal." He bowed with a flourish and said, "That concludes your first cultural lesson on Italy, compliments of the house."

"You're a little too late, Mateo. I read the exact same thing in the guidebook on the way here. In America we like to dip our biscotti in coffee, so you probably aren't dealing with ignorant tourists so much as people who trust their own taste and aren't easily swayed." Rose's smile was sweet even as her words dripped with sarcasm.

Mateo recovered quickly from the barb, spreading his arms wide and smiling.

"Ah, but what joy is there in life if you don't try everything at least once? You might miss something wonderful." Mateo picked up his tray, nodded his head to them, and walked back into the restaurant.

"Well, that was awkward." Rachel looked at her mom as if she had farted in front of the queen.

"I'm not as easily impressed as you are, Rachel. Just because he has an accent doesn't mean he's any more exotic than the next guy, believe me." Rose dipped her biscotti into the wine and took a bite. The softened cookie melted on her tongue as the sweet wine warmed her mouth.

Damn if Mateo wasn't right about the taste.

CHAPTER FIVE

"AND THE MOTHER, she is beautiful?" Chef Aldo stood stirring a giant pot of sauce, perfuming the kitchen with the aroma of tomatoes, onions, basil, and garlic. Mateo felt his stomach rumble.

"Yes, she is attractive. But this Rose also comes with thorns." Mateo picked up a spoon and dipped it quickly into the sauce for a taste before Chef Aldo could stop him. "I am still bleeding from our first conversation."

"How did you get to this age without learning to handle roses, Mateo?" Chef Aldo kept stirring as he spoke. "You do not grab them and force them to your nose. You approach the rose, look for an opening, and then gently clasp it as you lean forward to inhale the scent." Chef Aldo pulled the spoon out of the pot and mimed smelling a rose, closing his eyes and drinking in the imaginary fragrance as tomato sauce dripped on the floor.

"This sounds like you are trying to teach me something again. Remember, I am a very poor student, *maestro*." Mateo put his spoon in the sink. "The sauce is perfect, as usual."

"If you won't listen, then get out of my kitchen. I can't have you bleeding on the food because you don't know how to behave with a grown woman." Chef Aldo waved him away, done with trying to tame the savage yet again. Mateo stood at the corner and smiled at the game they played over and over again, the Italian trying to civilize the unruly Spaniard who was mistakenly left in charge. To hear Chef Aldo tell it, he was singlehandedly saving Tre Amici from certain ruin at the hands of Mateo and his Madrid-based business partners. Like many patriotic Italians, Chef Aldo thought anything not from Italy was inferior: people, products, and traditions. Mateo liked to remind him that Italian olive oil was largely made from Spanish olives, but only when he was certain of a quick getaway. Once, after suggesting they bring in some Spanish wines for the menu, Chef Aldo chased after him with a spoon. The rain was falling outside and Chef Aldo hated getting his bald head wet, so Mateo made a mad dash out the back door to safety. But Chef had the last word by locking him out of the restaurant. When Mateo was finally allowed to come back inside, soaking wet, he agreed they'd only serve Italian wines with Chef Aldo's food.

The back and forth between the two was like a father-son relationship, spiced with a bit of brotherly rivalry. Working with Chef Aldo was an unexpected pleasure, an ongoing lesson on life and cooking from a wise but scrappy bald man. Mateo wasn't sure the relationship would work out when he first arrived five years ago with his business partners, Ruben and Alejandro. Three new Spanish owners at an Italian restaurant was not a welcome change, but Chef Aldo was smart enough to know the restaurant couldn't survive another season with the current owner, whose health was in rapid decline. And once he realized these interlopers weren't going to micromanage his kitchen, Chef Aldo considered them only a minor annoyance. Over time, that minor annoyance turned into a comfortable friendship.

"I think our new guest might get thornier when Rachel reveals her big news. Maybe we should all go stay across the lake until she leaves." Mateo picked up the basil and began plucking the leaves for garnish.

"*Mio dio!* How does Spain still make *bambini* with this level of ignorance about women?" Chef Aldo sighed and put the spoon down. "You don't avoid a woman's anger, Mateo. You walk with her through it." He walked over to the counter to test the mound of dough sitting under a towel. Satisfied it was ready, he divided it into eight sections, sprinkled the counter with flour, and started rolling the first one flat. Today's menu included a meat ravioli with a pine nut sauce, one of Mateo's favorites.

"Easy for you to say, Chef. Your wife is always happy." Mateo watched him press out the ravioli and then take his famous filling and spoon it on each one. Once he finished, Chef rolled out another thin layer to put on top and then sealed the ravioli shut with the press. Like an artist at work, each ravioli was perfect.

"You think my Simona has no anger? Ha! Don't run away from fiery women, Mateo. Once you learn how to walk in the fire, you'll never have cold feet again." Chef Aldo bent over to continue making the ravioli, bald head gleaming under the kitchen lights.

Mateo crossed his arms and leaned against the refrigerator door, considering the perfect response to Chef's nonsense. He looked up when Lorenzo came through the kitchen door with news of a lunch reservation at 2 p.m. for ten people.

"Are Rachel and Rose still outside?" Mateo wasn't the type to hide from a woman, but he wasn't ready to go round two with Rose just yet.

"The *conquistador* is trembling in his armor from the threat of a thorny Rose!" Chef Aldo cackled to himself as he turned to drop a ravioli into a pot of boiling water, testing the final product. Lorenzo tried to hide his grin from Mateo.

"They are going upstairs now, Mateo. Signora Rose is taking a small rest." Lorenzo couldn't help but try to gain entry into the men's club of Mateo and Chef Aldo. "What is it they say in the American movies? The coast is clear." He playfully punched Mateo on the shoulder before going out to pour wine for the lunch guests.

Mateo lost a lot of his macho swagger when he became an adult. He didn't have to puff out his chest and win all the girls to prove himself like he did at university. But still, even at forty-three he couldn't become the butt of a joke about his manhood, especially now that Lorenzo was teaming up with Chef Aldo in the teasing. Work would become intolerable.

"*Maestro*, you are correct: I am a conquistador, and I will prove it. Before this Rose leaves Italy, she will be like your ravioli dough in my hands.

CHAPTER SIX

"GOOD MORNING TO you, good morning to you, you look like a monkey, and you smell like one, too!" Rachel sang the song to the tune of "Happy Birthday," waking Rose from a sound sleep. "Time for a shower!"

Rose groaned and rolled over, covering her head with a pillow. "Just five more minutes."

The song was one Rose sang to Rachel every morning of her life, up until she left home just a few months ago. The role reversal of their morning routine was strange, and it was only because of the jet lag. Rose was normally awake before the sun came up, but after soldiering through her arrival day with a short walking tour of Varenna and a hasty pizza for dinner, she crashed hard.

"Mom, Italy is waiting on you and I'm hungry. Let's go, sleepyhead!" Rachel reached for the duvet cover and yanked it back, just like Rose used to do to her after repeated calls to get up. Underneath the blanket, Rose was naked. Rachel couldn't hide her shock. "Oh my god, I'm so sorry!" Rachel quickly threw the blanket back over Rose and turned around, but not before her mother saw the heat flushing her face.

"Bet you won't do that again." Rose yawned and looked at Rachel's back. She still hadn't turned around. "It's okay, Rachel. Moms can sleep in the nude. It's not a big deal. Besides, how would you have known? This is the first time in the history of the world you've woken up before me."

Rose sat up on her elbows and looked at Rachel's back, thinking about all the mornings she woke the little pajama-clad body of her daughter. As a child, Rachel slept with her stuffed animal Bunny clutched to her all night. As a teenager, she often fell asleep under a mound of clothes on her bedspread, items that were tested and discarded as outfit options that day. Waking Rachel in those years was akin to going on an archaeological dig.

Rose knew that Rachel liked to sleep with a night light, to have a glass of water on the nightstand, and that she despised alarm clocks. The blinds were always open so she could see the moon and stars at night. And she always slept in socks.

Rose knew everything about Rachel, or at least she used to. And this distance between them was killing her. Why couldn't they just go back to the way it was?

"Rachel, I'm your mother. I'll always know more about you than you know about me." She paused. "And I'll always be more comfortable with that fact than you can possibly imagine." Rose reached for the robe on the chair next to her bed. "You can tell me anything and I'll understand." She wrapped the robe around her and walked over to Rachel, hugging her from behind and kissing her on the back of the head. The honey-scented shampoo reminded her that today their hair would smell the same again, just like it did back home. And even though it was a small thing, it was another step on the bridge back to normal. "I hope today you'll unload whatever secret it is you've been carrying."

"Can we just make a deal that you'll wear a nightgown while you're here and look like a mom? I'm totally gonna need therapy for what just happened." Rachel was working to lighten the mood, obviously not ready to talk about it yet, and Rose decided to indulge her. The door was open, and she had to wait for Rachel to walk through it.

"Rachel, I don't even own a nightgown, so you've got two options. You can spend all your travel money on therapy, or you can let me sleep as late as I want every day. Your choice." Rose turned around to walk back to the bathroom. "I'm taking my clothes off for a shower now. Should I sound the warning bell?" Rose laughed as she dropped the robe on the floor and shut the bathroom door.

"Gross, Mom! You are totally gross! And I'll be using your credit card to pay for the surgery to remove the scars from my eyes." Rachel's drama made Rose smile. *Just like old times.*

Inside the small bathroom, Rose examined the bathtub/shower combo. The tub looked more like a square pot, barely big enough for her to sit in, much less lounge. Rose thought of her spacious bathroom at home, constructed only twelve years ago. *How old is this building?* Probably older than the United States. The designer in her saw the limitations in modernizing centuries-old buildings and appreciated the result. But the tired and still jet-lagged woman would have given a small fortune to have a long soak in a tub right then.

Rose turned on the water and stepped into the hot shower, the water washing away the fog of sleepiness. With her hands flat against the tiles of the shower wall, she leaned into the high-powered spray, the water beating against her forehead as if trying to scrub her brain clean.

Rose stepped out and looked at herself in the mirror over the sink as she reached for a towel. Despite her hours at the desk, she still had a toned physique from all her years of gardening and hiking. And the work this summer had left her tan. The tan lines on her arms and legs from her shirts and socks gave her away as a worker, not a lounger. Rose turned to the side and touched the slight pooch in her belly, thinking maybe she should take it easy on carbs while she was here. But her arms were strong and her butt still firm, thanks to all the bending and carrying in her job. She hired subcontractors to do the majority of the physical labor, but she was still a very hands-on designer.

After drying off, Rose wrapped her auburn hair in a second towel while she slathered her skin with lotion. Living in the desert and working outdoors made this a daily routine if she didn't want to turn into a lizard, and she was glad she'd kept up with it over the years. She wasn't great about styling her hair or wearing makeup every day, but she never skipped the lotion at night or the sunscreen in the daytime. Her devotion to the routine paid off with great skin, and she loved it when people mistook her for Rachel's older sister, even if it drove her daughter crazy. Rose wondered if that would happen today.

Robe belt cinched, Rose stepped out of the bathroom to an empty apartment. Rachel had left a note.

Meet you downstairs for coffee. Please wear clothes.

~ R

Rose laughed, wondering what other ways she would shock her daughter on this trip by being a human woman instead of just a mom.

# # #

"This *spagnolo* we work for has not properly welcomed your *madre* to Italy. Let me make up for his failings as a gentleman and cook you a special meal." Chef Aldo was his usual charming self, a benevolent dictator of the kitchen and upholder of the Italian societal custom.

"*Grazie*, Chef. Mom would really like that. How

about Tuesday night?" Rachel wondered if her mom would still be speaking to her by then.

"*Certo*. It will be my pleasure." Chef Aldo took out a small notebook from his apron and licked the tip of his stubby pencil to make notes, mumbling to himself about ingredients and options. Rachel leaned against the counter and sipped the hot espresso, willing herself to remember this exact moment. Soon she'd be gone and likely never see him again.

Time was running out, and Rachel found herself taking mental pictures all throughout the day: Mateo with the towel thrown over his shoulder and chatting up customers from behind the bar, Lorenzo and the funny expressions on his face when he was in the zone on the dance floor, and even the baker who walked by the window every day with a trail of stray cats behind him, feeding them once they reached the marina with cat food he stuffed in his pockets. Rachel once asked him why he didn't just set out a bowl at the bakery and he told her it was bad for business, but ignoring the cats was bad for his heart. So every day they followed him down to the water when he closed up shop.

The village of Varenna had been just what Rachel needed, even though she didn't know it at the time. The pace of life was slow, but it was real living. Unlike her life back home, these people weren't waiting for anything. The people of Varenna didn't feel the need to work and work until they finally deserved a bit of happiness. They indulged in things that made them happy every single day. Rachel knew if she went back to the United States she'd be in college for four years, followed by work, followed by debt, and then one day she'd wake up and wonder where her life had gone. No, she wasn't going to follow that path, and the only way she knew to avoid it was to stay out of the country. Rachel just hoped her mother would understand.

The one goal since middle school had been to get out into the world, to live a life more like her Auntie Ivy, who worked for the US Embassy in London, but with less pantyhose and boring suits. Rachel wanted to travel, eat strange foods, fall in love with exotic men, and dance under the moonlight on a beach. The desert wasn't a lush enough life for her, and she'd always known it. So while her friends were falling in love with classmates and dreaming of college keg parties and getting married, Rachel was getting a passport and learning about visas. And now all that planning and research was going to pay off. Rachel smiled to herself, snapping back to the present.

"Chef, would you mind taking my mom with you to the market one morning? She'd love to see how you shop for a day's cooking." Rachel took the final sip of her espresso and set the cup and saucer on the counter. The caffeine buzz was in full swing, and she looked at the time on her phone. What was taking her mom so long?

"Of course. She can come with me on Tuesday when we shop for your special dinner." Chef Aldo walked over and stood in front of Rachel, both hands reaching up to her shoulders, brown eyes searching. "What are you worried about, *cara*? I see you have something heavy on your mind."

"You don't miss anything, do you, Chef?" Rachel reached up to pat his hand on her shoulder before grabbing it and holding tight. "Not to get too dramatic, but I'm afraid I'm going to break my mother's heart in order to follow my own." Rachel frowned, looking into his kind face.

"That is the way with parents and children, *cara*. Someone gets a broken heart no matter what you choose. The pain is in picking which heart to break." Chef Aldo gave her hand a final squeeze.

Rachel sighed. *Nothing like a little light morning banter to start the day.*

Mateo walked into the kitchen. "Good morning, Rachel. I seated Rose at the outdoor table with some coffee and a few of the brochures we had about the monastery and the gardens." He looked over the day's menu on Chef's chalkboard and picked up the chalk to change the board outside.

"Thanks, Mateo. I should get out there."

"Oh, did Chef tell you I wanted to have a special dinner for her?" Mateo tried acting casual, but this was not something she'd expect from him. Rachel looked over at Chef, who pretended not to notice.

"What kind of special dinner?" Rachel felt something shift in the room, like there was a secret she wasn't privy to.

"Just something to welcome her to Italy and celebrate your reunion. Do you think she'd enjoy that? I'd be happy to join you and tell her more about the villas and gardens. Rose will probably find them as fascinating as I do, given our similar training." Mateo looked over at Chef Aldo, who remained silent. Rachel wondered why Chef didn't mention that he was first to have the idea, taking credit as usual. Unless it wasn't his idea first.

"That sounds great, Mateo. Were you planning to have this dinner at the same time as Chef Aldo's special dinner, or should I book my mom for two special nights?" Rachel was beginning to get an idea of what was going on here and wanted to see them squirm.

"Chef has already mentioned the idea, has he?" Mateo glared at Chef Aldo. "We thought it would be the nice thing to do. So yes, just one special night. Have you already talked to Rose about it? Because I wanted to suggest it myself."

Rachel raised her eyebrows. "Mateo, are you asking my mom on a date?" She wagged them up and down, enjoying the red flush to his skin. "Hey, boss, you've got my permission, but that's the easy part. You'll have to ask her yourself." Rachel turned to walk out of the kitchen, pausing at the door just long enough to hear Chef's final words.

"Well, I didn't say I'd make it easy for you, did I, Mateo?" Chef went back to chopping.

CHAPTER SEVEN

THE BIRDS WERE loud. With few other competing noises, the sounds of chirping and squawking followed Rose and Rachel throughout their walk to the monastery. Below them the ferry occasionally sounded a horn, warning the pleasure boats away from its path across the lake to Bellagio. Rose stopped to catch her breath, still a little sluggish from the flight and the time change. The first leaves of the season were starting to change color. If she stayed a few weeks longer, Rose knew it would be an explosion of autumn color. Back home in Hobart, there were few trees until you got up into the mountains, and even then they were evergreens. Rose soaked up the many contrasts to her regular life.

A light wind swept a strand of hair across her lips, and Rose pushed it back behind her ears. They were almost to the Villa Monastero, a monastery founded at the end of the twelfth century. The brochure stated there were over two kilometers of gardens with thousands of plant species. Rose didn't know exactly how big that was, but a quick check on her phone showed it to be just over one mile. In Rose's landscape design work, she'd never created anything that large. She hoped to meet a caretaker during their visit because she already had dozens of questions.

Rose looked at Rachel to see if she was ready to resume walking. Annoyingly, she was just waiting on Rose to catch her breath.

"C'mon, Mom. Let's go!"

The garden was revealed to them at the entrance to the grand villa, and in Rose's opinion it was far more interesting than the building, which now functioned as a conference center.

Rose could see the lake from every vantage point in the long garden. The terraces gave depth to the view, and they were filled with all manner of plants due to the mild climate. There were palm trees, more of the vibrant bougainvillea, and even a formal rose garden that smelled like heaven. Rose thought back to the harsh climate of home and her struggles with any non-native plants. How much easier it would be to live in a place that allowed all manner of life to thrive!

Every corner held a delight, and the landscape designer in her silently thanked the centuries of gardeners just like her who molded and shaped this beautiful place over the years. There were quiet spaces for reflection, filled mostly with green plants like shade-loving hostas. Then there were public spaces, surrounded by a riot of colors to spark conversation and laughter. Still others contained small statues, bird baths, and non-floral accents to add texture and interest to the overall design. Rose couldn't imagine being in charge of this gorgeous space, not only creating the garden, but getting to carry out long-term plans and see her creations grow over time. That was one thing that didn't happen often in her current business—clients only wanted basic maintenance after she created their outdoor spaces. These areas didn't usually evolve and change unless a new owner came in, and then it was more like a complete renovation than a growth of her original idea.

Rose took out her notebook and sketched a few of her favorite displays, thinking back to a conversation with Violet about feeding her creative spirit. As usual, she was right. If Violet wasn't too pushy about it, Rose might even admit it to her when she got back. Something deeper pulled at her about this garden, the way it changed and evolved under the care of each successive designer. There was an immediate joy to being here, but also an appreciation of how it had been created over the centuries.

What would the Garden of Rose look like if it was mapped out for the past forty years of her life? No weeds, that's for sure—she was too meticulous for that. But there would be patches of bare earth, the parts of her life she just hadn't planted yet. Romance. Adventure. Risk. Was that a future-stage planting, or a design for someone else's garden?

Better watch it, Rose. Being in this old place is turning you into a philosopher.

The cobblestone path to the villa was good for

working off her morning pastry, and after they finished inspecting the garden and taking in the views of the lake, Rachel suggested they get some lunch across the lake in Bellagio. It was a bit of a thrill for Rose to get on the ferry just to go to lunch.

The horn sounded as the ferry approached the shore, and Rose watched the uniformed attendants expertly clip the heavy rope to the pier and back the ferry in. The small gangplank was lowered by switch and the passengers exited, mostly on foot, but a few were on bikes and motorcycles.

Rachel high fived the attendant and exchanged a few words in Italian as they walked on, already a regular on this route. The ferry pulled away from the dock with a loud blast of the horn, and Rose felt the breeze on her face as they made the short trip across the lake. Looking back to Varenna, she saw the multi-colored houses lining the main street, flowers streaming out the windows. The foothills of the Alps soared in the background under a bright blue sky.

How could Rose live on the same planet as this place? The difference was striking, the barren landscape of her life compared to the lush green of Italy. Maybe she should dust off her passport and travel more. With Rachel grown now, or at least trying to be, Rose had the freedom to see and do more. But she wasn't sure she wanted to do it by herself. Maybe Ivy or Vi would take a trip with her.

Coming back to the present, Rose remembered why she was here and wondered when Rachel was going to confess her big secret about Mateo. The two of them had definitely been playing it cool since Rose arrived. No one would be able to tell they were an item, not even their coworkers. Rose wondered if he was hiding his affair with Rachel or if it was her decision to keep it on the down-low. Or maybe it was all an act for Rose.

Rachel stood next to her at the railing as they watched Bellagio get closer.

"I'm really glad you came, Mom." Rose put her arm around Rachel's shoulder and squeezed.

"Me, too, Baby Girl." She kissed the top of Rachel's head and squeezed her shoulder as they waited for the ferry to dock.

Once they stepped off the boat, it was like a different world from the sleepy fishing town of Varenna. Shoppers carried fancy bags from high-end stores that lined the streets in Bellagio. People on vacation sat out under umbrellas at the numerous cafes, and the buzz of conversation was loud. This town was picturesque in a planned sort of way, like an investor came in and created the perfect quaint lakeside village for vacationers who still wanted access to their shopping and takeaway coffee. Rose might even get away with ordering a venti latte to go here.

Bellagio had a more touristy feel than Varenna. Still, there were more restaurants to choose from and it did give them a different view of Lake Como.

They walked to a restaurant Rachel liked and sat

outside in the warm sunshine on a lakefront patio. Rachel ordered their lunch in Italian. Rose immediately noticed how the waiter looked at Rachel, openly admiring her and trying to get her attention, though she hardly seemed to notice.

When he walked away, Rachel wrinkled her forehead.

"The Italian men are big flirts. Just wait until you're alone. They're only being polite to you because you're with me and they respect mothers. By yourself, you'd be fighting them off." Rachel pulled her sunglasses down from her head, blocking the afternoon sun.

"It's not the Italian men I'm worried about, Rachel. The one that concerns me is Spanish." Rose hadn't planned on starting the conversation like this, but the opening was too good. Besides, Rose was the parent here, and if she was finding it hard to start the talk then Rachel had to be struggling even more. "Tell me what's going on with you, why you're staying here, and what you couldn't reveal on the phone. If you want me to treat you like a grownup, you're going to have to act like one."

"Mom, you've got it all wrong." Rachel sighed, straightened her shoulders, and looked Rose in the face. "Mateo is a nice guy. If you gave him a chance you'd realize it. He just asked me today if he could prepare a special meal for you one night this week to welcome you. You're here twenty-four hours and already I'm your social secretary." Rachel was rambling, going off on a tangent to avoid the real subject.

Rose sat back in her chair, tilted her head, and crossed her arms over her chest. "Mateo asked you if he could make dinner for me? To butter me up, I suppose?"

"Mom, you don't get it. Mateo has nothing to do with what I'm trying to tell you! Will you listen to me?" Rachel's voice rose, and a few people nearby glanced over, wondering if there was an argument in the making or just an exuberant Italian telling a story.

"You're right, sorry. Go ahead." Rose uncrossed her arms in a bid to look more receptive, even if she didn't feel that way.

"Can we just enjoy a nice lunch together, Mom? Let's not talk about any men at all, okay?" Rachel's eyes pleaded with her to agree.

The waiter walked over with their wine and spoke briefly in Italian to Rachel. She started laughing and then thanked him.

"Too late, I guess. See that table over there with the two guys? They just sent this wine over and asked if they could join us." Rachel held up her glass to them, toasting from afar.

"Are they coming over here?" Rose asked. The men were in their forties, obviously fit and rich from their clothes and manner. Rose couldn't say they were her type, but she couldn't help but be flattered by the attention. Ivy would jump on the situation, while Daisy would be more interested in what they were eating. Rose shook her head at the thought of her friends seeing her like this in Italy.

"Don't worry, Mom. I told the waiter to tell them thanks but no. It's been too long since we've been together to share you with anyone else, no matter how good-looking and rich they probably are." Rachel clinked her glass with Rose's. "Here's to new beginnings."

Rose knew the moment had passed for their previous conversation, so she went along with the change in topic. She looked out over the water, taking in the boats floating in the harbor. After a few minutes, she spoke.

"So which yacht do you think we just turned down?" Rose cracked a smile as Rachel took off her sunglasses and strained to look at the fleet in the harbor.

"Definitely the one with the big flag. I think those guys are overcompensating for something. Probably a good thing we said no." Rachel slipped her glasses back on her head, and Rose reached across the table to clasp her hand. There was still a secret between them, but the gap was closing.

CHAPTER EIGHT

"SHIT!" ROSE PUT a hand over her eyes, taking a deep breath. A simple check of email back in the flat was supposed to reassure her everything was okay with her business back home. Not so.

Her biggest current clients, a couple named Henry and Mary, were waiting for new landscaping, a pool, a tennis court, and a pond, all to be started the minute the construction on their new house was finished. Henry and Mary were wealthy snowbirds from Minnesota who picked Arizona as their retirement location. They wanted a place that would attract frequent visits by their grandchildren and friends, and Rose was excited to have such a complex project to come home to.

But now this email from Henry.

Turns out Mary's back pain is actually stemming from her hips, so she's scheduled to have both replaced over the course of this year. We're staying in Minnesota until that's done, so we'll have to put the landscaping project on hold. We really want to be there to oversee it.

~Henry

This was the biggest project on her docket for the next six months, and she already had subcontractors and deposits out for the work, scheduled to begin in November. It was not a big problem for her to cancel the work requests since they were still a couple of months out, but it was a huge problem for her business cash flow as a whole. Rose hadn't recruited more work for the winter because this was going to tide her over until well into the spring, when she usually got a swell of business.

Rose never talked about her work problems with Rachel. She didn't want her daughter to ever worry about their security, even back in the leaner days when it was an everyday concern to Rose. And there was no one else here to talk to. Rose was starting to realize how alone she'd be once Vi moved and she couldn't just drop by her house. But she could still text her. *Big client canceled work. No $ for winter. Maybe I should jump in Lake Como? Talk me down from the ledge, Vi.*

Eight hours ahead meant Vi was just waking up and having her morning tea. Rose tapped her fingers on the desk waiting for a response. It didn't take long for Vi's text to arrive. *You've been in the biz for 12 years. One client cancel won't kill you. But I will kill you if you leave Italy early. Seriously. xoxo*

Easy for her to say. She had a big contract with a

department store for her new jewelry line. Rose sighed and thought about it. What was the worst that could happen? She'd dip into her savings, possibly lose face a little with her pool contractor, and call all her regular clients to solicit some winter work when she got back. Maybe she could get a spot on the local morning news program about winter landscaping and drum up some new clients. Rose's phone chimed again with a text alert from Vi: *You aren't working instead of eating/loving/playing, are you? If so, you don't deserve Italy. ;) I should have come with you.*

Rose laughed, thinking that very same thought. This trip would be easier with one of her friends beside her. But she had to get used to the idea that she was on her own.

The more Rose thought of potential solutions, the more reasonable she became about Henry's email. She replied back with sympathy on Mary's situation and best wishes for her healing. Vi was right. Rose could always find more work, and Mary's hip problem was a far worse one than her business. Rose had to get her head back on straight. She texted Vi back: *Thx Vi, you are a lifesaver. Promise not to leave 'till I've eaten my weight in pasta and seen George Clooney. Wish you were here. xoxo*

Rose lay back on the bed and looked up at the ceiling. When was this adulthood thing going to get easier? At forty she still felt like she was floundering most of the time, and here she was trying to instill some sense of direction in her daughter. Who was she to give advice?

Rose pulled the pillow over her face and screamed into it, kicking her legs on the bed. It was her go-to move for relieving stress, a way to get it out of her system without alarming her daughter when she was a child. Now it was to keep the restaurant patrons below —and Mateo—from thinking she was a crazy person.

Was he downstairs right now thinking about her special dinner? And what was the real purpose? She kicked again in frustration and screamed into the pillow.

"Mom, are you okay?" Rachel stood in the doorway, hand on the doorknob. Rose sat up on the bed, aware of how ridiculous this must look.

"Just working out a little aggression over work. Nothing to be alarmed about, Rach. At least I had my clothes on," Rose said with a smirk.

"Are you sure this is about work? Because I know you're worried about me. I just wish you wouldn't." Rachel closed the door behind her and sat on the bed next to Rose.

"Rachel, I'm your mom. I'll worry about you even when you're as old as I am. Older even." Rose reached around Rachel's shoulder and gave her a squeeze. "Tell me what's on your mind and I won't have to wonder about it anymore. I'll even go to this dinner Mateo has planned and promise not to poison his food." Rachel laughed at this.

"Chef Aldo would kill you for doing that. He takes his reputation seriously, you know." Rachel's weak smile was the first indication she was breaking down, ready to talk.

"C'mon, Rachel. Spill it. I've come a long way at your request. Tell me what's on your mind." Rose was tired of waiting, wondering if Rachel was planning to tell her on the last day when she couldn't raise too much of a stink. "You're too old for me to ground or spank, so let's have it."

Rachel sighed, obviously gearing up for the big reveal. Rose was also ready to hear it, her practiced responses to the problem of Mateo ready to roll off her tongue like a good and thoughtful mother.

"Mom, I'm not dating Mateo, and I never have. He has nothing to do with the decision I've been keeping from you. There is actually no man involved." Rachel took deep breath.

Rose cocked her head and gripped the bedspread with her right hand. She wasn't prepared for any secret other than Mateo, and Rose felt a little unbalanced. Had she missed a clue along the way?

"I've applied for a visa to work in Australia, and it came through. I'm taking a job with a tour company, and I'm leaving in two weeks to live and work in Australia." Rachel cleared her throat and straightened her back, going all in now that the secret was out. "The contract is for one year, renewable for up to three with this visa."

The color drained from Rose's face. "What about college? You're set to start in January! Have you applied for a deferment?" The comprehension was slowly dawning, but not fast enough.

"Mom, I'm not going to college now. I'm not moving back to the US. I'm going to Australia. This is a great opportunity, and I want you to be happy for me." Rachel's muscles unclenched, her spine relaxed, and her jaw released, now that the secret was finally out. Rose could see the stress leaving Rachel's body and crossing over to hers. Rachel did this to her, and it wasn't the same as the other childish disappointments, like a bad grade or breaking house rules.

"Two weeks, Rachel. Two fucking weeks? That's all the notice you give me for this huge decision, one you've apparently been working on for months? You didn't think I'd have an opinion on it?" Rose put her hand on her forehead, as if she could stop the flow of information into her brain.

"Mom, I didn't tell you because I knew what you'd say. Just because you disagree with it doesn't mean it's wrong for me. I can't live my life for you, and you've gotta stop living your life for me." Rachel bit off the last end of the sentence, as if it wasn't supposed to come out. Too late.

"Does Mateo know you're leaving? He's not going to be happy after giving you a free apartment all summer," Rose said.

"I haven't told him yet that the visa came through, but he knows I've been working on something big. Mateo owns a restaurant in one of the most popular destinations in Italy. Believe me, he's used to seeing people come and go." Rachel seemed to be saying it as much to ease her guilty conscience as she did to reassure Rose. "If you want to stay in Varenna I'll make sure the apartment is available to you, and if you want to leave I can talk to my friends at the tour company and find you another place. You should enjoy this beautiful country without me tagging along. Unless, of course, you want to come to Australia."

Rose stood up and smacked the wall with the flat of her hand, immediately regretting the action. These walls were probably three feet thick and backed with stone. Her hand throbbed. "Dammit, Rachel. Do you think life is all one adventure after another, a long trip with no need to work, or plan, or think of anyone else? If you keep living like this, you're going to wind up with nothing. You can't build your life without a foundation!" Rose didn't know how to get it into Rachel's head that she was making a mistake.

"Mom, I'm sorry. I really am. I don't want to hurt you or worry you or make you mad. But this is my life, and I can't live it by your rules. That's your life. And you're the only one who's ever planned on me coming back to go to college and settle down. That has never been in my plan, even when I was in the US. You're the one who filled out my college application, remember?" Rachel reached out and touched Rose on the shoulder as she said the most important thing, the statement she'd obviously been practicing for weeks. "Would you let anyone tell you how to live your life, Mom, even someone you loved?"

Rose felt the wind being sucked out of her lungs,

Rachel using her own words against her. This was her daughter, the one she thought was so opposite from her all these years. And looking across the table, Rose saw the familiar defiance and stubbornness she viewed every single morning in her own bathroom mirror. The only difference was that Rachel's view of what was right for her was completely different than Rose's. Rachel was comfortable with a lot more uncertainty than Rose.

"Rachel, I can't stand the thought of you being so far away. I can't help it; I'm your mom." Rose was fighting a losing battle, it was clear.

"Mom, I'm not nearly as rash as you think. I have a job. I know some people there. I am not venturing off to a penal colony at the end of the earth without a plan." Rachel locked her fingers with Rose's, squeezing tight.

"I knew from the moment you started walking that I'd never have a moment's peace. Before I could ground you or take away your allowance when I didn't like your behavior, but now I have to just watch you go." Rose dabbed her eyes with her fingers, resolving that she would not let Rachel go under a dark cloud. She wanted Rachel to feel like she could always confide in her, even if things went wrong, so Rose had to make peace even if she hated this decision.

"Well, if we only have a short time together we should make it memorable, shouldn't we?" Rose ground her teeth in silence, smile plastered to her face.

CHAPTER NINE

AUSTRALIA! ON A whim! Rose was glad Rachel hadn't met a scientist from a research station in Antarctica or she just might be going to the actual end of the earth instead of the next closest thing.

Rachel went downstairs to tell Mateo she was leaving, and Rose was pretty sure they'd have to leave the apartment. Mateo was going to be upset with Rachel for ditching her job after his generosity toward her, and Rose didn't blame him. She went online to look for last-minute hotel deals and the train schedule to Milan.

Well, at least I got to see one garden, Rose said to herself, bookmarking a few of the pages she'd need to plan their departure.

Rose folded her clothes and began repacking, thinking that she was just as crazy for coming to Italy as Rachel was for going to Australia. She should have stayed home, worked on her business, and maybe signed up for Internet dating or a community college night class to spice up her life. Rose could have been drinking wine and hashing out the details of Rachel's latest decision with her friends, not thinking about Italy and creativity and even meeting a new man. She picked up the new lacy panties and bras Violet insisted she bring to Italy, predicting wild days and nights of pleasure with mysterious men. *I certainly didn't get my money's worth on those,* she thought.

Rose looked up at a knock on the door. "Come on in and tell me how it went," she said, bracing for Rachel's tears or anger. Instead, it was Mateo who opened the door.

"Hello, Rose. I'm sorry to bother you here, but I'd like to talk to you." He looked around at her underwear strewn about the bed. "We can go downstairs if you'd be more comfortable." Mateo was handsome, the afternoon sunlight though the window highlighting the streaks of gray in his wavy dark hair. That would make Rose's eviction just slightly worse, being shooed out of the apartment by such an attractive man.

"Um, no, this is okay. I was just packing up a few things." Rose gestured at her suitcase and realized she was pointing with a lacy peach bra and panty set that was designed for seduction, not support. *Damn you, Violet.* Rose turned and put the delicates on the bed behind her, out of sight. She closed the lid on her suitcase and motioned for him to have a seat on the chair next to the bed.

"Rachel just told me she was heading off for Australia and you weren't very happy about it." Mateo gauged her reaction, deciding how to move forward with the conversation.

"Well, I can't imagine you're too happy about it either, losing an employee so suddenly, and right after she settles her mother into your apartment," Rose said.

"I've been in this business for five years, and one thing I know is that you can't count on anyone to stay forever, especially if they aren't from Varenna. Lorenzo will probably own this place one day, but almost every other person who works for me is from somewhere else, and none of them will stay. I'm used to seeing them come and go. Rachel is an adventurous young woman, and I'm betting Australia is not the last stop on her journey." Mateo said that last line with a smile. Rose realized for the first time that he never was into her daughter. She'd misread all the signs because it was easier to blame someone else than to see Rachel forging her own path, becoming her own woman. Rose felt like a fool.

"If you're trying to make me feel better, you're doing a lousy job," Rose said with a smile. "I know my daughter is growing up and I have to let her go. But I worry about these rash decisions and how she'll handle the consequences. Did you know she didn't even want to tell you by herself that she was leaving? She wanted her mother to go with her! How grown up is that?" Rose felt an ugly cry building inside, but she blinked quickly to stop the flow. That kind of wailing was best done in private.

"We all learn by experience, and you're a good mother for making her realize the consequences of her decisions. But you have to give Rachel some credit: she did it even though it was hard for her, and now she is free to follow her heart. I envy that. Don't you?" Mateo shifted the conversation away from Rachel.

"I wouldn't know, Mateo. I've never been able to follow my heart because I always think about everyone else. First with Rachel and being a single parent, and then with building my business. I didn't have the luxury of jetting off to Australia on a whim or following my heart on anything but the most serious issues, like raising my daughter and building a financial future for us. That's it." Rose's shoulders sagged.

"Well, I just wanted you to know that the flat is still yours while you're here, and I hope you'll both stay. There is no reason to leave before Rachel's new job starts. Spend some time together. Family is important, Rose." Mateo stood, looking down at Rose and surveying the mess of clothes on her bed.

"Thanks for your understanding, Mateo. I didn't mean for us to cause you any problems." Rose was still covering for Rachel as if she were a child who spilled a drink on a friend's carpet.

"It's no problem at all, Rose. Besides, how would you have ever tempted me up to your bedroom to show me your underwear if Rachel hadn't done this?" Mateo started a slow smile, seeming to enjoy Rose's discomfort.

"It's obvious my daughter has had some seriously bad influences since she started traveling, Mateo.

From now on, I'll blame you for her poor behavior." Rose smiled as he walked out the door, and then began crying the minute he shut it.

# # #

"I guess you know I told him." Rachel stood in the doorway of the flat.

Rose looked up at Rachel, much of her anger washed away by the ugly cry. She should be proud of having such an adventurous daughter, and who was she to say that her own way was better? And if the worst consequence was having to buy a ticket back from Australia, Rose would gladly do it.

Rachel walked into the room and sat on the bed next to Rose.

"I'm sorry mom. I know I'm being inconsiderate of you for going to Australia, but if I don't take this opportunity I might not get another one like it. I don't want to wonder what it would have been like for the rest of my life, but it also kills me to hurt you like this." Rachel rested her head on her mom's shoulder, and Rose stroked her hair.

"Don't worry, Rachel. I'm going to be fine. I don't like it that you're going to Australia, but I love it that you're making your own way, even if it isn't the way I'd do it. Don't worry about me; I'll be fine." Rose smoothed her hair and held her like she did when she was a little girl. Rachel was excited and scared at the same time, just like on her first day of school, and she needed Rose to be her rock. Rose could do that.

"I applied for a visa to Australia months ago when I first heard about this job opportunity. I was worried I did all that work for nothing, though the paperwork said I had a year from the date of issue to enter the country. I really didn't think it would happen! But I was prepared to find another way if this one didn't work out." Rachel was nervous to tell her mother this had been her plan for so long, but it all came spilling out.

"I'm actually happy to hear that you've been thinking about this for a while and taking steps to make it happen. I'm less worried now that I know it's not a whim that came up last night. But I have to be honest, Rachel, I'm not happy about you being gone this long or being so far away. I'm going to miss you." Rose was surprised and proud that Rachel did the paperwork on her own to get the visa, and she wondered if she hadn't overlooked a streak of responsibility in her.

"How soon do you think they'll let me have vacation time?" Rachel mused out loud.

Nope, the responsibility gene still hadn't kicked in. But there was plenty of time for that. Rose smiled and kissed the top of Rachel's head.

"When you do leave for Australia?" Rose asked.

"The flight leaves in two weeks from Milan, but I have to get there early to meet with my boss and greet the tour group. We can enjoy Milan for a few days before you leave, maybe do a little shopping." Rachel talked as if Rose would leave just because she was, but Rose surprised even herself with her decision to stay.

"I think I'll do some traveling on my own after you go, maybe explore more of the gardens in Florence and Tuscany for a few days days before heading to London to see Ivy." Rose stopped with that one statement, gauging Rachel's reaction. She watched the realization build in her eyes. "You don't need me tagging along in Milan while you learn a new job, and frankly I wouldn't have a good time adjusting my vacation to your work schedule."

"You can't stay by yourself! You don't know Italian or have a place to stay. Come with me to Milan, Mom. I promise we'll have fun." Rachel grabbed her hands and looked her in the eye, searching for the reason she was staying.

"Rachel, it will be another year before I can even try to swing something like this again." She took deep breath and continued. "You were right: life is for living and I've been ignoring mine for too long. This is the perfect time to relax, unwind, and figure out what I want to do with the rest of my life. Now that you're grown, I don't know what my life is supposed to look like, so it's high time I figured that out."

"Oh my god. You're trying to have one of those Lifetime movie experiences, aren't you?" Rachel put her hand over her mouth. "Single woman goes to Italy and falls in love...cue the sweet music." Rachel grinned. "It would be so much more interesting if you'd just shag Mateo on a table in the restaurant and make it more of an HBO kind of thing."

"Rachel, don't be so crude. My sex life is none of your damn business!" Rose's lips curled up and she slyly looked to the side. "Besides, I'm more of a Showtime kinda gal anyway." Rose started laughing, and after a moment of surprise Rachel did, too.

This was the first conversation where Rose felt like they were interacting as adults instead of mother and daughter, and Rose wasn't sure she was ready for it. It was awkward, but appealing. She thought she could warm to it.

"Mom, I'll try not to gross out that you're thinking of seeing my boss naked. He is pretty hot for an old guy, I guess." Rachel hugged her tight.

"You know, I think we're both gonna be okay, kiddo. I was worried about at least one of us." Rose smiled and squeezed Rachel tight before sitting up on the bed.

"It's a good thing you came here first. My new boss at the tour company has a pot belly and smells like cigars. Mateo is a much better choice."

"Rachel, you realize that I'm not dating any of your bosses, right? I can find my own man." Rose rolled her eyes.

"Whatever you say, Mom. But I think I have good connections in the old guy department. You know how much they're after me." Rachel jumped off the bed before her mother could grab her and spank her.

CHAPTER TEN

MOM, I'VE GONE out with Lorenzo. Rest up and we'll meet back here for lunch. If you need anything, just go downstairs and ask Mateo. Remember, he's not the bad guy, I am. Be nice.

~ R

Rose lay back in bed and held the note up in front of her. A good night's sleep hadn't necessarily changed her opinion about Mateo, even if he wasn't after her daughter. What was a Spaniard doing in Italy alone at this age? He must be running from something. *Be real, Rose. What's an American doing in Italy alone at this age?*

The phone buzzed on the nightstand: three emails from Violet and a text from Ivy. The good thing about having four close friends who were more like sisters was that they were always there to support her. The bad thing about having four close friends who were more like sisters was that they were always there to support her. Rose sighed, wondering how much longer she could put off dealing with their questions.

The phone buzzed again. This time it was Daisy, just saying hi. Lily was working in Africa, so she didn't expect to hear from her anytime soon.

There was no way to put it off, so Rose composed a text message to all of them: *I arrived in Italy thinking I'd be saving Rachel from a bad love affair with a middle-aged Spanish man. (And P.S., when did middle-aged men get to be the same age as us? Something is not right about that.) Turns out she's not screwing Antonio Banderas, but she is moving to Australia to work for a tour company...in two weeks. No college for Ms. Know It All. Feeling like a total failure as a parent, but I guess it's time for her to make her own decisions.*

Rose looked at the screen. What were they going to say to her in response? The best defense was a good offense, so Rose continued typing. *Planning to enjoy the rest of the trip, eat a lot of carbs, and drink wine that doesn't come from a box. Who knows? Maybe I'll even have a fling before I get back on the plane. You'd like that, wouldn't you? Will send a few pics later. xoxo*

Rose hit send and put the phone on the nightstand. Time to get up and face the day. After all, it couldn't be any more shocking than yesterday, could it?

As she stepped from the hot shower another wave of fatigue hit. How did glamorous jetsetters actually live like this? All Rose wanted to do was crawl back in bed, but it was already past noon. What she could use was a strong cup of coffee, maybe even two.

The alert on her phone meant new text messages.

From Ivy: *Rachel is a big girl, and so are you. Need a pic of you having fun soon or I'll have to come rescue you. Not joking, FYI.*

And from Lily: *Good job beats any boyfriend, IMO. But then I'm the cynical divorced one right now. Let it go and have some fun, Rose. Rachel is smart and she'll be okay.*

Vi and Daisy were likely still asleep, so she'd have to wait for their opinions until later.

Rose rubbed her eyes and leaned against the counter at the bathroom mirror, settling her eyes on the pendant around her neck. The wild rose mocked her, glinting at her neck while she sat in the safety of her room, her biggest adventure of the day deciding whether to have one or two cups of espresso.

Rachel was heading to Australia for a new job. Violet had pitched her jewelry design to one of the biggest department stores in the United States and gotten a deal. And even Mateo had left behind his home in Spain to come to Italy. Everyone around her was taking chances, getting a little bit wild, while Rose watched from the sidelines.

Rose frowned, leaned into the mirror, and examined the lines around her mouth. They were definitely trending down. She smiled, an exaggerated clown smile, and saw the difference in her face. *Not bad. Maybe I should get a job at the circus.*

After some makeup magic, Rose decided she'd been a little too harsh. Yes, she had problems taking chances. But she was successful and smart and still a pretty good-looking woman, and a swipe of mascara and lipstick highlighted that fact.

Rose pulled on her favorite dark brown pants that hugged her figure without pinching. She turned to look in the antique mirror in the corner of the room, glad for all the squatting and lifting she did for her job because it kept her butt in great shape. Then she pulled on a navy V-necked shirt that skimmed her waist and drew attention to her face and cleavage.

"Today is the day I start taking risks," Rose announced to the empty room. She clasped her wild rose pendant and looked around for her jacket and purse. Even in her rebellion, she wanted to be prepared.

# # #

Mateo wiped down the counter at the bar, the repetitive movement pulling him into an almost meditative state. How do you de-thorn a rose?

The bragging to Chef Aldo was foolish. Mateo's pride was his downfall and always had been. But then again, he normally didn't have trouble attracting women. The last few years had been dry in terms of a relationship, but he had female companionship whenever he wanted it. Mateo knew how to seduce a woman's body, but he was well out of practice at seducing a woman's heart. Carla made sure of that.

And now he had to convince this Rose to go out with him or lose his pride in the process. Chef Aldo was the village busybody, and he'd relish the idea of telling everyone in town about Mateo's failing in the romance department—and how the failure was due to not following Chef Aldo's advice.

Mateo looked up as the door to the upstairs apartment opened and Rose walked in. She was attractive with her auburn hair loose, eyes alert and sparkling even before coffee. Mateo could feel the sunshine coming off her and surprised himself by his reluctance to speak. Normally he was confident in any situation, but with Rose he felt off-kilter, hyperaware of his every thought and move.

Mateo was the only one working at this time of day and there were no customers in sight. Rose looked around for a table, but then seemed to realized it would be ridiculous to sit away from the bar when there was no one else there. Mateo wondered if Rose felt the tension as much as he did. And then he hoped she did.

"Did you sleep well, Rose? I personally picked out that bed myself." Mateo let that statement linger, enjoying the thought of Rose sleeping on his bed, even if it wasn't the one he used anymore.

"Well, you certainly know your beds then. I slept like a baby. Now I need a little coffee to wake up." Rose took a seat at the bar, oblivious to his innuendo.

"One espresso coming up." Mateo threw the towel over his shoulder and turned his back to Rose, preparing to construct the perfect cup of coffee. First he tapped the handled filter into the trash to dislodge the grounds from the last cup. Then he wiped out the filter and finely ground more beans to fill it. As he tamped down the grounds, he looked over his shoulder. "I'm impressed that you didn't order a cappuccino. Every tourist we get wants a cappuccino no matter what time of day, which gives every Italian a heart attack. The unstated rule is no cappuccino after ten o'clock in the morning." Mateo paused, remembering how well his first cultural lesson had gone with the biscotti, and then grinned. "But you don't care about those rules, do you?"

He inserted the filter into the espresso machine and placed a small shot glass under the spout. With a press of a button the nectar began flowing, two ounces of dark coffee with a perfect layer of *crema* on top, reminiscent of a Guinness beer. Mateo had made thousands of espressos in the past five years, and he was a master. He poured the contents into a small white cup, added a packet of sugar to the saucer, and then turned around to place it on the bar in front of Rose with a small spoon.

"It's an American trait to be a little contrary. We're a country of individuals, even though we're mostly doing the same thing. Are you a typical Spaniard?" Rose took a sip of her espresso without adding sugar, making a soft noise of satisfaction after she swallowed.

Was Mama Bear starting to warm up, to engage in an actual conversation? Mateo leaned against the counter toward her and smiled, feeling his confidence return.

"Not if you ask my *mamá*. I'm a single Spanish man in my early forties living in Italy. She's waiting on grandchildren." Mateo realized he'd never thought of himself as a rule-breaker before, even though there was plenty of evidence. He liked that description.

"So what would your mom tell me about you if I asked her?" Rose took another sip, acting as if they'd always been friendly. Being on her good side felt like admission to a secret club, one he was sure he'd get kicked out of very soon. Visions of imposing nuns, ready to snap his knuckles with a ruler when he looked like he was having too much fun at school, came to mind.

"My *mamá* would complain that I know too much about taking care of myself for my own good, and that's why I'm single. She'd tell you that I live too far away and that I should be designing buildings in Spain instead of serving coffee in Italy. And then she'd ask if you were single, and if you said yes she'd pretend like she never said any of those things and tell you what a warm and wonderful man I am and that I'd make a great husband and father. This is why I don't let my *mamá* fix me up." Mateo flashed his best smile at Rose. When she smiled back he pulled the towel off his shoulder and began wiping down the bar again, an excuse to not look directly at Rose after that intense moment of connection.

"Tell me how an architect from Spain ends up running a restaurant in Italy." Rose took another sip of espresso and looked at him with those intelligent hazel eyes, genuinely curious about him.

"I came here with two friends on a holiday, we saw this little place for sale, and we decided it would be a good investment for three guys who had more money than sense. I was between contracts, so it was decided that I should open it. And I've been here feeding the tourists ever since." Mateo left out the part about Carla, his heartbreak, and his near-monastic love life since he'd been here. "Sometimes I think my business partners forget about me, but then they come to visit and drink up our stock of wine. Makes me feel loved again."

"Your business parters are back in Spain?" Rose's forehead crinkled, revealing a small vertical crease just above her nose. This was her look of concentration, and it was obviously one of her most common. Mateo's friend Alejandro had the horizontal version of this wrinkle, the one that came from worry. The forehead moves in a different way for the two emotions, and Mateo could tell Rose was a thinker, an analyzer. He liked that.

"Yes, Alejandro and Ruben have real lives, as they keep telling me. I'm here babying our investment until it grows up, and then who knows what's next?" Mateo didn't tell her that he'd been thinking about what was next a lot these days. The restaurant business was great, and they were running at a profit, but Mateo craved another challenge. He just didn't know what it was yet.

"So how long until your baby investment is grown?

Even though my business is successful, I'm not sure how I'd ever know it was grown." Rose paused for a moment before adding, "It's not so different from raising a child in that way." She frowned into her cup and Mateo quickly spoke to keep her from thinking about the situation with Rachel.

"You could say that the business is already grown, and I'm just being an overprotective parent. It's still a good fit, I like the people I work with, and as long as I go for a run every day I can keep Chef Aldo from wrecking my figure." He patted his right hip and grinned, leaning on the bar with his left elbow as he watched her sip her coffee.

Rose's face turned pink and she quickly moved her eyes from Mateo's hip up to his face. He felt a faint rumbling of desire, almost as if she'd actually touched him.

"Speaking of Chef Aldo, what's the best dish to try while I'm here? I don't get much Italian food where I live, unless you count Olive Garden."

"I have heard of this place, but I don't understand. Olives are grown in orchards or in groves. A garden is for flowers and plants. Maybe this is a translation problem for me?" Mateo cocked his head as if he were seriously analyzing the problem.

"I don't think I've ever heard anyone question the name before, but I think you're right." Rose giggled. "Maybe I'll call them when I get back and let them know about the mistake."

"I would be most grateful if you'd help me correct

that problem, Rose. But to get back to the matter of authentic Italian food, let's talk about your special dinner tomorrow night." Mateo hoped she still wanted to come after all the drama of yesterday.

The vertical line appeared above Rose's nose again.

"Oh, I completely forgot!" Her eyes were wide, probably realizing how rude that sounded. "I mean, after everything that happened I didn't think you'd still want to do it."

"Of course I do. Nothing has changed for me." He said it with as much intensity as he could muster. "I still want you to experience the best of what Italy has to offer." He paused before adding, "and maybe even a little Spanish surprise." When Rose's face turned red, he knew he'd made an impact.

Mateo turned to the pastry case and brought out a flaky, buttery *cornetto* and placed it on top of a napkin on a white plate. He set it down in front of Rose, waiting for her to speak.

"Oh, well that sounds nice. Thank you." Rose was frustratingly neutral. "What kind of food can I look forward to?"

"Being the boss around here doesn't get me much, you know. Chef Aldo runs the kitchen the way he sees fit. He's in charge of the feast, so you will just have to show up and and see what happens. One thing I can promise is that you won't be disappointed," Mateo said.

Rose's eyes went wide for just a moment before she recovered.

"I'll hold you to that, Mateo." Rose hopped off the stool with a smile, picked up her pastry in the napkin, and waved goodbye as she walked out into the sunshine.

CHAPTER ELEVEN

CHEF ALDO WHISTLED as he walked down the street, bags of bread and tomatoes in his hands to replenish the stock from the day's lunch rush. The tourist shoulder season—early fall and late spring—was an unpredictable time. While he generally knew how many people to expect, the weather often changed behavior patterns. A slightly cloudy day made people stay nearby, savoring morning coffee and pastries, hoping for the sun to peek out before starting their day. A bit of rain caused travelers to stay in Varenna, napping or reading in their hotels and often coming to the restaurant for both lunch and dinner. For Chef Aldo, checking the weather forecast was as essential to his meal planning at this time of year as looking at the reservation list.

Today had been a busy one, with a bicycle tour group extending their stay in Varenna due to a mechanical problem with their transport van. Those people worked up a hearty appetite before they arrived, and Chef Aldo had to serve each person double the portion of an average diner. His supplies dwindled to a dangerous level over the course of their afternoon stay, and since the weekly vegetable market didn't arrive until the following day, he was hoping the bicyclists' van would be fixed before dinner.

Chef Aldo scanned the street for the rugged bicycles used by the groups who rode around Lake Como for fun. There were no bikes, but sitting at the table outside the restaurant was a striking woman, auburn hair tucked behind her ears as she studied a map. *This must be the famous Rose,* he thought. Her pen was poised over a notebook as she made notes, occasionally sticking the instrument in the corner of her mouth. Rose's intensity reminded him of Mateo, and he knew in a split second that she would not be motivated by the usual scent of romance like most people. This woman needed a challenge, and Chef Aldo would have to dare her to take a chance on Mateo. He sighed, feeling the enormity of his responsibility to bring them together. Rose and Mateo were like two peas in a pod, though they didn't know it yet. Time to get to work.

"Buon pomeriggio!" Chef approached the table with a wide smile. "You must be Rose, and I am most definitely Chef Aldo." Rose looked up at him, shading her eyes from the sun. "Please accept my apology for the delay in welcoming you to Varenna. Mateo likes to keep me in the kitchen when beautiful women come around because I make him look like a caveman in comparison." Chef Aldo grinned, showing off his slightly oversized white teeth, the pride of his

appearance.

"Nice to meet you, Chef Aldo. I can see why Mateo would feel threatened." Rose returned his smile with a sly one of her own, appreciating his joke.

He judged her teeth to be good, but not nearly as large as his. Satisfied at his continued dental supremacy, Chef Aldo gave a firm nod of his head and set his bags on the vacant chair.

"Mateo tells me that you have accepted my invitation for a special dinner tomorrow night. It is only fitting that you should sample the best of Northern Italian food while you are in my restaurant. How else will we tempt you to return?" Chef Aldo could see her stiffen at his words, wondering whose idea it really was to invite her to dinner. He enjoyed stirring the pot, whether in the kitchen or while creating recipes for other peoples' lives.

"Rachel and I are looking forward to the special dinner tomorrow night." This Rose was a polite one, but also clueless. Chef Aldo cocked his head to the side.

"You will dine only with Rachel? I was hoping Mateo would join you and share more stories about Varenna, but he's probably made other plans. Every person in this village wants to set him up with their daughter or sister or cousin, not to mention the women on holiday who come through here looking for a summer fling." Chef Aldo paused, letting the visual sink in.

"Quite the player, is he?" Rose had a superior look

on her face, as if Mateo was now proven to be what she'd thought. Time to add a little spice to this pot.

"A player? I think that means a *casanova*, no? In that case, no. But he is a single man in his forties with a good head of hair and a successful business. That makes him almost a god. Even though he is Spanish, many Italian mothers would have him join their families without blinking." Chef paused, watching the wheels turn in her mind. "Mateo likes it here, but I do not see him growing old in Varenna. So he does not take a *Varennesi* as a wife."

"Well then, I guess it's good for him that the female tourists throw themselves at him. Sounds like the perfect job for a commitment-phobic man." The finality of her statement threw him. Chef Aldo expected her to get a little jealous, or at least a little curious. He had to change his recipe a bit.

"Mateo is a very poor catcher of these flying women. I think he waits for the best one." Chef Aldo let that sink in, but only for a moment. "But enough about Mateo. We should be talking about my food, which you will be eating tomorrow night. Would you like to join me on the shopping trip to the market tomorrow? I think you will like it."

"I would love that, Chef Aldo." Rose extended her hand toward his and grasped it, standing to kiss him on both cheeks. "Thank you for the warm welcome."

Chef Aldo turned red with delight, as he did every time a woman kissed him, and told her they would leave the restaurant at 7:00 a.m.

The restaurant door opened and Rachel emerged with a tray of salami, olives, nuts, and cheese: an afternoon *merende*, meant to keep hunger at bay until dinner time. Behind her Lorenzo was holding a bottle of red wine and two glasses. Rachel set the tray down and turned to kiss Chef Aldo on both cheeks.

"I've just had the pleasure of meeting your mother, Rachel. Now I see where you get your beauty and brains. You are a lucky woman to have such a mother." Chef Aldo continued to charm.

"Chef, I don't know how your wife handles your outrageous flirting." Rachel squeezed his shoulders after their warm greeting.

"Rachel, I may cook in a restaurant, but I only eat at home." He winked at her before picking up his bags. "And now I must get to the kitchen. Rose, I will see you tomorrow morning. Enjoy your *merende*." Leaving the wine on the table, Lorenzo and Chef Aldo walked into the restaurant together. Before the door shut, Chef Aldo could hear Rose's question to Rachel hanging in the air.

"So what is the story with Mateo?"

Yes, the recipe was coming along nicely.

CHAPTER TWELVE

ON TUESDAY MORNING, a bleary-eyed Rose walked into the restaurant from the upstairs apartment to go to the market with Chef Aldo. Shades were still drawn over the front windows, casting shadows against the espresso machine and the tiny white coffee cups lining the back shelf behind the bar. She'd hoped to find Lorenzo or Mateo already at work so she could have a coffee before leaving. Chef Aldo was an intense man, and Rose would need fortification to keep up with him.

The bells on the front door tinkled as the key turned in the lock and Mateo walked in. He didn't see her standing there next to the bar, being so focused on his normal routine. Mateo pulled up the shade on the front door, flipping the sign from "chiuso" to "aperto." Then he turned on the lights and walked to the front of the shop to open the rest of the shades. Brilliant sunlight streamed in, bouncing off the polished wood tables and chrome surfaces in the restaurant. Rose felt like a voyeur, wanting to continue watching in private but knowing the polite thing would be to announce herself. She cleared her throat just as Mateo turned around. If he was surprised, he didn't show it.

"Good morning, Rosa." Mateo trilled the "r" in her name, the sound of a purring motor. "I didn't see you standing there. Would you like a coffee? I was just about to make one for myself."

Rose liked the variation on her name, a more exotic version than the one she'd been hearing for forty years. She hoped he'd continue using it.

Mateo shrugged off his jacket and reached for the hanger in the small closet to the side of the bar. Rose thought back to her morning routine at home, arriving at work to the smell of dark roasted coffee in the machine thanks to the timer she set the night before. If it was cool enough for a jacket, she draped it on the back of her office chair. Rose started work within one minute of walking in the door, right after pouring her coffee. Here at the restaurant, Mateo went through a steady pace of activity, a sort of meditative path to the start of his day. Rose knew even without asking that he'd never drink anything from a drip coffeemaker on a timer.

"Thanks, Mateo. A coffee would be great. I'm just waiting for Chef Aldo so we can go to the market." Rose settled on the stool at the bar, staring at Mateo's back as he tapped out the grounds to make espresso at the giant machine. He looked up and Rose could see his expression in the mirror. They locked eyes.

"You're going to the market with us?" Mateo was surprised, but not unpleasantly so. Or at least Rose hoped she had interpreted his expression correctly.

"Oh, I didn't know you were coming, too." Rose cringed a bit, hearing how rude it sounded after she said it. She quickly continued. "Chef Aldo invited me to shop for the food we'll be eating this evening. It sounded a lot more fun when he invited me than it did at six o'clock this morning when my alarm rang."

"Chef likes to arrive early. I usually go with him so we can split the list and get the best selection of produce and fish. No matter how good a cook he is, if the raw ingredients are second-rate, it will be reflected in the food." Mateo was matter-of-fact, willing to accept an early wake-up call to ensure the best food for his key employee. As a business owner, Rose could respect that kind of commitment to producing a quality product. Maybe he was a *casanova* with an MBA. "I hope you don't mind that I'll be joining you."

"Of course not, Mateo. I just didn't realize, that's all." Rose felt like an idiot. They stopped talking while the espresso machine buzzed. Mateo turned and placed the finished product in front of her, a small shot of dark espresso that went to work in her bloodstream with just one sip. "You're quite the dedicated restaurant owner. I don't know of many who would go food shopping with their chef." Rose paused before taking another sip. "Honestly, though, I don't know many restaurant owners. But I do know a lot of architects. How did you make the transition?"

"Chef Aldo would tell you I still haven't." Mateo raised his eyebrows as he sipped his own espresso.

"But I think of food much the same way as I do buildings. There is a plan for how it will be used, a solid foundation to create upon, good building materials, and a pleasing final look. It's all the same, really."

"So is it easier or harder for you to be a restaurant owner?" Rose asked.

"Easier in many ways, because I have the chance to recreate my success every single day. Harder in some ways because I have the chance to recreate my success every single day." Mateo set his cup on the counter. "In my old career, I came in, designed a building, and then walked away after completion. Owning a restaurant is more of an ongoing commitment, and I like the idea of growing something over time."

Rose grew bold from the caffeine.

"A handsome single man with a thriving restaurant who likes commitment? Better not let the word get out or you'll be mobbed." Rose looked him in the eye, waiting for his response. She was testing Chef Aldo's opinion.

"Did I say commitment? Please don't quote me or every *mamá* in Varenna will be on my doorstep again, their poor daughters in tow." His eyes softened and he leaned on his elbow at the counter. "I feel sorry for them, actually. The daughters want true love, and their mothers want security for them. These young women resist the matchmaking as much as I do. You should always hold out for love. I'm still young enough to remember that. Barely." Mateo crinkled his forehead in fake concentration.

"True love, huh? Forgive me for being a blunt American, but that sounds a little sappy. I'm not sure I felt that way even when I was Rachel's age." Rose surprised herself with the admission. "Don't get me wrong; I love love. I'm just not sure we're all cut out to have that soulmate experience. I'm probably a lot more like the *mamás* in this village, though I tend to prefer creating my own security rather than waiting on someone else. Call me a realist."

"What is the difference between a cynic and a realist?" Mateo picked up their empty coffee cups and put them in the sink. Rose raised an eyebrow in response. "A cynic makes herself feel better by calling herself a realist."

"Looks like I'm not the only blunt one in the room, Mateo." Rose wrinkled her forehead in concentration, cocking her head to the side while analyzing his latest comment. "And you know what? You're probably right. I'm a bit more cynical than I was a few years ago. Love hasn't always been generous to me." Rose was uncomfortable with this line of talk, so she decided to turn the tables. "It sounds like you have a different experience, Casanova. Spill it. Why are you holding out for true love?"

Mateo's face drained of color, and Rose could see she stepped in further than she should have. They were talking in generalities before, and she just brought up something personal. Rose didn't know if he'd answer her question or tell her it was none of her business. Which technically, it wasn't. Mateo surprised her by responding.

"Five years ago *El Croquis*, the premier Spanish architecture magazine, had just done a big profile of me. They called me the most creative architect to come out of Spain since Antonio Gaudi, a flowery compliment I do not actually deserve. But there was a lot of press, a big photo spread, and a description of me as the talented architect with movie star looks." He snorted. "My friends never let me forget that line, you can be sure." Mateo shook his head and continued.

"I didn't think anyone outside the architecture world would notice, honestly. I had a fiancée named Carla, my career was riding high, and then Spanish celebrities started coming around. I went to parties with futbol players and actors and even once a fancy dinner with the King of Spain. It was crazy. Sometimes I felt like I was living inside a warped Dalí painting."

"Sounds like you had everything you wanted. Please don't tell me you got caught cheating in front of the paparazzi." Rose watched him visibly recoil, instantly regretting her flip comment.

"I did have everything I wanted, and no, I did not cheat. Not all men do, you know." His faced hardened.

"I'm sorry, Mateo. I shouldn't have said that." Rose lowered her voice, removing the snark.

"Carla cheated on me, with a man not as famous, successful, or handsome. She left me because she found true love. And I realized then that as happy as we'd been together, there was something more out there. Something Carla found, and something I should still be looking for."

"Mateo, that's terrible. I can't believe she cheated on you." Rose didn't know what else to say.

"This many years after the fact, I don't hold a grudge. But I do wonder what Carla found that was better than what we had and why I haven't found it yet. So that's why I'm a believer in true love, even though I've been kicked around by it a little myself." Mateo looked up as the door to the restaurant opened. Chef Aldo was whistling as usual.

"*Andiamo!* I spotted the chef from Bellagio outside. We have to get to the market before he picks the best fish." Chef Aldo waved them both to the door.

# # #

Chef Aldo toured the market stalls like a king surveying his subjects. Once he found the best produce, he circled back to order, reminding the grocers in no uncertain terms not to hide bad tomatoes underneath the good ones—or at least that's what it sounded like to Rose. The intensity of Italian communication was still overwhelming, what with all the gesturing and raised voices. She couldn't tell if people were arguing or chatting most of the time. Rose hoped it was chatting, because otherwise the entire market was going to turn into a street brawl.

They ordered a wheel of parmesan cheese as big as a steering wheel, and Rose mentally calculated how much that would cost at home as well as how long it would take to use it. Chef Aldo told her he would go through that much cheese in just a few weeks at the restaurant.

At the fish stall, Chef Aldo explained the different varieties fished from Lake Como: lavarello, which was a small whitefish normally fried or sautéed in sage and butter; along with shad, which was a fish more suitable for salting and marinating; and then the more familiar types like trout and pike. Back in Arizona, Rose usually avoided the fish counter at her grocery store, reasoning that people living in a landlocked area should not be preparing fresh seafood at home, especially when fished out of a refrigerated case in a tray of styrofoam and covered with plastic. But here with Chef Aldo, on the shores of Lake Como at an open-air market, she was ready to try them all.

Rose walked next to Chef Aldo and Mateo followed behind, the aisle too crowded to walk three abreast. As Chef Aldo narrated their tour in between shouting greetings to friends, she felt her heart expand. At this moment, in this place, Rose was as far from her regular environment as she could imagine. She was in Italy! For a moment she lost herself in thought, easy to do because she couldn't understand most of what was being said around her. Of course Rose knew she was in Italy; she had been for days. But in that moment, she felt a strange combination of freedom and permanence course through her whole body, a deep seating of her soul. She'd stopped thinking about Rachel's life so much and started focusing on her own. Her friends were right; she needed this trip.

Rose's feet were connected to the earth where the produce grew. The breeze on the lake ushered the scent of marine life to the shore, a pleasant combination of fish, fresh air, and algae that she absorbed into her body with every breath. Rose drank red wine grown from nearby vines, many of which were older than she was. And the gardens surrounding her were designed by people who'd been doing her same job centuries before computer programs, excavators, and dump trucks. There was a continuity in Italy she hadn't experienced before, a connection between the past and present, the earth and the people, the sea and the air. For the first time in a long time, perhaps ever, she felt grounded. The sensation was as fleeting as it was intense, and Rose grasped at the wisps of the feeling as it left her body.

What was that all about? And where do I find it again?

Rose wasn't the woo-woo sort, at least not in the mainstream way. She was far too practical for that. But as a landscape designer, Rose knew that flowers bloomed differently—or not at all—depending on where they were planted. Now that she'd been planted in Italy, she was feeling new sprouts of growth, a different reaction to the sun, the water, and the soil than back in her native Arizona. Rachel's decision to live and work in Australia instead of going to college weighed less heavily on her in Italy than it would have at home. Over here, it seemed an acceptable risk, an option a reasonable person could take. In Italy, Rose could let go of control a little bit more. Being honest with herself, she could let go of the *act* of being in control, because she never really had been in the first place.

What other changes would the soil, water, and sun of Italy make in Rose? She wondered at the possibilities, feeling more open and less anxious than usual. Even Mateo, the man she originally thought was a lecherous jerk after her daughter, was starting to intrigue her. Here was a guy publicly humiliated by love, and yet he still wanted it. Rose in America would have mocked him for his naiveté, but the Rose blooming in Italy was curious and wanted to learn more. How do you maintain your thirst for vibrant love when you've been in a desert, surrounded by weeds, and deprived of water?

At once Rose was awakened from her reverie by Mateo, who touched her upper arm to guide her over to a quiet corner while Chef Aldo chatted with a friend.

"Want to know a secret?" Mateo asked.

The Rose growing in Italy did find herself curious about what was going on in his mind. Would he talk more about his breakup with Carla, and his ideas about true love? Would he reveal some centuries-old European wisdom about life and love? Maybe even kiss her? She shuddered at the last thought, wondering where in the hell that came from.

"I'll never tell...I promise," Rose said, feeling the need to prove her trustworthiness. She held her breath, waiting for his revelation.

Mateo pointed to the stall in front of them, stacked with bottles of olive oil.

"The olives in that oil mostly come from Spain. It kills me that Italy gets all the credit for great olive oil when it comes from our trees." Mateo shook his head and looked at her, obviously waiting for her reaction.

Rose giggled, at first a quiet whisper of a laugh and then a full-on comic bark. Thirty seconds prior she had waited for him to impart the wisdom of the ages or to kiss her, and instead he wanted to reveal a secret about the poor marketing practices of Spanish olive growers. Rose bent over, hands on her knees, while tears streamed from her eyes and she struggled to catch her breath. Mateo looked on with alarm, probably worried she was having some kind of meltdown.

A few moments before she had been rooted to the earth, feeling at one with Italy and all her non-Italian ancestors. Then she looked for deep meaning in a comment from a man she previously wanted to castrate. And in this moment, it all came streaming out of her, a load of stress and worry that had been years in the making: building her business in a male-dominated industry, raising her daughter alone, watching Rachel grow up and leave, seeing her friends go off on adventures without her, and feeling like love had passed her by.

The dam broke, and all that tension came flooding out, destroying everything in its path. Poor Mateo didn't know he was drowning in her release.

Rose stood up and reached into her bag for a tissue, first wiping her eyes and then blowing her nose. She knew she looked a mess, but Rose felt lighter and better than she had in memory.

And she had Spanish olives to thank for it.

"I'm so sorry, Mateo. I had no idea your secret was going to affect me like that." Rose grinned, wondering what his reaction would be. The owner of the stall poured a small bit of olive oil into a sample cup and offered it to Rose, and she waved him off, feeling the laughter coming on again. If the mere news of Spanish olives being rebranded as Italian was enough to set her off, what would drinking the stuff do? It was all she could do to hold it in, unsure where this giddiness was coming from but feeling the waves of relief from it all the same.

Mateo ran one hand through his hair and put the other on his hip, staring at her.

"It is a relief to me that you understand the severity of this problem, Rosa." He said it with a straight face, but it took only a second for him to break character and grin.

"I couldn't tell you why I did that, but I can tell you it felt damn good." Rose again wiped a tear from her eye as the laughter subsided. "There is something about this place that moves me in a different way, and I'm feeling a little bit unbalanced." She quickly added, "But in a good way." No need to make him think she was coming unhinged, even if that was the truth.

"Balance is overrated, Rosa. Sometimes you just have to let go and venture out into the void if you want to get to your destination." Mateo offered his arm and Rose put her hand in the crook, feeling the tightness of his bicep press against her fingers. Just ahead of them, Chef Aldo stood with his arms crossed, foot tapping, waiting for them to catch up.

# # #

The group text was simple, in the same shorthand style the five friends had been using for years to communicate. *411: Complete meltdown at market in front of Mateo and Chef over olive oil. Looked like a dork, but it felt GOOD. Big dinner tonight at restaurant. Should have packed a muumuu to go with my sexy undies. xoxo*

The first response came from Ivy, who was in the same timezone: *Let it all go! And then check out the boss for yourself, Muffin Top. :) See you in London soon.*

Rose took a pinch of her waist and thought about the dinner coming up tonight. No way she was going to turn down a specially prepared meal like that, even if it meant a little spillover from her pants. That was one gift of turning forty: finally accepting her body and knowing that the balance was an overall thing, not a daily thing. Rose would work off any weight she gained after she got back home.

Daisy was next, probably still in bed as she typed: *Send me food pics! And man pics! And YOU pics! Hugs to you and Rach.*

Rose could picture Daisy's enthusiasm, her typical joy at every little thing in the world and an almost obliviousness to the big stuff. It was a strange combination, but it worked.

Rose threw the phone on the bed and decided to get ready for dinner. She and Rachel had gone for a run in the afternoon along the waterfront, working off a lunchtime bowl of pasta, and she was happy to have made some room for tonight's feast. There was so much food to try here that Rose had a hard time figuring out how she'd fit it all in.

The water pressure was good, but a long shower was not in the cards in this old building. Whether it was a small boiler or ancient plumbing lines she didn't know, but Rose made her shower quick to preserve hot water. As she toweled off she thought of her conversations with Rachel since she revealed her big secret, the slow gathering of understanding and acceptance that was coming from her decision to move to Australia. Rose was still a long way from liking it, but she had made considerable progress in learning to keep her opinions to herself. Rachel was growing up, and barring any life-threatening situations, she'd have to let her navigate her life the way she wanted to.

Rose had three dresses hanging on the hook of her closet door, and she stood in front of them for a while wondering which to wear. She didn't want to go overboard, but she didn't want to show up too casual, either. The dark purple one would better hide stains, and she was a notorious food dropper. The deep orange one showed off her hair, but it was a little snug. The red one was probably way too sexy to wear at a dinner with her daughter, but she knew it looked great on her. Rose could feel her overthinking begin, so she went with the comfort of the purple.

Rose admired the result in the mirror. The way the dress criss-crossed her breasts and wrapped around her waist made her look curvy while still holding in the evidence of her carb indulgence. Even she had to admit it was one of her best looks. At her neck, Violet's wild rose necklace caught the light, reminding her she had a reputation to live up to.

Standing in front of the full-length mirror, Rose snapped a photo to send to her friends with a short text message: *Eat your heart out, Italy. I look great AND the dress expands. Bring it on!*

Rachel knocked on the bedroom door and opened it, catching her mother in the act of laughing at her own photo.

"Wow, Mom. You look great!"

"I'm just looking the part of a woman traveling in Italy, my dear." Rose flung out her hip and ran her fingers through her hair dramatically.

"Okay, Sophia Loren. Let's get you to dinner." Rachel turned to walk out the door.

"How do you even know who Sophia Loren is? Aren't you too young for this kind of cultural information?" Rose was teasing her, but also a little impressed that she knew of the Italian movie star.

"Oh, Mom. I'm learning all kinds of things on this journey. You have no idea." And before Rose could ask what she meant by that, Rachel opened the door of the apartment and started downstairs to the restaurant.

CHAPTER THIRTEEN

MATEO WATCHED THE restaurant start to fill up, Lorenzo expertly managing the tables and Chef Aldo's food coming out of the kitchen with perfect timing. Mateo loved it when things flowed so well.

Most diners didn't appreciate the rules of a well-run Italian restaurant, and he had only learned them himself five years ago. The wine was served with food, always. It was the same in his native Spain, but since he'd never worked in a restaurant before he hadn't appreciated the reasoning behind it. As Chef Aldo often said, "Food without wine is a corpse; wine without food is a ghost; united and well-matched they are as body and soul, living partners." For a long time Mateo thought Chef Aldo was a poet trapped in a chef's body, and he spent hours at the old man's side learning about Italian food and customs. One day Lorenzo revealed Chef Aldo was actually copying verbatim the wisdom of the gourmand Andrè Simon. Leave it to the young to shatter the illusions of the old.

Still, Mateo admired the Slow Food movement, a new thing in other parts of the world but very much a way of life in Italy for centuries. Eat local foods, in season, with an appreciation of what it took to bring them to the table. When stated so simply, it seemed a shame that it even had to become a "thing" for people to follow. But fast food was killing the enjoyment of eating, and Mateo considered it part of his mission to show diners how a good meal with friends and family could replenish the spirit. He only hoped they would take this lesson back to their home countries.

One of his favorite things about Italy and his home country of Spain was the enjoyment of a meal with other people. In Italy the saying was, "*a tavola non s'invecchia,*" which meant that one does not age while at the table. Eating was about more than just food. Dining with other people was about the exchange of ideas, the nourishment of your soul and relationships, and a way to properly appreciate the life cycle of the items that went into the making of the meal. Dining time should always be at least twice as long as it took to make the meal, something it was hard to convey to tourists. They always seemed in a rush to feed their bodies, and in the process never got the benefit of feeding their spirit.

Mateo looked around the restaurant, which was half-full. Not so bad for the start of the slow season, especially at the early hour of eight o'clock in the evening. He knew more people would be trickling in over the next hour, but the only one he really wanted to see was Rose.

The idea of her eating in his restaurant gave him a

thrill, and not just because he was making progress on his bet with Chef Aldo. He wanted to know what was going on in her head, why she'd laughed so uncontrollably at his comment about the olives. There was something simmering beneath that crown of auburn hair.

Mateo wondered if Rose would invite him to join them for dinner, since he'd so stupidly said the special dinner was for her and Rachel. He'd already given the heads up to Lorenzo to manage the house if he sat down at their table, something he sometimes did when VIPs came to dine.

At that moment, the door to the upstairs apartment opened and Rachel came out. Mateo waited for Rose to follow but didn't see her. Rachel walked over to the bar and put her elbow on it, chin resting on her hand.

"You look like you lost something, Mateo. Anything I can help with?" She was torturing him, and he knew it.

"Just scanning the room like I always do, looking for signs of trouble. It seems I have found some right here at the bar." Mateo wouldn't give her the satisfaction of admitting his longing.

"Mom went back to get her scarf. Don't worry, she'll be here." Rachel smirked at Mateo and turned as the door opened again. Rose walked in the restaurant and even the noisy Australians at the front table stopped their conversation for a moment too long to be considered polite.

Rose smiled nervously at the attention and then

walked over to Rachel and Mateo at the bar.

"You should probably get that door fixed so we don't make such a noisy entrance into the restaurant during mealtimes," she said.

"Oh, I don't think it was the noisy door, my dear Rosa. You look stunning tonight. I may have to dim the lights to keep people focused on their food." Mateo tried imagining Rose with her hands in the dirt or wearing a hard hat on a construction site. He thought of the landscape designers he worked with back in Madrid, regretting that none of them ever looked like Rose.

Lorenzo walked over to show Rose and Rachel to their table, one in the corner of the room away from the bar. He lit the candles as they sat down, informing them that Chef Aldo had prepared a special menu that night and he would bring out the food as it was ready, so there was no menu for them to choose from.

"It is a slower night than usual. Signora Quinn, if you'd like I can invite Mateo to join you for dinner to better explain Chef Aldo's creations and Italian culture. He is a filthy Spaniard, to be sure, but we have cultured him over the years." Lorenzo smiled and looked over at Mateo by the bar, who gave him a look of warning. Ever since that dare from Chef Aldo, Lorenzo had grown bolder toward Mateo.

Rose looked over at Rachel, who shrugged her shoulders as if she didn't mind. Rose paused a little too long at the offer, and Mateo didn't realize until she answered that he'd been holding his breath.

"Lorenzo, thank you for the offer. We'd love to have Mateo join us for dinner." Lorenzo brought another chair over to the table and set the glassware and flatware from the sideboard. Mateo gave him credit for trying not to make it look too planned.

Lorenzo wagged his eyebrows at Mateo as he walked away from the table.

"The lovely ladies in the corner requested that you join them for dinner. I promised them that an uncultured savage such as yourself had been tamed by the Italians and that you'd be happy to share what you've learned. Don't embarrass us or we'll have to ship you back to Spain." Lorenzo placed the tray on the counter, untied his apron, and straightened his shirt. As the acting manager, he had to look the part.

"Thank you, Lorenzo. I'll do my best. If it gets to be overwhelming, just flip the closed sign over on the door. I'm okay with losing a bit of business tonight." He gave Lorenzo's shoulder a squeeze as he rounded the bar to walk over to the corner table.

# # #

"I see Lorenzo sat you at the corner table next to the window, no doubt to attract every man on the street to this restaurant. I should give him a raise for being so smart." Mateo stood at the table, waiting to be formally invited to join them.

"The main man we're interested in attracting tonight is Chef Aldo." Rose smiled and motioned for him to sit down with them.

As if the chef overheard them, they soon had plates of prosciutto-wrapped melon seasoned with mint, balsamic vinegar and lime in front of them along with their first glasses of wine.

"This is the *antipasti* course, and Chef Aldo has chosen one of my favorites. I think of this as summer in a bite." Mateo liked playing this role of teacher to Rose and wondered if she liked being his student. "Go on, try it."

"Mmm, delicious." Rose closed her eyes and made a slight noise as she ate. The sweetness of the melon was offset by the sting of the balsamic, then wrapped in the salty goodness of the prosciutto, topped off by the refreshment of the mint. Mateo knew Rose tasted summer, too.

"Mom, you're doing it again," Rachel said under her breath. She looked over at Mateo and said, "Mom can't eat without making noises. If she's starting this early, it's going to turn into a concert before we're done." Mateo was a little put off at Rachel's comment, but Rose still hadn't said anything.

"I think Chef Aldo would be pleased to know you enjoy his food so much. I know I am." Mateo smiled across the table at Rose, enjoying the way she looked in the candlelight.

Rachel stared into her plate, probably feeling like the third wheel on a date. That's certainly what Mateo considered her.

As they all continued eating their bites of summer,

Mateo tried to explain the Italians' preoccupation with digestion.

"This country is ruled by its guts. The fear of indigestion is what drives the food rules the Italians live by. Balance and harmony are the goals. The cool melon we just ate was offset by the salty prosciutto. Without this balance, the Italians fear indigestion or illness in the body." Mateo wasn't sure how far to take this discussion of indigestion over dinner. Would Rose be as fascinated by the roots of these customs as he was?

"I like knowing what works and what doesn't. I think there's a lot of freedom in knowing where certain boundaries are." Rose sipped her wine, noting just how much better it tasted when paired with a handsome man.

"No way, guys. Think about it: someone had to push the boundaries to figure out what works and what doesn't. And no one gives credit to that person for experimenting enough to sort this all out. I'm much more interested in eating my melon with a bunch of different flavors to find out what I like." Rachel continued being a contrarian.

Mateo and Rose smiled at each other. They both remembered the fire of youth and the need to rebel, but they were also just old enough to realize that it wasn't necessary to spend all one's energy testing every single boundary. Where Rachel wanted to test everything, they wanted to test the right things.

This, Mateo thought. *This is why I want a woman*

like Rose. She gets it.

As their plates were cleared, Mateo explained that they were getting smaller portions than normal because Chef Aldo wanted them to experience every course, something they would not normally order.

"This is why the Italians don't get fat," Rose said, thinking about the muumuu she forgot to pack.

Next up was the *primi*, or first course. Plates of risotto alla milanese were placed in front of them, and Rose commented on how yellow the dish was. She said she'd always had white risotto.

"Your risotto is yellow because it is seasoned with saffron, which is what gives it that earthy scent. You'll also notice the dish is served with Parmigiano-Reggiano cheese, from the wheel we bought this morning. Lots of customers ask for extra cheese, which is something many outsiders don't understand about Italian cooking. However the chef serves it to you is how it should be eaten. The meal is complete as delivered. We get people in here all the time who ask for extras and it drives Chef Aldo crazy. If the dish needs it, he provides it." Mateo couldn't wait to hear Rose's reaction to the texture and flavor of the risotto. He wondered if he should tell her the onions were softened in a pan with bone marrow rather than butter.

"So if you're a control freak, you should be a chef," Rose said to Mateo as she took her first bite.

"Well, I don't know about that. But leaving it up to an expert means you don't have to bother yourself with the details. I don't have to think about what else I need for my meal and I can instead concentrate on my dining companions and feeding more of my soul. It's more about priority than control." Mateo thought about his instruction to Lorenzo to close the restaurant if it got too busy for him to manage alone. He was definitely exercising his priorities tonight.

"So the Italian way of life is to give your guests exactly what you think they need to enjoy themselves. What do you think I need, Mateo?" Rose only had a couple of sips of wine, so Mateo knew it wasn't the alcohol talking. Before he had to answer this question, though, Rachel stood up from the table.

"Hey, guys. I'm already full; I had a big lunch today and I'm a little tired from our run. I'll pop in and let Chef Aldo know I'm done and leave you two to enjoy the rest of the meal." She threw her napkin down on her chair and beat a hasty retreat, not even pausing for a response.

"Okay, honey. I'll see you upstairs later. Love you." Rose reached for her wine glass and asked Mateo again, "So what is it that you think I need, Mateo?"

CHAPTER FOURTEEN

"THE FIRST THING every smart man learns is not to predict what a woman wants. What he should do instead is listen to her and then follow her wishes. The trouble comes from guessing." Mateo raised his glass toward the kitchen. "Luckily for us, Chef Aldo does not have to guess about what two adventurous eaters will like."

After finishing the *secondi*, a course of fragrant pan-fried lavarello fished from the waters of Lake Como and simmered in dry white wine, Rose and Mateo enjoyed a dessert of frittelle di mele, or apple fritters. These flat donut creations were sprinkled with sugar and melted in Rose's mouth.

Talk was less bold and more thoughtful once Rachel left, as if they knew the stakes were higher without an audience. They laughed comfortably with each other as they told funny stories from the past.

"No, really. I grew up in a sort of informal commune. My mom and her friends had all been part of this farm. They had this idealistic view of how the world should be, and they were going to make it happen. The problem was, they weren't so good with money back then and they lost the farm before it could make a profit." Rose shrugged her shoulders as she took another bite of her apple fritter.

"It's hard to know the consequences of your actions when you're that young. Or maybe even when you're older," Mateo said.

"Well, I have to hand it to my mother. She didn't let the experience spoil her ideals. She and her friends just created their own kind of commune right in the middle of town, sharing houses and child-rearing duties and even money when needed. Over time there were husbands and other kids and jobs and regular life, but I always felt like I had five mothers and four sisters and a lot of love. I wish Rachel had the same thing, but none of my "sisters" ever had any kids. Just me," said Rose.

"Our families looked different, but my childhood was much the same, a big extended family where everyone fought and loved and stuck their noses into each other's business. Every single adult in my family was a parent to me, and most of them still think they are." Mateo smiled warmly at the thought of his family in Madrid.

"Now you're here in Italy and your family is back in Spain. And my sisters are spread all over the world. We see each other about once a year in person, and the rest of the time it's just text and email. I definitely miss them, but they can be nosy!" Now that Rachel was leaving, Rose realized just how much she needed her friends.

"You are telling them about your adventures in Italy?" Mateo grinned. "I hope you've said good things about us. About Italy, I mean."

"I've been instructed to send pictures of me, men, and food. If I don't, they won't ever believe I came here. They'll give me a hard time about it until I'm eighty years old." Rose took another sip of wine.

"Do you have your phone with you, Rosa?"

Rose reached down for the phone in her purse on the floor. "But we already ate everything! There's nothing left to photograph." Rose threw her hands wide over the table, barely missing her wine glass.

"You have left a bite of your fritter, and you are sitting at a table with a man. You have the trifecta— you, food, and me—all in one shot." Mateo scooted his chair closer to hers as they posed for a selfie. Rose could feel the heat of his body next to hers, a not unpleasant sensation. She wanted to lean into him, to inhale the scent of his skin and hair. *Must be the wine getting to me,* she thought.

"You know, this feels like a date. And I haven't been on a date in a long time." Rose's voice dropped to a sexy murmur as she felt her daring coming back.

"You've come a long way for a date, Rosa." Mateo spoke softly, trilling the "r" in her name the way she'd grown to love.

"Or maybe you've been waiting a long time for me to arrive. Women can be so slow to get ready, you know." Rose traced the rim of her glass with her finger while looking into his eyes.

Lorenzo walked over with two small glasses of Fernet-Branca and silently laid them on the table. A signal passed between Lorenzo and Mateo, a brief sign that he was locking up and going home. Soon Rose and Mateo would be alone.

Rose picked up her glass and swirled the dark liquid. She raised her eyebrows at Mateo, waiting for the explanation.

"This is Fernet-Branca, a type of amari. After dinner, the Italians believe that an alcohol with bitters will help stimulate your saliva and start the digestive process. Remember what I said earlier: Italy is ruled by its guts." Mateo smiled and lifted his glass, taking the first sip.

"Hmmm. It tastes a little bit like cough syrup to me. Not unpleasant, but certainly not like the Vin Santo I had with the biscotti when I arrived," Rose said.

"Well, I like to end all my dates with a good dose of cough syrup." Mateo brought the topic right back to a date.

"I hope that's not all." Rose decided to follow the Italians' lead and go with her own gut on this one. "If you don't kiss me, how will I know it was even a date?"

Mateo leaned over and put his hand on the back of her head, gently pulling her toward him. His lips were soft, contrasted by the friction of his sexy beard. Rose opened her mouth slightly, tasting the medicinal flavor of the Fernet-Branca they'd both ingested. It was strong, but not unpleasant. Perhaps the cure for what ailed her?

She felt his hand gather her hair at the back of her neck, holding it tight as he explored more of her mouth with his own. This man was a delightful kisser with just the right touch. Rose vaguely wondered how he became so good at it.

When they pulled apart, Mateo brought his hand around from the back of her head and used his finger to brush away the remnants of sugar still on her upper lip. He licked the sugar from his finger.

"Delicious," he said.

A warm glow spread over her, little hairs standing at attention all over her body. The heat settled in her pelvis, and Rose decided she had never wanted a man as much as she wanted this one now. The night had been a revelation, a rejoining of the adult human race after years of mostly parenting and working. Rose felt as if she'd been plunged into a pool of warm water after shivering in the cold.

But her daughter was upstairs, Lorenzo was at the bar, and she was not going to sleep with a man she hated just a few days ago, no matter how sexy he was in this moment, in this light. It was too much, the risk a little bigger than she was ready to take. Rose stiffened, breaking the connection with one move.

"This has been a wonderful evening, Mateo, but I should go upstairs while I'm still in control of myself. Please give my compliments to Chef Aldo. And thank you for joining me. I mean, us." She made sure to refer to Rachel, hoping he understood her hesitation. With all the care and attention Chef Aldo took to feed her and keep her from upsetting her delicate digestive system, her gut still clenched at the thought of opening herself up again.

"Of course, Rosa. I enjoyed it, too. Though you should know I think control is overrated." Mateo's desire for her was evident.

"I'll keep that in mind, Mateo." Rose stood and picked up her scarf and purse, knowing if she touched him again she'd change her mind. She quickly made her way over to the bar where Lorenzo was finishing up.

"Thanks for everything. I'm off to sleep now. Good night." Rose quickly opened the door and leaned against it, trying to compose herself before climbing the stairs to the apartment. She could hear the muffled voices of Mateo and Lorenzo behind her.

"If you were Italian, you'd still be at that table with her." Lorenzo was trying to be funny, but Mateo wasn't laughing.

"If you were smart, you'd mind your own business," Mateo grunted. The howl afterward was likely the result of a playful punch on the arm.

Rose put her hand over her mouth to keep from laughing, and then she slipped off her sandals so she wouldn't make any noise on the stairs. At the top she opened the door to find Rachel reading a book in bed.

"You were so right, Mom. That evil guy Mateo

clearly has an agenda, and I certainly hope you can do something about it." Rachel smiled at her mom, and then turned out the light.

# # #

Lying in bed in the dark, Rose reached for her phone. She couldn't talk to Rachel about her pseudo date with Mateo, but she could talk to her friends.

Rose typed: *You asked for pics of food, men and me. Will this do?*

She attached the picture of her and Mateo with the almost empty plates at dinner and clicked send, waiting for the responses.

Daisy was first: *Hey, we didn't get to see what you ate!*

Violet was next: *Um, yeah, I think we just did, Daisy. Hope you wore your new undies!*

Ivy jumped in: *Hope he tore those undies off with his teeth!*

Daisy: *Do you guys even care about the food at all? Barbarians.*

Ivy: *D, there is eating, and then there is being eaten. ;-)*

Daisy: *You had to go there, didn't you, Ivy?*

Ivy: *The more important question is, did MATEO go there? Ha!*

Lily chimed in: *Just landed in Ghana and LMAO at this exchange. Way too tired to play it cool and everyone is staring while I snort. Good for you, Rose!*

Violet finished the exchange: *You look gorgeous, Rose. Wildness suits you. xoxo*

Rose snuggled deeper under the blankets, keeping the light of her phone from waking Rachel. She was lucky to have these women in her life, this irreverent and loving crew of friends who'd be with her 'till the end, whether she liked it or not. Rose wouldn't trade this made-up family for the world.

Rose responded to all: *You guys are the best. No sex, but great food and convo. Plus a kiss. You were all right: I needed this trip. Will keep you posted. Nighty night.*

CHAPTER FIFTEEN

SIMONA GREETED CHEF Aldo at the door of their home, kissing him softly and taking his coat.

"I have soup on the stove. Are you hungry?" In their own home, Simona did all the cooking and food shopping. Chef Aldo was simply her husband Aldo once he walked through the door.

"Simona, I am always hungry for anything you have to offer me." Chef Aldo grabbed her in a big hug and squeezed, feeling the cushion of her body against him. "You smell like sage, my love. You know that drives me wild." He nuzzled her neck while she giggled.

"Come inside, Aldo. Tell me about your evening." Simona grabbed his hand and pulled him toward the dining room, table already set. She ladled the steaming soup into his bowl. "How was the big feast?"

"I will humbly admit it was some of my finest work, Simona. If those two cannot find love over these dishes, there is no hope for them." Chef Aldo picked up his spoon and took a sip of the soup. "Mmm, delicious as usual. This is the perfect amount of onion to flavor the soup. You always know how to please me." He winked at her and reached under the table with his free hand to squeeze her knee.

"What did Rose and Mateo talk about?" Simona sliced a loaf of bread fresh from the oven, the warm smell of yeast filling the room. Chef Aldo's favorite place in his home—besides the bedroom—was this very room, the place where he and Simona connected over food and drink. Over the years, they'd laughed, fought, and made big decisions in this room. And not coincidentally, it was often the room they shared right up until bedtime on the nights they made love. Chef Aldo adored his wife, her strong will encased in a soft body, a devilish sense of humor behind the face of a saint, an interesting woman who was interested in everyone else. He still couldn't figure out how he landed her so many years ago, he with the big teeth and already balding head at twenty, but he knew his life would not be half as good without her.

"I couldn't hear them talk, but Lorenzo told me Rachel left right after the *primi*. Rose and Mateo were laughing and at one point he saw them kiss. It must have been my apple fritters. They can make anyone fall in love." Chef Aldo reached for his wine, the warmth of the liquid coating his tongue.

"Be careful who you serve the apple fritters to, my love. I wouldn't want anyone else to fall in love with you. I don't know if I'm tough enough to fight them off anymore." Simona pretended to be scared for just a moment, and then released one of her funny little laughs, a combination of hiccuping and snorting. It was so terrible it was adorable, and one of the quirks Chef Aldo loved most about his wife.

"I would bet on you in any fight, Simona, but you will never have to worry about that." Chef Aldo patted her hand on the table. "I told you Rachel is leaving for Australia soon, no? Rose is upset that Rachel is not going back to America for school. I don't know if Mateo and Rose will be able to connect as long as Rachel is still here to worry her mother."

"Maybe Rose will stay after Rachel leaves for Australia? I would love to see Mateo find a good woman. It is no good for him to be alone." Simona shook her head for emphasis.

"Lorenzo served the two of them the *digestif* when I left, and there was no one left in the restaurant. Maybe the romance has already begun." Chef Aldo wagged his eyebrows up and down salaciously.

"Speaking of romance, I've already turned down the bed. Why don't you take a shower while I clean the dishes and I'll meet you there?" Simona cleared the table while she spoke.

"An excellent idea. Let's stop wasting time talking about someone else's love when our own is so much more interesting." Chef Aldo kissed her cheek and then raced up the stairs, humming in anticipation of the night's dessert.

CHAPTER SIXTEEN

SHIT! RACHEL THREW her phone down on the bed. Just when things were starting to mend with her mom, this had to happen. Damn the Italians and their preference for talking instead of emailing. If her new boss hadn't put her on the spot, she could have figured a way out. But on the phone? Ugh. Who actually talked on the phone anymore? Neanderthals, that's who.

Rachel paced the room, knowing her mom would be back any second. *At least the call didn't come while she was here,* Rachel thought. She replayed the conversation in her mind, wondering what she could have done differently.

"Rachel, what do you think about starting your new job early? The tour leader you were assigned to has been diagnosed with mono, so we need to put you on a different tour that starts next week. You are ready to start, no?" Carmine waited patiently for her to agree, and Rachel could hear him puffing on a cigar in the silence. Nonsmoking rules were still a relatively new thing in Italy, and in Carmine's office they would never be enforced.

Rachel didn't know how to respond. She was quick with her wit in a conversation, but she was not yet quick on her feet with negotiations. She stammered, trying to think of what her mom did when clients tried to change things. Unfortunately, she hadn't paid such good attention over the years.

"Um, so what does that mean in terms of schedule?" Rachel knew as soon as she said it she shouldn't have gone to logistics so quickly. Carmine must have thought she was already agreeing.

"You'd leave from Milan in three days, but I'll need you here tomorrow morning for orientation and then the next day to meet your group at the hotel. Then the flight to Sydney to meet the tour leader." Carmine stopped for an audible puff. "And remember, the time difference is ten hours, so it would be smart to start adjusting yourself now so you won't be too jet-lagged to help guide the group." Carmine laughed. "You know how hard it is to manage us Italians even in the best of circumstances!"

Rachel laughed along with him, mind racing as to how to explain this to Rose. Rachel didn't feel like she could turn this down, not at the very start of her job, and she desperately wanted to live in Australia. The tour would be the first of many, but in the future she'd meet all her guests at the airport in Sydney, refreshed and relaxed and, most of all, experienced.

When she decided to apply for this visa and job earlier in the summer, she imagined days off on the beach and work days of fun leading Italian people around Australia. It was going to be a low-stress job, a way to have fun at work. As it was now, she hadn't even officially started and her stomach was in knots. By the time the call was over, Rachel agreed to all of Carmine's terms and said she'd see him tomorrow for orientation with the group. Some negotiator she was.

As Rachel sat slumped in the chair thinking over her situation, Rose opened the door to the apartment, grinning from ear to ear and holding a piece of paper in her right hand.

"Chef Aldo gave me his fritter recipe! Violet is going to die when I make this for her." Rose walked over to her suitcase at the end of the bed and tucked the recipe into the outside pocket. "I was thinking we'd take a little ferry ride around the lake and find a place for lunch. I still can't get over using a boat like a bus!" Rose turned around and looked at Rachel, waiting for a response. "Honey, why you are you so quiet?"

Rachel took a deep breath. There was no way out of this but through it, so she blurted the news as fast as she could.

"My new boss just called. They want me to start the job tomorrow because the other tour guide has mono. I didn't know how to say no." Rachel's eyes watered, worried about her mom's reaction.

Rose paused, then sat down, pursing her lips. She took a deep breath and let it out, then shrugged her shoulders.

"Real life 101, kiddo. Things don't always go the way you planned." Rose put her hands on her knees and stared at Rachel, who then began to cry. Rose moved next to her and hugged her, stroking her hair like she did when Rachel was a child.

"I thought you'd be mad at me!" Rachel wailed.

"Well I'm certainly not happy, but I'm not mad at you, Rach." Rose pulled the hair away from Rachel's face and wiped the tears away with her thumbs. "But there's one thing you should know."

"What is it, Mom?" Rachel's voice was serious, matching the tone of her mother's. Rose pointed at Rachel's side of the room, covered with clothes and shoes.

"If you think I'm gonna help you pack that mess, you'd better think again."

# # #

"You move like a turtle, Mateo!" Chef Aldo raised his arms, right hand holding a giant wooden spoon that dripped tomato sauce on the floor. "I will be an old man by the time you win Rose's heart."

"Chef, I don't want to continue the bet. And it's not because I don't think I can de-thorn this Rose; it's because I think I can. And I don't want it to be like that." Mateo picked up some basil on the cutting board and sniffed, filling his nostrils with the scent of Italy.

"He finally starts using that brain in his head," Chef

Aldo said to no one in particular. He stuck the spoon back in the pot and stirred. "What will happen if he starts using his heart, too? *Mio Dio*, he might actually find happiness!" Chef Aldo played to his invisible audience, speaking as if Mateo wasn't even there. After all these years Mateo was used to Chef's drama, and he leaned against the counter to enjoy it.

"I don't know if it will turn into anything at all, but I'm willing to try. There's still ten more days before she leaves, and I think we can make a lot of progress in that time—at least enough progress to see if it is worth continuing." Mateo knew Chef was waiting for some credit, a token of appreciation for the work in preparing that first dinner together. He threw him a bone. "Chef, thanks for making the special dinner last night. That's what changed my luck, you know."

"Of course I know that, Mateo. I'm just glad you recognize it." Chef Aldo wiped his hands on his apron. "Now get back into the restaurant and take care of business. We can't go broke while you're in here pouring your heart out to me." As usual, Chef was long on talking and short on listening.

Mateo walked into the restaurant and surveyed the crowd. Half-full on a weekday afternoon in late September wasn't too bad. Lorenzo had things in hand, so he stepped behind the bar to check reservations for the evening. Mateo looked up when he saw the door to the upstairs apartment open. Rose walked in, wringing her hands.

"Rosa! Can I offer you some lunch before you go

out, or are you cheating on Chef Aldo with another restaurant today?" Mateo's smile faded when he saw she wasn't in a joking mood. "What's wrong?"

"Mateo, I have some news. Do you have a minute?" Rose's voice was steady but quiet. Mateo walked them over to a small table by the cleanup station and they sat down.

"Rose, you look so sad. What happened?" Mateo reached out and put his hand over hers. She smiled at him before withdrawing her hand and putting it in her lap.

"Mateo, I've had a wonderful time in Italy, and you've been so generous to me and Rachel. I had hoped to get to know you better...you know, after I got over the desire to kill you." Rose gave a nervous laugh.

"You still can. I'm not going anywhere. And if I do I'll walk really slow so you can be sure to catch me." Mateo flashed his brilliant smile.

"That's just it. I'm the one going. Rachel just found out that her new job starts a week earlier than expected. She's leaving for Milan today, so I'm going first thing tomorrow." Rose frowned, followed by a sigh. Mateo was so glad he didn't have children, because at this moment he wanted to throw Rachel in the lake for making Rose so unhappy. He took a deep breath and instantly reversed his decision, thinking Rachel just became his best ally in winning Rose's heart.

"Why do you keep trying to break up with me

when I haven't even asked you out on a proper date yet? There is a lot more medicine in my cupboard." Mateo grinned, reaching across the table to touch her arm. "Just because Rachel is leaving doesn't mean you have to, Rose." Mateo's voice was steady, delivering his invitation with as much care and compassion as he could muster. He knew if he oversold it he'd sound sex-obsessed, but if he soft-pedaled it she wouldn't think he meant it.

"What else would I do? The whole reason I came to Varenna was to see Rachel," Rose said.

"And you have. Her leaving and you staying are two unrelated things, Rose. Rachel doesn't need you to leave when she does. It won't matter to her because she'll be in Australia. She's following her heart, and you can follow yours." Mateo reached across the table and put his hand on Rose's forearm. "I'd love it if you'd want to stay here, with me, even for a little while."

Mateo's heart beat rat-a-tat like gunfire in his chest, waiting for her response.

"You want me to stay here just to spend time with you?" Rose's words hung in the air.

"Well, not just to spend time with me. Italy has a few things to offer as well, I'm sure." Mateo spread his arms wide. "I felt something this week, Rosa, and I know you did, too. We'll both regret it if we don't see where it leads. I don't want to add to my list of regrets, do you?"

"Stay in Varenna? On my own?" Rose talked out loud, seemingly more to herself than to Mateo, turning the idea over in her mind.

"Yes, I want you to stay so we can get to know each other. I know it sounds a little strange, but the flat is vacant until October 15. I think we can have a really nice time together. And there's no reason for you to rush home and miss all the beauty and culture in Italy just because Rachel decided to go to Australia. She made her decision, so you need to make yours. What do you say, Rosa? The flat is yours to use, and you can come and go as you please, no strings attached."

Rose tilted her head and narrowed her eyes, the faint vertical line above her nose showing her brain at work. When the line softened, she looked him in the eye and said, "I was hoping there would be a few strings, Mateo."

Mateo took the hint and came around the table, pulling her up from her chair and putting his arms around her. He leaned forward, brushing his soft whiskers against her face as he pressed his lips into hers. The kiss was soft and gently curious, a promise of more to come.

"You know we've only kissed in your restaurant. Don't you find that a bit strange, especially given that you've been in my bedroom already?" Rose's voice was low and husky, just inches from his face.

"Please don't tell Chef Aldo. If it is in any way related to food, he'll take all the credit." Mateo laughed and squeezed her tight before releasing her.

"It's settled then. I'll stay for a while and we'll see

what happens. No rules, no expectations, just playing it by ear," said Rose.

"Oh, but there is one rule I'll have to insist on," Mateo said.

Rose raised her eyebrows, wondering where he was going with this. "And that is?"

"I may not have kissed you in your bedroom, but I did see what you were packing. You'll have to wear those lacy panties, Rosa. Even if I don't get to see them, I want to know you have them on." Mateo squeezed her again and then walked back to the kitchen, a new spring in his step.

CHAPTER SEVENTEEN

HOW DO YOU say goodbye to your daughter and hello to a new adventure? While Rachel packed her bags, Rose sat on the bed, legs crossed like a teenaged friend. The angst and drama after her arrival had dissipated over the time in Italy, the highs and lows mellowed out to an even keel.

"You know, I'm starting to think you don't want to live with your mother for the rest of your life, Rachel." Rose handed her a stack of folded T-shirts.

"Really? I was trying to be subtle." Rachel smirked at her mom, enjoying the camaraderie of the evening.

"Why do you have so many T-shirts? I counted twenty-five." Rose could remember when everything Rachel owned had been bought by her.

"Most are to remind me of an experience, like a concert or a place I visited. And some I just like. Remember, the seasons are flipped in Australia. I'm leaving fall in Italy to arrive in spring in Oz. If I don't want to do laundry every week, I'll need a lot of T-shirts." Rachel said it like it was the most practical thing in the world.

"Why wouldn't you do laundry every week, Rachel?" Rose was genuinely curious to hear her answer.

"Mom, I'm traveling for work for two weeks at a time. On my days off, I want to go to the beach and make new friends. I do not want to obsess over my laundry when there's fun to be had." Rachel's logic did make a certain amount of sense, though Rose couldn't imagine not doing her laundry for weeks at a time.

"You are turning into an extraordinary woman, Rachel. I admire the way you think. But please don't turn into a dirty hippie while you're gone." Rose pretended to sniff her folded clothes and hold her nose.

"If only you could be one of those indulgent, hovering moms who comes over once a week to clean my house, cook a week's worth of meals, and do my laundry. Or, better yet, pay someone else to come do it. That kind of meddling I can handle." Rachel walked into the bathroom to pack her toiletries, including the honey shampoo Rose smelled when she first hugged Rachel on arrival.

"Fat chance, kiddo. I'm a meddling mom in the most modern sense of the term. I'll only nag you and hover around your life with texts and emails. You can wear dirty clothes and keep a filthy house and I'll never know unless you invite me for a visit—in which case I hope you will clean house before my arrival." Through all the joking, Rose was fishing for a clue to what their relationship would be like going forward.

Rachel turned around and sat on her suitcase, barely zipping the overstuffed bag.

"I was hoping you'd come to visit on my first vacation next year. I'll try to find a more attractive boss by then for you, because Carmine is pretty gross with his big belly and cigar breath. I can send you pics before you buy your plane ticket to make sure it's worthwhile." Rachel grinned, obviously enjoying this new level of friendly banter in their relationship.

"I'm not too picky. Something along the lines of Hugh Jackman would be just fine." Rose pursed her lips. "Seriously Rachel, does it freak you out that I'm going to stay here for a while?

"Mom, it's weird as hell. But it would be weird no matter who you went out with. Mateo is a good guy. He's a whole lot more interesting than that dud Steve you used to date." Rachel pulled her bag off the bed, informally weighing it in her hands. Rose knew without a doubt she'd be paying overage charges. "I'm glad you're dating, Mom. Really, I am. You should get out more, though I think Italy is probably too far to drive for a relationship. But still, have fun while you're here. That's what vacation is for."

"You know, I think we're both going to be just fine, Rachel." Rose stood up to hug her tight, not wanting to think about the fact that it could be a year before she'd see her again.

"I never doubted I would be, Mom. And I never doubted it about you, either." Rachel let go and turned toward her purse. "Oh, I almost forgot. I have something for you. Close your eyes. Hold out your hands."

Rose felt the package drop and opened her eyes: a box of condoms, ultra-sensitive and ribbed...*for her pleasure*.

"Rachel, I'm still your mother!" Rachel fell back on the bed laughing, only stopping when Rose continued in a sly voice. "Besides, what makes you think I didn't bring my own?"

"Ewww! Mom, you are so gross." Rachel covered her ears.

"Don't forget, Rachel. I've been a woman a lot longer than you have." Rose smacked her on the leg. "Hop up and let's lug this bag downstairs. You don't want to miss your train. Destiny awaits."

With the subtlety of a freight train, the two women managed to get Rachel's suitcase down the stairs. While Rachel said goodbye to Chef Aldo and Lorenzo, Rose walked over to the bar and sat down, watching her little girl prepare to leave.

"You look like you could use a drink. Or maybe four." Mateo reached out to touch her arm. "This can't be easy for you, Rose. But you know she's going to be okay. Rachel is a smart and resourceful young woman, just like her mother."

Rose put her hand on top of his and smiled.

"It's not an easy day for me, but it isn't as bad as I thought it would be. You're right. She's a good kid. I did all that I could to raise her, and now it's up to Rachel to gain her own experiences." A few tears rolled down her face, the kind of bittersweet cry that doesn't require sobbing. "I really am okay. Promise."

Rose stood and walked over to Rachel, ready to walk her into her new life. And then, Rose would do the same.

CHAPTER EIGHTEEN

MATEO LIVED IN the heart of Varenna, a second story flat overlooking Lake Como and the mountains beyond. The town buzzed with activity below as people went to dinner at the various restaurants, and Rose could see why Mateo chose this place to live instead of the more isolated villas up the hillside.

"I'm happy you accepted my invitation, Rose. There are just too many eyes in Varenna, especially at my own restaurant. I want us to have the time and space to get to know each other." Mateo put his hand on her lower back, guiding her to the door of his building.

"And here I thought you were just trying to seduce me in my emotional state." Rose fluttered her eyelids before bursting out with a laugh.

"Oh, that can certainly be added to the schedule, *cariño*," Mateo said with a sly smile. He tossed his key on the table and walked into the small but sleek kitchen to pour them some wine and light a few candles.

Rose fluttered with excitement at the new

nickname, which she liked even better than Rosa. She really had hit the romantic jackpot to be in gorgeous Italy with a sexy Spaniard. People wrote books about this kind of experience, and here she was living it. Rose imagined herself as the heroine of a romance novel, Mateo her sexy love interest. Now that would be a page-turner!

Rose wore a green dress with a halter neckline that she bought in Varenna, one that hugged her curves at the top and flowed over them at the bottom. The fit was supportive enough that she didn't have to wear a bra, but she added a lightweight gray cardigan for modesty. If she made it to the cover of a romance novel, she'd definitely take off the cardigan.

The wild rose pendant shone at her chest just above the swell of her breasts, and Rose caressed it as she looked around the flat, taking in the spare but sleek design. While minimal, Rose could see he paid attention to textures and quality. The modern white leather Barcelona chairs complimented the slender tan couch and small round glass coffee table. The fuzzy gray rug underneath the table gave sharp contrast to the rich wooden floor below. The fireplace in the corner was empty on this early autumn evening, but she admired the dark chimney over the heavy wood mantel. Rose looked at the cashmere throw on the back of the couch and imagined wrapping herself in it as she drank coffee on cool winter mornings.

Mateo interrupted her thoughts with the delivery of a glass of wine. He then walked her through the living area to the double doors leading to a balcony outside. On the table was a domed plate of olives, cheese, and cured meats. Mateo uncovered them with a flourish.

"When did you have time to do all this?" Rose asked.

"You forget that I own a restaurant. Chef Aldo will feed your belly tonight while I take care of everything else." Mateo smiled.

They toasted and sipped their wine, looking out over the lake at the mountains beyond.

"The sunset view must be stunning from here," she said.

"Yes, but I am so often at the restaurant at this time that I miss it. Maybe you will encourage me to spend more time on this balcony in the near future." As Mateo said the words, Rose was thinking the same thing.

They sipped their wine and talked comfortably about the scene in front of them, the expansive lake and the people below. The evening was growing cooler, and when Rose wrapped her arms around herself to stay warm, Mateo put his arm around her shoulder and drew her close to him.

"I hate to leave such a beautiful spot, but I'm getting cold, Mateo. Can we go in?"

"Your wish is my command, Rosa. I have a feast waiting for you inside." Mateo smiled, and Rose wondered if there was a double meaning of that phrase.

Rose took a seat on the couch, placing her wine on

the table and unwinding the scarf from her neck. The music had transitioned to Spanish love songs. Rose couldn't understand everything they were saying, but she could pick out a love song in any language. As the evening grew darker, the candles cast more shadows in the room. Mateo busied himself in the kitchen, plating the pasta dishes like a pro and carrying them to the table.

"That smells delicious, Mateo." Rose shrugged off her cardigan and walked over to the table. Mateo stood at the table with a bottle of wine in his hand.

"And you look delicious, *cariño*." Mateo poured more wine before taking a seat across from her.

The dinner conversation leapt well ahead of where they were just that morning, as they talked about deeper subjects than expected on an official first date.

Rose told Mateo about some of her past relationships, including the local politician Steve. He laughed when she told him Steve put her on his email fundraising list after they broke up.

"Dear Concerned Citizen, can I count on your support even though you've kicked me out of your life? Your donation means no hard feelings, right?" Mateo showed no trace of jealousy at her stories, only an interest in what she had learned from those relationships. Though he did seem to enjoy the breakup portion of each story the most.

The banter with Mateo was easy, and they talked more about why he came to Varenna in the first place.

"I was the only one between jobs and without a

relationship, so it made sense for me to open the restaurant after we bought it. After that, I just stayed on. It was a weird time of transition in my life, without Carla, and this became a quiet place for me to hang out, away from the nosy attention of my family. I think I just needed some time. But maybe I've gotten myself stuck in transition." Mateo took the final sip of wine from his glass and looked at Rose. "The breakup really did a number on me, made me question everything I thought I knew. I'm just now starting to trust my judgment again." Mateo slid his hand across the table and grabbed hers.

Rose blushed at his blatant honesty, not quite sure where to focus her attention. This is what she had missed in the superficial relationship with Steve and every other man in recent years, and now that she had it, she wasn't sure what to do with it.

Mateo stood and pulled her up close to him, circling her waist with his arms as she reached her arms around his shoulders. They kissed gently at first, the same curious exploration as in the restaurant, and then with a pressing urgency.

Rose and Mateo moved backward as one unit from the table over toward the couch, still kissing and caressing each other. Rose kicked off her shoes when they stopped and clenched her toes in the shaggy rug. Every nerve in her body was on high alert, waiting for some kind of signal. With one more deep, searching kiss from Mateo, Rose pulled him down to the couch with her.

Rose straddled him, feeling the soft cotton of his pants on her bare legs. Mateo moaned softly as she kissed him, the heat of their bodies together raising the temperature in the room.

Mateo grabbed her hips with both hands as he scooted forward on the couch. He put one hand on the arm of the couch and stood up while Rose gripped his waist with her legs. Rose squealed in surprise, clenching her legs tight around him as he gripped her ass with his hands. No man had ever handled her like that.

Mateo took a few steps forward as Rose nuzzled his neck. He smelled like fresh soap mixed with a fine layer of sweat, a combination that spoke directly to her own body chemistry. The message: *We belong together.*

As Mateo walked across the room and toward his bedroom, a small sound, so tiny it could barely be heard above the music. Rose stiffened.

"What's that noise?" she asked.

"What noise? I don't hear anything." Mateo's breathing was labored, his eyes heavy with desire.

"Dammit. That's my phone. It's probably Rachel." Rose awkwardly unwound her legs and plopped down to the floor. Her dress was stuck in the waistband of her peach panties, the ones Mateo asked her to wear, and she quickly yanked it free to cover herself. Rose hurried over to her purse and picked up her phone, keeping her back to Mateo. A text from Rachel: *Made it to Milan. Have fun with my boss...but not too much! Will call tomorrow. -R*

"Everything okay?" Mateo tucked in his shirt while she wasn't looking, smoothing out his appearance.

"Um, yeah. Rachel's in Milan, no problems. I just worry, you know." Rose slowly put her phone in her purse, wondering what would happen next. She was standing barefoot on the carpet, a completely different sensation on her toes than just moments before. Rose turned around and sat on the couch, elbows on her knees and chin in her hands. "I guess I sorta killed the mood, didn't I?" She looked down at her feet, embarrassed more by her sudden display of passion than the awkward way she ended it.

Mateo walked over the couch and sat next to her.

"I'd give you a solid 9 for the dismount. Had you done it without a clothing malfunction, you'd have scored a perfect 10 in the Mateo Olympics. Besides, I blame Rachel entirely." He said it matter-of-factly, waiting for Rose to get his humor. She was grateful to him for giving her an easy way out of the embarrassment.

"Yes, we should blame Rachel entirely. Though without her we'd never have met, and I'd never have had a chance to show you my smooth moves." Rose picked up her cardigan and put it back on.

If they'd been a couple, this would have been the moment they started kissing again, resuming the passion from before. But Rose still didn't know what they were, or if they'd be anything at all. The silence lingered.

"Why don't I make us a coffee? I'll walk you back to the restaurant and we'll have it there." Mateo was either the gentlest gentleman on the face of the earth or he was letting her down easy. Rose was anxious to get away, to examine her thoughts and motivations a little more deeply. She might have just ruined everything, or she might have dodged a bullet. It was so hard to know, to trust her instincts when everything around her was changing.

Rose knew she couldn't sit across from Mateo and drink coffee, not after grinding his pelvis and then throwing cold water on their date. That face, those eyes, that hair—he was appealing to her, but she wasn't sure if it was real or just an overload of emotion from the day. This was moving way too fast, though what she was waiting for she had no idea. Rose needed a quick chat with her friends to figure out what in the hell was wrong with her.

"That sounds nice, Mateo, but coffee will just keep me up. Do you mind if we call it a night after you walk me back? I think the day was just too much for me." Rose hoped he would agree, but not too much. She wanted to know if he wanted to see her again as much as she wanted to see him. "Besides, you've given me a lot to dream about already."

"Of course, Rosa. Next time we'll start our date earlier like the old people in the village. Perhaps a dinner at 4 o'clock in the afternoon, followed by a game of cards and a stroll along the water to feed the pigeons with our day-old bread? Then we can watch soap operas on television with the volume turned all the way up until we fall asleep snoring in our chairs." He smiled at her as she jabbed him in the side with her elbow.

"I don't think old people can move their hips like we just did, even at 4 o'clock in the afternoon." Rose winked at him as she picked up her purse and they walked out into the cool evening.

CHAPTER NINETEEN

"MY, MY MY. Look at what the cat dragged in." Violet clucked at Rose, grinning at her disheveled appearance on the laptop screen. She took a sip of tea and continued. "I was wondering when you'd check in live from your frolicking in the Italian countryside."

Rose couldn't help but laugh, feeling immediate comfort in the presence of her good friend, even if she was thousands of miles away.

"Oh Violet, I think you might be right. There are cobwebs down there, and I'm starting to worry they'll never get brushed away!" Rose pulled her hair back from her face with her fingers and wrapped an elastic band around it.

"Tell me what's going on, Rose. It can't be as bad as you think." Violet calmly sipped her tea from her sunny office in Arizona, quietly enjoying the drama of Rose's situation. For years Rose had been the steady one, working hard, raising her daughter, and only indulging in safe and casual love affairs, relationships destined to fail because there was so little connection. Violet liked seeing her a little deranged by life and love, knowing she was shaking loose from the ties that were holding her in place. Ever since they were kids, Rose had looked out for everyone else, waiting for who knows what to go after her own desires.

"Where do I start?" After a long sigh, Rose told her the entire story of Rachel, ending with her leaving to Milan that night.

"Okay, so your baby has flown the coop, you two had a moment of understanding before she left, and it sounds as if you're in a good place. So why the crazy hair and wrinkled clothes? You should have turned off the video if you only wanted to talk about Rachel, my dear." Violet smiled, waiting for the real story to come out.

"Mateo came to my room after Rachel's announcement and asked me to stay in Italy. There is definitely a spark between us, no doubt. So he asked me to stay for a while just to see where this takes us, no strings attached." Rose paused, letting that sink in.

"No strings? Was that his suggestion or yours?" Violet asked, already knowing the answer.

"I'm doing this my way, Violet. But I am doing it. Just give me a little space, okay?" Rose felt her defenses rising.

"You're right, Rose. I'm just trying to understand. Keep going." Violet backed off, seeing this was a little more serious than she thought.

"I agreed to stay, which surprised the hell out of Rachel, let me tell you." Rose shook her head at the memory.

"I can imagine. It surprises me, too, frankly," Violet said. Quickly she added, "But in a good way!" She didn't want to derail Rose's sense of adventure.

"Tonight he asked me to dinner at his place, which is a great flat overlooking the lake. Really, the guy has such good taste. I shouldn't be surprised, I guess, but for some reason I think of bachelors living like overgrown college students." Rose thought back to his apartment and how it perfectly reflected the man he was: tasteful, strong, and spare but sensual.

"Maybe it's the guys you've been dating." Violet said it before she thought about it, a rare misstep for her. Thankfully Rose was a little lost in her own dialogue and stepped right over the dig at her social life.

"Anyway, it was perfect. The food, the conversation, the setting, everything. And then at the perfect moment of the evening, right when we'd told each other a little bit of what was broken in us and why we were still searching for love, he said he was ready to move forward. And then we started kissing." Rose relived the moment in her head, not even really seeing Violet on the screen in front of her.

"Okay, now this is getting juicy. Did you like it? Is he as sexy in action as he is in the photos? God, that hair. It has to be thick and wonderful." Violet's imagination was in overdrive, and Rose couldn't get to the details fast enough for her.

"Violet, it was the hottest, sexiest date of my life. We made out on the couch for a while and then he actually stood up with me straddling him and started walking toward the bedroom. It was like a damn movie with a romantic Spanish soundtrack!" Rose fell back onto the bed, remembering how good it felt to have him hold her so tight. She wanted to blend into him, to become one.

"So what happened? Why are you calling me from your room at midnight when you should be afterglowing in his bed with gelato or meatballs or whatever it is they do in Italy after sex?" Violet hoped Rose didn't say anything to ruin this relationship before she even had sex, because now Violet was invested in knowing exactly how good Mateo was. Rose sat up again and stared at the laptop screen.

"As he was carrying me to his bedroom, my phone buzzed. I knew it was probably Rachel, and I suddenly felt like a jerk, having a date while Rachel was traveling at night, getting ready to fly off to Australia and start a new life. It's hard to let go of being a mom, Vi, even though she's grown."

"Oh my god, Rose. Please tell me you didn't check your phone when he was mid-stride in taking you to his bed." Violet clutched her pearls in suspense, even though she wasn't wearing any.

"It was worse than that, Vi. I plopped to the floor like a clumsy elephant, and my dress was all caught up in the waistband of my underwear. It was not one of my finer moments." Rose rubbed her face with her hands, further smearing mascara across her cheeks.

"So how did you leave it? Surely you didn't walk

out after that?" Violet was slightly panicked, gripping her tea cup.

"Oh, Violet. It was so uncomfortable. There I was, digging my dress out of my undies and smoothing my hair while searching through my purse for my phone. And the longer I stood there checking the message with my back to him, the more I felt the heat leaving the room. I just don't know if I'm ready for this. There is no safety net, and it scares the hell out of me." This wasn't about Rachel at all. It was about being in control of the situation and having a way out. Vi was glad Rose could see it.

"Rose, you don't get a safety net with love. There is always a chance of loss, of heartbreak, of losing your way. That's the flip side of all the good stuff, you know. You can't have one without the other." Violet was patient with her.

"He asked me to have coffee with him at the restaurant after he walked me home, and I begged off. Honestly, I didn't think I could stand the intensity. It's just too much! He turned it into a joke, saying we could go out like old people next time, eating dinner at 4 p.m. so I didn't exhaust myself. Do you think that was his way of letting me down or that he's still interested?" Rose sighed and felt the emotional exhaustion of the day catching up with her.

"If the evening was as hot as you described, I can't imagine he'd lose interest even if you were wearing granny panties under that dress." Violet sat her cup of tea on the desk and leaned toward the screen to show her seriousness. "Take a deep breath, get a good night's sleep, and then try this again on a day when you haven't been on an emotional roller coaster. You deserve a good man, Rose, even if lasts only as long as vacation. You've been out of the game too long, and it's time to get back in it and remember what it's like to open your heart as well as your legs."

"Yes, ma'am! Open heart, open legs, sexy undies, and turn off cell phone. I think I've got it." Rose knew Vi was only trying to help, but it was just too much. All she needed right now was to forget about the embarrassment of tonight, the loss of her daughter to adulthood and Australia, and the fact that all her friends seemed to know more about love than she did.

"It's been an exciting week for you, my wild Rose. Get some sleep and things will look better in the morning. Call or message me if you need me, okay? And don't forget about that talisman I sent with you. Touch the necklace when you feel out of sorts and it will calm you. I put a little magic in that wild rose just for you." Violet tried to show Rose how much she loved her with a smile, and she hoped it transmitted through the screen. "Love you, girlie."

"Love you, too, Vi. Thanks for talking me down and giving me a magical device. I have a feeling I'm going to need it." Rose touched her necklace as she signed off and then fell back on the bed, immediately falling into a deep, dreamless sleep.

CHAPTER TWENTY

"HOLA, AMIGO. CÓMO estás?"

Ruben's voice sounded casual on the phone, but Mateo had known him long enough to know he wanted something. For one thing, Ruben was never one to call. Mateo usually had to track him down, and then he only responded in cryptic texts. Ruben was an in-person kinda guy, which was strange since he made his living in the high-tech world. Or maybe that was exactly why, that he wanted to preserve his offline relationships in a totally offline way. Mateo had given up on trying to figure him out and just adapted to his way of communicating.

"Hey, Ruben. What's up?" He left the conversation open, waiting for Ruben to get around to the real topic at hand.

"Alejandro and I were thinking of coming to Varenna next week for a visit. Is the flat open?" Ruben was tapping his pen on the desk loud enough for Mateo to hear it. His smooth and confident friend was nervous about something.

"No, I have someone there right now, but it's the

end of the season and you guys can easily find a place to stay. The flat under mine is for rent if you want me to arrange it for you. How long are you staying?" Mateo waited for his response, wondering if he'd tell him what was going on.

"We were thinking of a few days. It's just me and Alejandro, so the flat under yours is fine." Ruben was still tapping his pen on the desk.

"No problem." Mateo paused for a moment before asking, "Is this a holiday or are we talking business?"

"Oh, you know, a little of both. It's raining like crazy in Madrid right now, so it will be good to get away."

"All right, I'll see you guys soon, then. Call me when you get to the train station and I'll meet you at the flat." Mateo wondered what he had in store for the weekend.

"Yeah, that's good. One last thing, did you hear about Carla?" Ruben's pen stopped tapping.

"No, you know I don't keep up with her." Mateo rubbed his face with his left hand, knowing the information was coming whether he wanted it or not.

"Carla's getting a divorce. Apparently she caught her husband cheating with a woman at work. I guess what goes around comes around. Just thought you'd want to know." Ruben began tapping the pen again at a faster pace. "You should also know she's asking about you." The news was delivered, and he was ready to get off the phone.

"Thanks for letting me know, Ruben. I'll see you

guys in a few days, okay?" Mateo set the phone down on the bar, thinking for a moment about Carla. A small part of him was happy about the pain she was feeling, wanting her to hurt like he did five years ago. But it was only a small part. And none of him wanted to reach out to her, to console her, or to reconnect with her. He knew she'd recover and move on with her life, just like he had.

"Whoa," Mateo said out loud. "I think I might be cured." For so long he'd been hiding out in Varenna and licking his wounds. He never thought there would be a day that he'd no longer have to.

Mateo thought back to the night before, the heat of Rose's body on his as she straddled his lap. He'd never forget the taste of wine on her lips or the tiny little moans she made as they kissed, and he hoped they'd have a chance to do it again. When Rachel's text interrupted them last night, he was upset at first. But it only took a moment for him to change his mind.

Mateo was no prude about sex, but he knew there was a lot of potential in this relationship and he didn't want to mess it up by rushing it. That was a younger man's mistake. They had plenty of time for sex, but she only had one daughter, and it had been an emotional day for them both. Mateo didn't want their first time together to be linked to her worries about Rachel. He didn't want anything in the outside world to be in the bedroom with them, so he was committed to waiting for the perfect time. He just hoped it wouldn't be too far away.

CHAPTER TWENTY-ONE

"GOOD MORNING, *CARIÑO.*" Mateo smiled at Rose as she walked through the door into the restaurant. He threw his towel over his shoulder and turned to the espresso machine, asking her if she wanted her coffee with or without milk this morning.

"Cappuccino, please. And good morning to you, too, Mateo." Rose felt a little shy, but his warm manner was going a long way to make her feel more comfortable.

When Rose woke up that morning the apartment was quiet. She texted with Rachel, making sure all was well before she even got out of bed, and then she lay back thinking about her day. She was all alone in Italy with a sexy, interesting man, for a few weeks. She didn't have to work, take care of Rachel, or think about anything other than relaxing and enjoying herself. She couldn't remember the last time this happened, or if it ever had. All her life had been full of responsibility, and she realized the lack of it now was a big reason she felt so out of control the night before. It was like being untethered, free to float wherever she wanted to go, and it was unsettling in a good way. Rose decided to embrace this feeling and push the boundaries a bit, easing into her discomfort until it no longer felt uncomfortable. Or at least she intended to try.

"I enjoyed your company last night, Rosa. Would you like to join me today for a bike ride along the lake and a little lunch? We can't keep eating the best of Chef Aldo's cooking without a little exercise, you know." Mateo smiled, hoping she'd say yes.

"A bike ride sounds great, Mateo." A little exercise would help clear her head and work off some of the incredible food she'd been eating. Rose decided to rent a bike for the rest of her time here, giving her the ability to get away from the restaurant and apartment without assistance. Without Rachel here, she'd need to create her own entertainment or risk falling harder for Mateo than she should. Or at least faster than she should.

Rose spent the breakfast hour journaling at a corner table, trying to make sense of some of her feelings without looking up at Mateo every sixty seconds behind the bar. She liked how he took command of the restaurant without being a tyrant. His method of management was firm but understated, making his wishes known and expecting his employees to carry them out. Rose wondered if he'd be the same in the bedroom, and when she'd find out for sure. Rose stared off into space with her pen resting against her mouth, oblivious to the smile forming on her lips. Mateo caught her attention and her face burned red. She quickly looked down at the table, her journal open in front of her.

The pages were neatly organized, just like most of her life. Rose was a sporadic journal writer, only using the book to help her bring order to a confused situation. She journaled a lot when she first opened her business, working out the financial and logistical details and working through her feelings of fear. Who was she to say she was a landscape designer when she didn't have a proper degree? Rose had a lot to overcome within herself, even though she had years of practical experience working in plant nurseries, with landscaping new homes and buildings, and as a certified master gardener. Rose also had the experience of creating her own home and garden, an adobe oasis in the desert. But still, it was hard for her to hang out her own shingle and ask people to pay for her expertise. Rose's journal was filled during those first few years with pages of self-doubt alongside burgeoning confidence and outward success. The journal kept her sane because she got those crazy thoughts out of her head and onto the paper. As her business grew, her need for the journal decreased.

Then Rachel started middle school, and Rose started journaling again to navigate the hormone surges and dire emergencies of puberty without becoming a casualty of them. Those were the years when she could have used a co-parent. But she made the decision long ago to do it on her own, for better or worse, so she dug in her heels for the onslaught of the teenage years. Rose had her good friends from childhood to lean on, but over time they moved away and the help came in the form of long-distance calls and emails. The journal kept her sane. Now the journal was her testing ground for a new romantic life, one that didn't involve a teenage daughter to care for or a business to build.

Rose finished the last of her coffee and went upstairs to get ready for the bike ride. She decided she'd dive full on into whatever this thing was with Mateo for the duration of her trip. How bad could she get caught up in just a few weeks? And after that she'd decide what to do next. Rose knew the Late Bloomers would approve of her plan, mainly because at least she'd have sex again. Ivy for sure would want details just to verify that she actually did it. Daisy would want to know what he fed her, and Lily would want to know where they were going next. It was scary how well she knew her friends—and how well they knew her.

Rose looked in the small wardrobe for a suitable outfit, something that would be comfortable enough for bike riding but still attractive enough for a date. She settled on a cute blue skort she often used for hiking back home, a comfortable shorts/skirt combo that gave her a free range of movement while still showing off her legs. Paired with this was a sleeveless white top that criss-crossed her breasts and showed off both her cleavage and her wild rose necklace. Last was a soft cashmere cardigan that begged to be touched, and she buttoned only the few middle buttons to emphasize her waist and the curvy delights above and below it. The effect of it all together was casual but sensual, and she knew Mateo would approve. Rose added her sunglasses and a big floppy hat to her bag before taking one last turn in front of the mirror and walking downstairs to meet Mateo.

The minute he saw her, she knew she'd chosen well. Mateo's eyebrows went up and he stopped talking to Lorenzo mid-sentence. Every time he looked at her that way she felt like the sun was beaming on her.

Mateo had traded his pants for fitted cotton shorts and his fisherman sandals for deck shoes. Those legs were powerful, his lean muscles flexing under his skin as he walked. Mateo had on a small backpack and a jaunty straw hat. Rose thought of the men back home wearing such an outfit and how ridiculous it would look. But on a sexy Spaniard bike riding around a lake in Italy? It was perfect. Rose was glad to have packed her camera and hoped to take a photo to share with her friends later. Would the outfit translate outside the scenario? Ivy would definitely tell her.

"All right, let's get our bikes and head out." Mateo reached out and touched her lower back, caressing the softness of her sweater, and gently ushered her toward the door. He smiled down at her, and she was excited to share the day together and hoping to regain some of the spark from the previous night.

CHAPTER TWENTY-TWO

THE BIKE RENTAL shop was just opening, and Mateo greeted the owner as a friend. Rose watched him negotiate the day's rental for two bikes and take the route maps. He had an easy manner, joking with the shopkeeper and listening as he pointed out places of interest along the way. The other man kept looking over at Rose and smiling, and it dawned on her that Mateo probably didn't do this often. She wondered when his last date had been and decided she'd ask him when they started to ride.

After adjusting their bike seats and showing them how to use the bicycle gears, the shopkeeper waved them off and wished them a good ride. Rose wondered how they were going to navigate the many steep steps and narrow roadways in Varenna, and her question was answered almost immediately.

"We're taking the ferry across to Bellagio and going from there." Mateo pointed across the lake, and Rose remembered going there for lunch with Rachel. "I thought we'd ride southwest along Lake Como to Torno for lunch, which is about twenty-three kilometers. Are you okay with that?"

"I'm an American. I speak in miles, not kilometers." Rose smiled, wondering if he realized just how lost she'd been since arriving in Italy. She never knew how far away anything was because all the signs were in kilometers and meters, not miles and feet, and combining that with the different language and customs meant she was always off-kilter at least a little bit and sometimes a lot. As a control freak, this was hard to get used to.

"In that case, it's about fourteen miles. Don't worry; we can reset our bikes to travel in miles instead of kilometers." Mateo winked at her. "You told me you were fit, and I've seen the proof, so I thought you'd be able to handle it. Besides, we'll gorge ourselves at lunch and take a cab back if we have to."

They took the steps down to the dock, arriving just as the ferry was pulling in. The horn sounded in the quiet morning air, a sound Rose thought was overkill for the tiny ferry with a small queue of passengers waiting to board. They stood next to their bikes and watched the deckhand expertly throw the ropes to the pier and release the gangway before opening the gate to allow walking passengers on, a job these guys did dozens of times every single day. Still, it was brand-new to Rose, who spent more time in the dirt than on the water, and she was fascinated at the everyday casualness of traveling by boat. To the people who lived here, it was no more exciting than a bus ride. Rose and Mateo walked their bikes on, secured them to the racks and stood together at the deck for the fifteen minute ride across the lake to Bellagio.

The air was warm on Rose's skin, but she felt a slight coolness to the breeze and knew that Italy was closer to fall than summer. In other words, it was a perfect day for a bike ride. She hoped this date would end better than their last.

When the ferry pulled into the dock on the other side of the lake, they picked up their bikes and rolled them off. The town was a shopping mecca for tourists, but it didn't take them long to leave it all behind once they hopped on their bikes and began peddling. The day was lazy and there were few cars on the road, giving them a chance to ride side by side along the lake.

Rose enjoyed Mateo's company, and the view of him ahead of her when a car forced them into single file was equally enjoyable. He had a strong upper back that rippled under his shirt as he rode. Rose was happy to see his strong calves flexing as he pedaled, a personal favorite of hers. Too many men worked on their arms and thighs, leaving a puny little calf below. She loved that he was well-proportioned all over, or at least she hoped he was well-proportioned everywhere.

They stopped a few times along the way for photos, and Rose tried not to be too obvious about it. But she knew her friends would demand to see them together, and she had to admit the faint glisten on his skin from the ride was sexy as hell. She could just imagine Ivy growling with delight when she saw the photo.

After a couple of hours, they arrived in Torno. Mateo led them to a lakeside restaurant with unobstructed views of the lake. They locked up their bikes outside and Mateo walked over to the manager and did the usual Italian triple kiss on the cheeks. They were obviously friends, touching each other on the shoulder and talking warmly. Rose hung back a little, not sure what to do.

"Rosa, I'd like to introduce you to Daniele, the manager of this restaurant and a friend of mine. Daniele, this is the beautiful Rosa from America." Daniele immediately took Rose by the shoulders and gave her the three kiss greeting, pulling her so close she bumped into his large belly.

"*Bella donna!* How can you consort with such a base man as this? You realize he is a Spaniard masquerading as an Italian, do you not? Ah, no matter. I will personally watch over you during lunch to make sure he minds his manners." He made a slight bow and then led them to a table on the edge of the terrace overlooking the lake. Rose looked at Mateo and raised her eyebrows, enjoying this outsized personality of Daniele and the easy way Mateo interacted with his friends.

"*Grazie mille*, Daniele," Rose said as she sat down. "I appreciate your concern for my well-being. I'm still trying to decide whether to trust this man with my affections. Perhaps we can discuss it after lunch and you can give me your opinion?" She dazzled Daniele with a smile, and Mateo pretended he was offended at the suggestion he was less than worthy. Daniele, of course, jumped in with gusto. His favorite part of the job was grand displays of courtesy to his guests and making them feel special. He should have been an actor.

"Oh, signora, we have much to discuss. I will be off now to get your wine and *antipasti*, but you should know that your companion is not playing fair. He has already called ahead and arranged for a special meal from my chef and a bottle of my best Barolo. I'd say he's working hard for your approval." Daniele winked at her and gave Mateo a friendly shoulder squeeze before walking away.

"If you keep feeding me like this you'll have to take me back to Bellagio to go shopping for bigger clothes." Rose grinned at Mateo, loving the attention he was lavishing on her.

"If that means an opportunity take your measurements beforehand, I'm all for it." Mateo smiled at her, and she could see he enjoyed the daytime flirting as much as she did. It was easier in the light of day, in public, to express their mutual desire for each other. Rose wondered if it would ever be comfortable enough to take it all the way when the sun went down.

Lunch was roasted duck, the skin cooked to a perfect crisp and the meat inside so juicy and tender she carved it with just her fork. The meal paired well with the intense Barolo wine, and Rose's mouth was in sensory overload trying to identify all the flavors and textures of the meal.

And did they talk! The conversation flowed during the meal as if they'd never had that awkward moment last night. Rose drank in his stories with her wine, and he tasted her history with every bite. They were as entwined as two people could be when sharing food, and Rose wondered why it got so complicated when they left the table. She thought about it for just a moment before wondering if it might be due to the guiding hand of a chef. If only they had a chef with them at all times, a menu of what to do, they might not mess up so much. Rose imagined Chef Aldo directing them in the bedroom. With all the rules the Italians had about eating and drinking and digestion, she could just imagine what a chef would recommend —and in what order. What would Chef Aldo consider *antipasti*, and could they go back to it after they'd sampled some of the main dish without a reprimand? The thought made her laugh out loud, and she quickly covered her mouth with a napkin.

"What's so funny?" Mateo asked, cocking his head. After her meltdown over the olive oil, he was probably bracing for the worst.

"I was just thinking how well we connect over a table of food and wine and how it only gets difficult when we stand up." She winced a little at her phrasing, remembering when Mateo stood up the night before with her legs wrapped around him and how that ended. Rose wondered if Mateo felt the same way about their connection or if it was just her.

"Then we shall never leave this table. I will ask Daniele for sleeping bags, though I have to admit it will get cooler here over the next few weeks. We may want to move over to a bench table to keep each other warm. I am willing to do whatever it takes." He winked at her and signaled to Daniele they were ready for another glass of wine.

"While the thought of watching the stars with you from this location sounds very appealing, I do wonder what it is about food and wine that makes us so much more comfortable with each other than we are in other situations. Or is it just me?" Rose decided to ask so she'd stop obsessing about it. Or at least she hoped she'd stop; that all depended on Mateo's answer.

"I have always been a man who knows what he wants, at least until these past few years. I let that part of me go for a while and just took what was offered, and as I told you last night, I'm finally ready to choose for myself again." Mateo paused while the waiter came over to pour more wine, and Rose waited, too, not wanting to divert his attention from her question. "When you arrived, all my senses lit up again. I want to choose, to have the very best, and to enjoy every last bit of it. That means food, wine, conversation, the beauty around me, and most of all, you. We connect over the table because I want to savor you like a good meal, a fine wine, or a deep conversation. I choose you, Rosa, but I'm a little out of practice and that's why it gets awkward sometimes." Mateo paused for effect and then challenged Rose, "Now, *cariño*, tell me why you think we do so well at the table."

Rose was stunned at his response, glad for the distraction of a fresh glass of wine in front of her. She rocked the stem with her fingers and watched the swirling red liquid form rivulets down the glass as she formulated her response.

"Can I tell you a little secret, Mateo?" Rose took a deep breath, gearing herself up to reveal more than she ever had to any other man before.

"I'd love to know a secret about you, Rosa," he growled as he leaned forward on the table. Mateo was doing his best Antonio Banderas impersonation, though he didn't know it. Rose felt herself blush as she thought of hearing that same tone of voice in the dark of Mateo's bedroom.

"For years I've worked hard to establish my business and raise my daughter. I even built a house and garden on top of a hill, or at least had a big hand in designing it. So I do know what I want, at least the big things. But for a long time I've overlooked the everyday desires of my life in order to reach these bigger goals." She looked up at him, judging his worthiness to hear her secret by the expression on his face, and then plunging forward. "This trip to Italy is my official unleashing of Wild Rose." She sat back in her chair, waiting for his reaction.

"Wild Rose? I'm not sure I understand." Mateo looked at her quizzically.

"You are looking at Wild Rose, or at least the combination of her and my existing personality. For years she's been my ideal way of living for some day in the future, the woman who enjoys the sensual moments of every day, the woman who loves and lives with abandon and isn't afraid of risk or looking stupid to get what she wants. She's the one who appreciates what she already has instead of always looking ahead to the next goal. She's the woman I always said I wanted to be, and you're getting the first look at her." Rose stopped to gauge his reaction.

"If she's always been with you, then she isn't really a different you, just a part that hasn't gotten as much play as the hard-working mother parts. And let me just say, I'm honored that you would introduce this part of yourself to me. I'm going to enjoy getting to know all the sides of your personality, Rosa." Mateo reached his hand across the table to link fingers with Rose.

Rose swallowed, even though there was nothing in her mouth. She felt as if she were taking a step forward with a blindfold on, at the edge of a cliff, a little bit scared and a little bit exhilarated at the same time.

"The good food and wine is something Wild Rose always wanted and I rarely gave her. A deep connection with a man is also something she craved. So is relaxation and beauty and adventure and laughter. All of those things I get at the table with you, and it's easier to indulge in the other senses because we're already eating and drinking. But I'd like to become more comfortable with using all my senses away from the table, too." Rose squeezed Mateo's fingers and smiled, relieved that he felt the same way.

"I think it's time for us to test our wings, little bird. Shall we step away from the table and see where it takes us?" Mateo stood, still holding her hand, and waited for her to stand up and join him. "If we make it all the way back to Varenna without awkwardness, then we've passed the first stage. And I promise to reward you with a kiss on the dock. How does that sound?"

"I like the sound of that very much, Mateo."

They stood up to leave and Daniele came out to say goodbye. He leaned in and stage whispered to her that if it weren't for his wife of forty years and his happy marriage, he'd gladly steal her away from Mateo. She giggled at his dramatic admission, in full earshot of Mateo, and enjoyed seeing this camaraderie. Friends were important to Rose, and she liked that Mateo felt that way, too.

The bike ride back was slower and with more stops as they worked off a big lunch and two glasses of wine. They stopped to watch the swans in the lake and take photos of the mountains surrounding them. And when they finally arrived in Bellagio, they boarded the ferry for the short ride to Varenna. This time they snuggled together at the railing, Rose completely wrapped up in Mateo's arms as they looked out over the lake. She couldn't stop thinking that she was here, on a ferry at Lake Como, with a gorgeous man who wanted her. The sun was shining, the birds were singing, and a picturesque village of brightly-colored houses at the base of mountains was her view. This was a long way from home, a completely different way of living, and for once Rose didn't have to design or arrange anything. She could simply be in this moment, with this man, in this place, soaking it all in.

Rose sighed with contentment and Mateo leaned down to kiss her neck, his hair brushing her cheek as his whiskers gently poked her skin. The horn sounded as the ferry pulled into the dock, and as the deckhand lassoed the boat to the pier, she turned to face Mateo and claimed her kiss.

"Hey, I said you got the kiss on the dock, not the boat," Mateo whispered. You cheated.

"Are you complaining? Because I planned to get another one in ten steps when we get off the ferry." Rose looked up at him, feeling his warm breath on her cheek as they embraced again.

"My complaint will never be about having too much of you, Rosa. I can promise you that." Mateo unlocked their bikes and put his hand on her back again, guiding her off the ferry. Once they were on shore, Mateo stopped and tilted her face toward his. "Can I have my kiss now?"

When Rose nodded, he pulled her tightly to him, taking her feet off the ground, and pulled her hair into a loose ponytail in his hand. His lips pressed into hers, then gently parted to explore with his tongue. Mateo lifted her higher and tighter toward him, only breaking free when the ferry workers started applauding and whistling.

Rose dropped to the ground and straightened her hair, cheeks bright pink from the attention.

"One full date without awkwardness, and we even got a standing ovation. I think we're making progress. Perhaps we can continue this over dinner at my place tonight?" Mateo was obviously making the most of the time they had together.

"I'd like that very much, Mateo. Though I'm not sure food is what I'll be hungry for." Rose's mouth curled up slightly at the corners as she turned and walked her bike up the stairs ahead of him, making sure he had a nice preview of what she'd be serving him that night.

CHAPTER TWENTY-THREE

BEHIND MATEO, ROSE saw candles flickering on the tables and heard Spanish music playing on the speakers. He kissed her on each cheek and ushered her into his apartment with his arm on her back, closing the door softly behind them.

"You look like a ray of sunshine in that dress." True, the deep orange dress was the color of the setting sun, but the heat came from his touch. Rose was sure there would later be a brand where his hand rested on her back.

Rose wore her auburn hair loose, letting it fall to her shoulders in waves. The wrap was one she bought in Varenna at a local shop, a large flower print that reminded her of summer. When she dropped it from her shoulders Mateo smiled, admiring the light sprinkling of freckles on her shoulders.

"Thank you, Mateo. You look very handsome yourself. *Muy guapo.*" Rose blushed a little, trying out the kind of romantic Spanish words she never used back at home with her clients and subcontractors.

Mateo's dark, wavy hair was shiny and tamed,

evidence that he'd used some kind of hair product. Rose appreciated the effort, loving that he knew how to groom himself well. He was wearing a button-down shirt of crisp white cotton, highlighting his tanned face from the day's bike riding. His shirt clung to his body, outlining his broad shoulders and tapering to his flat waist. His flat-front trousers were gray, and they narrowed over his calves to his black leather monk strap shoes.

Rose was close enough that she could smell his aftershave, a heady concoction of musk that emphasized his own pheromones. She closed her eyes to inhale it, leaning in to nuzzle his neck and timidly licking his neck like an animal. There was no awkwardness tonight. Her breath caught in her throat at the thought of what they would be doing together.

Mateo gripped her upper arms with both hands, as much to steady himself as to stop her. He bent his neck down until they were touching foreheads, and they both slowed their respiration, matching each other breath for breath. The pacing was hypnotic, and Rose felt herself blending together with him.

"Tonight I have switched to a Spanish theme. I hope you like it. It's just too hard for me to think about loving you in Italian." Mateo spoke quietly, just above a whisper, as he pulled her closer to him, his breath warm on her cheek. "I am a Spaniard to my bones, and I want you to know me as completely as I want to know you."

Rose shivered at his intensity, then softly said in his

ear, "I've never been seduced by a conquistador." Every hair on her body stood at attention, little flags announcing her immediate surrender. Rose wanted to stay forever in this limbo of wanting him and knowing she would have him, a perfect space of longing.

"No conquistador has ever discovered a treasure as rich as the one in my arms. Make no mistake, I will discover every hiding place tonight, *cariño*. Every single one." Mateo gently bit her ear, sending a bolt of pleasure through her heart and down to her center.

"Tell me, Señor Conquistador, about your plan to conquer the Fortress of Rose. She is well-defended, you know." Rose took a step back from Mateo, smoothing her dress down as if it were armor. Rose was at the height of her sexual and mental awareness, tingling with every smell, touch, and sound.

"First I start by softening the walls of your fortress with the Spanish love songs. The singer you hear now is Enrique Iglesias. He's one of the most famous in Spain, and so is his father, Julio. The two of them are probably responsible for most of the sex that has happened in my country in the last forty years," Mateo said. "He also sings in English, but his Spanish songs have more passion and desire." Rose listened to the slight tremor in Enrique's voice, every word like a secret confession to his lover.

"Hmmm. Do you think this Iglesias Effect works outside the borders of Spain?" Rose stepped closer and put her hand on Mateo's chest and pretended to groom him, smoothing his shirt down to his waist. It was a stealth move to feel his chest and abs, and she was not disappointed. His muscles were tight, tensed for action, and Rose knew she was responsible for his excitement.

"Ah, that is the test of the evening, I suppose. I have faith that my countrymen's talents can cross borders in the name of love." Mateo smiled at her and leaned down for a kiss. She was a little thrown by his use of the word *love*, but she didn't show it. Wild Rose was in charge tonight, so there would be no overthinking everything as usual.

As they kissed, Rose allowed herself to imagine what life with Mateo would be like. She'd wake up every day next to this face, this body, and she'd probably never again eat frozen pizza or drink wine out of a box. She imagined Mateo at her house wearing only tight boxer briefs and an apron, pulling together a gourmet meal with just four ingredients and one pan after exhausting her in the bedroom. He seemed like that kind of guy. She lightly moaned at the thought, tenderly breaking the kiss by putting both hands on his chest. She looked at him with half-lidded eyes.

"I believe you have breached the walls, Señor Conquistador." Rose looked up at him with desire, enjoying every moment of her impending capture.

"Ah, then let me commence to stage two of my attack." Mateo was obviously enjoying the slow seduction as much as she was.

He showed her into the living area, where

flickering candles displayed a selection of small plates of food on the round coffee table. The savory scent of cooked meat reached her nose and made her stomach growl with anticipation. The plates were all white with two tiny forks on each one. There were two cloth napkins on the table, and she spread one on her lap. Mateo stepped into the kitchen and returned with two glasses of red wine. He sat next to her on the couch and raised his glass in a toast.

"To us," he said, as he looked into her eyes. They clinked glasses and drank, with Rose making one of her little noises of satisfaction as the spice and cherry flavor of the wine slid down her throat.

Mateo had a little smile at the corners of his mouth as he said, "I see that you approve of my choice of wine tonight."

"My friend Violet calls it my Sensual Tourette's Syndrome." Rose blushed a little. "I can't help my body's response to good food and drink; I've had this tic ever since I was a kid. I used to get really embarrassed when people commented on my noises, but now I accept it as a hopefully adorable quirk." She grinned, hoping he'd agree. "It's getting a real workout here in Italy, much more so than in my regular life back at home."

"Tonight we will attempt to hear every noise you can make, *cariño*." Mateo pointed to the table and began describing the small dishes, which he called *tapas*. "This is an assortment of small snack plates, what we in Spain would enjoy with our wine a few hours before a proper dinner." Rose could tell he was proud to share his traditions with her and listened attentively. "I've made a few of my favorites, including a seafood paella. Normally we wouldn't eat paella at night, but I'm making an exception for you." He put some rice and bit of scallop on a fork and fed it to her.

"Mmm." Rose chewed the food and closed her eyes, focusing on the earthy taste of the saffron combined with the pan-charred bits of rice and tender seafood. She opened her eyes, silently begging for more. Mateo fed her two more bites from the small plate. "I think this is my new favorite," she said as she swallowed the last one.

"Oh, but there's more. Now we move to the *albondigas*, which you would incorrectly call meatballs. I can promise that you've never had one taste like this." Mateo forked an entire meatball and moved toward her mouth. She flicked her tongue on it, wanting to taste the savory roux before the pork, and she heard Mateo groan at the visual. As she bit through the meatball, she was surprised at the lightness of it. Mateo was right; this wasn't a typical meatball. Rose then took the rest of it into her mouth, groaning with pleasure.

"How do you make them so airy?" she asked, between chews.

"I gently mix them so they don't get too dense, and then I keep the portions small, bite-sized enough to tempt you to eat more." Mateo's eyes were hungry as he looked at her.

He reached down to the table and brought up a plate of sliced Ibérico ham and Manchego cheese with some salted almonds. He fed her bites of each as he continued talking.

"Until just a few years ago, you couldn't even get Ibérico ham in the United States, but we've been eating it for centuries in Spain. It is simply the best in the world and hardly anyone who's ever tried it will dispute that fact. The true aficionados of Jamón Ibérico don't even like to classify it with other hams." Mateo paused for effect. "Like so many other pleasures, the best in the world comes from Spain."

Rose felt the flavors of the acorn-fed black pig melt in her mouth, the smooth, paper-thin texture in contrast to the rich marbling of fat. Mateo was right; this wasn't like any ham she'd ever tasted.

"So I can buy this in the US and think of you every time I eat it?" Rose delighted at the thought, though she was surprised to see Mateo's expression cloud over.

"No, you may not eat this alone in the US. You will only eat Jamón Ibérico with me." His jaw was set, and there was to be no negotiation on this point. Rose felt herself cave in again, willing to submit to any of his demands tonight. His faced softened, and he continued. "This is a small sampling of the food and wine in Spain, and I want to share so much more with you. You must come to Spain with me. You'll be practically grunting a new language when you eat a juicy roast pig, drink a sparkling Cava, or taste a paella made over an open flame on the shore of the Mediterranean Sea."

Mateo made a small sound of longing, thinking of the food and wine back home in Spain. "And in Spain you'll try the range of our wines. You know we have more vineyards than any country in the world, right? We're the unsung heroes of wine and olive oil, with the French and Italians getting all the credit." Mateo was excited to share his love of Spain with Rose, and she wondered if she'd ever visit Madrid with him. A tour of the country's best foods and wine with a handsome man didn't sound like a bad way to spend a few months of her life.

"You should be working for the Spanish tourism department, not running a restaurant in Italy," Rose said. Mateo's expression flashed a different kind of longing, but only for an instant.

"I'll give it to the Italians that they know how to cook and the wine is good, but I still prefer my Spanish food. I hope you will, too," Mateo said. The look he gave her made her long for Spain, too, just to experience it with him. "The wine tonight is a Gran Reserva Rioja, made with Tempranillo grapes grown in the cool hillsides of North Central Spain. It is one of my favorites, and I have a case of it delivered to the restaurant every few months just so I can have it anytime I want."

"You miss Spain, don't you?" Rose pushed a little, wondering what happened in the moment before. Was there something behind his longing she didn't know about? She remembered conversations with Violet before she left about Mateo's background and what a forty-something single Spanish man was doing living in Italy. Was it more than the breakup with Carla?

"I do miss it, and I know I will return some day. But right now, I'm in Italy with a beautiful woman, delicious wine and food, and nothing to interrupt us until morning. There is nowhere else I'd rather be in the world than right here, right now." Mateo said it with finality, closing the subject of Spain and the outside world for the moment, and Rose decided not to push it again tonight.

"I don't know what it is about you, Rosa, but I want to know everything about you." A slow smile crept up as he continued, "But not all at once. I want to savor everything about you, slowly and completely." His breath grew ragged as he spoke his passion out loud, making it even stronger by putting it in words. He leaned in to kiss her deeply.

Rose explored his mouth with her tongue, tasting the full flavor of him. Of all the delights from Spain in her mouth this evening, he was the most delicious. They sat next to each other on the couch, kissing, stroking, and squeezing each other like two teenagers alone together for the first time in a borrowed car. Rose quickly grew frustrated with the limitations of being side by side and pushed herself up to straddle Mateo. Her dress rode up on her legs, and she felt the goosebumps erupt as he put his bare hands on her naked thighs. His hands were hot, like fire on her skin, marking her with his passion as he pulled her legs tighter around him.

Rose ground her pelvis into his lap, feeling him grow hard underneath her as they devoured each other's lips. She felt an animal-like pull from inside her, a definite lack of manners and propriety. Rose grabbed his thick hair with both hands, pulling his face into hers as they kissed, raking her fingers gently down his face and across the coarser hairs of his trim beard.

Rose wiggled her toes so her sandals fell to the floor, and extended her right leg to the arm of the couch for leverage and pulled Mateo down on top of her. The desire to feel his weight on her was overwhelming. Rose wanted him to sink into her, to feel every pound of his flesh on her and in her. They wiggled together on the couch until they were perfectly synced, adjusting to this new position without ever leaving each other's lips.

Mateo lifted himself on one elbow while continuing to kiss her and caress her thigh with his other hand. Rose squeezed his bicep as it was flexed to hold him over her, feeling the curve of his muscles underneath her fingers. Mateo's other hand went higher and higher up her thigh, eventually gripping her bare ass in his hand and then extending his fingers under the band of her purple lacy thong. He traced his fingers along the entire side of her waistband, tormenting her with his promised thorough exploration of her body. Rose didn't think she could wait any longer. She wanted him inside of her.

Mateo brought his hand up to her hair, cradling her head as he kissed her and slowly pulled her to a sitting position on the couch. He then stood in front of her, physical evidence of his desire bursting against his pants right in front her face. She drew in her breath quickly. It was time. Mateo offered his hand down to her and then pulled her to her bare feet. She felt the plush carpet beneath her feet again, remembering the last time she was in this moment. This time, she didn't want to hold on. Rose wanted to jump with both feet.

The strap of her dress fell from her right shoulder and Mateo leaned down to kiss the freckles there. Then Rose took a step back, ready to show him the treasures of the Fortress of Rose. She pulled the left strap down, watching Mateo's eyes as he followed her every move. Enrique continued singing, and Rose felt the rhythm settle inside her body. She slowly turned her back to Mateo in time with the music, pulling her hair to the side so he could unzip her dress. His fingers were achingly slow, and when the zipper was down he retraced its journey down her spine with the flat of his thumb, skimming over the hook to her bra.

Rose took a deep breath and turned, letting the dress fall to the floor. She stood before him in her matching purple lace thong and sheer, pushup bra. The candlelight cast shadows over the curves of her body, the play of light giving her the look of a goddess.

"*Dios mio*," Mateo panted.

Rose reached for his hand as she stepped out of the

puddle of dress and led him toward the bedroom. She stopped midway to turn back, satisfied to see he was entranced by the rear view.

In the bedroom, the door to the balcony was open, letting in the cool evening air. Rose stopped and Mateo came from behind to embrace her, tracing his hands over her body and nuzzling her neck. Her nipples jumped to attention as Mateo freed her from the bra, exposing her breasts to the breeze. He turned her around so he could lean down to kiss her left breast, suckling with his hot tongue as he gripped both breasts with his hands. Rose looked to the ceiling and closed her eyes in pleasure as he caressed and licked her, teasing her gently with his teeth.

Mateo's hands moved down to her waist, and as Rose opened her eyes and looked down, she felt the short whiskers of his beard journeying down her stomach until he bit into the waist of her panties. He looked up at her with them still in his mouth, waiting for permission to enter the inner sanctum. Rose moaned with desire, his permission granted.

Mateo brought his hands to her waist, fingers gently digging underneath the band of her thong and pulling it away from her body, and then caressing her thighs as he pulled it down to her feet. His mouth moved from her panties to the wet center of her being. He kissed her there, drinking in the taste of her and smelling the sweet aroma of her body. Rose moaned, putting her arm out to the wall to steady herself. The room was pulsing with the musky scent of pheromones and sweat. Still on his knees in front of her, he reached up to her waist and pulled her down on the bed. He peeked up from his work to lick her abdomen, looking her in the eye and saying, "*tranquilo*." Rose lay back on the bed, following his command to relax.

Mateo sampled every nook of her most private place with his tongue. Rose clenched her teeth and dug her head back into the bed. Two urges fought for dominance, the desire to have him bring her to orgasm with his mouth and the need to have an orgasm with him inside her. Logic briefly re-entered her brain to remind her that with this kind of passion, she could probably have both.

Rose giggled out loud at the thought, causing Mateo to rise up from his exploration. "Am I amusing you, Rosa?" He held her thigh out from her body and kissed the little concave area that connected her leg and groin. Rose had never been kissed there before, and she decided that was one of the greatest disasters of her life. He softly licked the space he'd just kissed and looked to her for an answer to his question.

Rose pulled herself forward and rested on her elbows so she could see him. Mateo's lips were wet from her, and she was overcome with a desire to kiss him. Rose pushed herself forward on the bed and then down to his lips, kissing him with a feverish intensity. She could taste herself on him, loving the way he was now marked with her scent. He was hers.

"I was giggling at my options for pleasure this

evening," she said.

"Oh, you are making these plans without consulting me?" he teased.

"Well, I thought we had enough passion to try at least two ways, with you being a conquistador and all." Rose smiled, tracing her finger down his cheek as she kissed him again. Mateo growled at her suggestion, pushing her back on the bed with his right hand and going back to his exploration. She wrapped her legs around his neck, thighs resting on his shoulders as she raised her hips to offer herself to him again.

The room spun around her, shrinking and expanding every time she opened her eyes. Rose gripped the duvet cover in her fists as the pressure began building, little cries escaping from her mouth when his tongue flicked her most sensitive region. Just when she thought she couldn't take it anymore, Mateo slowly inserted a finger. Rose immediately clenched around him, tightening as she moved closer to her peak.

With his tongue still caressing her, Mateo expertly added another finger, further tightening the space and filling her up. As his fingers slid in and out, Rose climbed to another level of pleasure, and then another. Her breathing was shallow and ragged, and finally she held her breath, anticipating the release. Rose screamed his name as her entire body tensed, her hips rising off the bed and almost crushing him with her thighs. A fierce pleasure started from the center of her being and rode out to the furthest reaches of her body, wave after wave, while Mateo kept his mouth at the nerve center, teasing out every last sensation and drinking it in as if he were dying of thirst.

As the waves slowly began receding, Mateo left the most sensitive areas alone and began kissing her inner thighs, squeezing and massaging them as he alternated legs, waiting for Rose to revive after her "little death."

"Mmm, Mateo. You have conquered me." Rose was in a delicious dream state, fully relaxed yet anticipating more pleasures to come. She rose up on her elbows again, surprised to find Mateo was still fully dressed. Rose felt powerful and sexy to be naked in front of him, fully exposed, as if he'd arrived just to service her needs.

Rose sat up and clenched the hair on both sides of his head, feeling the thick waves in her fists. Rose pulled him to her face to kiss him, and he pulled her up from the bed with him as he stood. She fumbled with the buttons on his shirt as they kissed, eventually freeing them all and sliding the shirt off his broad shoulders as she caressed his lean muscled arms. The feel of her breasts against his bare chest was like electricity, the bolt going straight to her still sensitive center. His moan told her he felt the same way. Rose mashed herself into him, feeling the muscles across his upper back and shoulders dance under her fingertips. He cupped her ass with both hands and pulled her tight against him. His pants were now in the way, preventing the full contact of skin.

Rose wanted to see, feel, know all of him. She unbuckled his belt and button quickly, taking care to slowly unzip his pants. Rose looked up at Mateo as she pulled the belt slowly through the loops of his waistband. She reached around to grab the loose end of the belt from her left hand and lassoed him into her, kissing him deeply as she slowly wound the belt around each hand. *Must keep this in mind for next time*, she thought.

Rose tossed the belt to the corner of the room and dug her hands inside his tight boxer briefs. His skin was hot, and the rise of his ass perfectly filled the palms of her hands as she gripped him. *My god, he's perfect*, she thought, as she continued kissing him.

Rose pushed his pants down as far as she could reach without breaking their kiss, and Mateo took care of the rest, almost tripping to get his pants off when he forgot to take off his shoes. He then flung his pants to the corner with a side kick worthy of a star soccer player. He walked Rose backward to the bed and sat her down as he stood before her, displaying himself for approval just like she'd done earlier.

The sweat was already glistening on his chest, impervious to the cool breeze from outside. Enrique Iglesias pleaded through speakers for his lover not to say no, and Rose knew she would never say no to Mateo, at least not tonight.

She looked him over from head to toe. Mateo's

shoulders were strong, his arms with the sinewy muscles of a runner. His torso tapered to a V, the waistband of his underwear laying flat against his abs. His runner's legs bulged from his boxer briefs, a Calvin Klein billboard brought to life. Mateo was bursting from the constraints of his underwear, so Rose reached forward and grabbed both sides and gently slid them down to his knees, where she let go and they dropped to the floor.

Mateo flexed his fingers, looking a little bit above Rose's head while waiting for her verdict. A slow smile spread across her face, and instead of telling him how she felt she decided to show him. Rose fell to her knees and took him into her mouth, her hands raised above her to feel his abs. He groaned as she pulled both hands down to help pleasure him, rotating her grip to give him the most intense pleasure as her mouth worked to take him all in. Mateo's hands plunged into her hair, clenching it and holding on for dear life.

Rose took Mateo from her mouth but kept her hands on him, squeezing and turning as she stood to face him. He leaned down to kiss her and she released him as they both fell back onto the bed, quickly rolling to the side so they could explore each other better.

Mateo's lips immediately found her breasts, sucking and caressing them while her legs gripped tighter around him.

"I want to feel you inside of me," she whispered.

Mateo obliged, kissing his way back up to her lips. She rolled onto her back and Mateo leaned over her, his biceps bulging and his hair damp with sweat.

"Are you ready, *cariño*?" he asked.

"God, yes," she breathed.

Mateo reached over to the bedside drawer and pulled out a condom, ripping the package with his teeth and standing on his knees between her legs as she watched him slowly roll it on. Having already had him in her mouth, she knew it was going to be a tight fit.

He leaned forward and rested above her on his left elbow, looking into her eyes as he guided just the tip inside. Mateo bent down to suckle at her breasts for a moment, cupping the left one in his right hand and gently biting at her nipple at the moment he slid further in. Rose yelped at the simultaneous pain and pleasure, and he raised his head to look at her, grinning.

"Did you like that?" he purred.

"Please, do it again," she asked.

Mateo leaned down again to gently lick her breasts, waiting for the right moment to nip at her again and push himself further inside. As he did, she yelped in surprise again.

"I want to feel you inside me, all the way," she pleaded.

Mateo raised his lips to hers and kissed her as he plunged himself all the way through to the inner sanctum of the Fortress of Rose. She cried out in pleasure, feeling like she couldn't take another moment, while never wanting it to end. Mateo began slowly thrusting himself into her, the pleasure building with each stroke.

Mateo rolled over onto his back, pulling her up on top of him in one swift move. Rose felt him fully inside of her, but from the top she was in charge of the rhythm and pace. His hands were on her hips, pulling her down onto him as she rode, faster and faster, feeling another orgasm build with the friction against his pelvic bone. The sheets to his bed were tangled around him, and he looked like a god below her. Rose leaned down to kiss him, maintaining the rhythm that was bringing them both to the peak. Mateo's chest was slick against hers, droplets of sweat that cooled against their hot bodies when hit with the breeze coming in from the balcony door. Rose felt the familiar swell of anticipation and tightness throughout her body. She could see his pleasure peaking, too, and she wanted them to come together.

Rose reached down, rubbing herself until she became so tight she knew he couldn't hold back. Neither could she. Rose peaked just before Mateo, roaring at the final climax and riding the continuing waves of intense pleasure that radiated out from the center of her body to her fingers, toes, and scalp. Even her hair felt the release.

"I can feel you!" Mateo exclaimed, as her body clenched around him. He looked up at Rose as she arched her back and yelled out, riding the waves of pleasure until they faded to small ripples, sweaty tendrils of hair sticking to the side of her face and beads of perspiration running between her breasts. The sight of her body above him and the bold way she touched herself only spurred his passion.

"*Dios mio!*" Mateo yelled at the moment of release, tensing his entire body just moments after Rose finished, thrusting until he was spent.

She leaned down to kiss his neck and chest as he let go of the last of his sexual energy, riding it with him all the way to the end.

In the exhausted silence afterward Rose lay down on top of him, slick with sex, and smelled the scent of their lovemaking in the air. Gradually their breathing slowed, and as they returned to mortal status again, Rose lifted her head and looked Mateo in the eye.

"I think Spanish music should come with a warning label," she cooed.

"I'll have to send the Iglesias family a thank you card and a gift for tonight," Mateo said.

"Perhaps we should dive into the *tapas* and wine to restore our energy. You've given me quite a workout, Señor Conquistador." Rose gently untwined from him and rolled to the side, looking over at his perfect form. He winced a little at their uncoupling as the cool air hit him, already missing the warmth of her body and their physical connection. Rose kissed his chest, her hair falling over him, as she stood up. Mateo was rewarded with the sight of her standing before him, breasts full, hair tousled, and the glow of sex radiating from her skin.

"You look beautiful in the moonlight, *cariño*. I'll never get tired of looking at you," he said.

"Yes, but eventually you'd hear my stomach growling, and it would distract you from the vision. Let's eat." Rose gently pinched his thigh and he sat up, grabbing her waist and kissing her on the belly button. She could feel his whiskers against her stomach, the most vulnerable part of her body, and for the first time in her life she didn't recoil.

"There is a robe in the bathroom if you want it, though I wouldn't mind you staying exactly as you are. I'll go pour us some more wine and meet you in the living room." Mateo stood up and slapped her on the ass. "My god, you will be the death of me, woman," he said as he walked out.

Rose smiled and walked into the bathroom, thinking how glad she was that Wild Rose decided to stick around through all the years of sexual famine, because tonight she planned to gorge herself on this man.

And after a bit of food and wine, that's exactly what she did.

CHAPTER TWENTY-FOUR

MATEO WAS SO intoxicating, Rose had to take a break from him for perspective. The intensity was overwhelming, and to keep herself together she decided to take a few days on her own to see the sights. Besides, Mateo had a restaurant to run, and she knew he was neglecting his duties to spend more time with her. They were both adults, and while they tried to pretend they had more control over their libidos, the only thing that worked was physical distance. Rose tried not to think about the day she'd leave Varenna and Mateo permanently, wondering what would happen with this relationship. Was it even a relationship?

Rose spent two days exploring Lake Como on her own. She wanted to take in the sights, sketch some local gardens, and breathe in the creative inspiration she sorely needed for her work back home. As much as she wanted this man in her life, she had to remember she was in Italy. She didn't want to spend her entire trip in her flat or inside his restaurant. She may never be here again, so she wanted to see as much of it as she could. And even if Mateo could leave his work entirely and join her, she liked being on her own for a while. The distraction of Mateo made it hard to appreciate anything but him, and the space she felt away from him allowed other pleasures to seep into her life.

Rose bought a six day ferry pass so she could come and go around the lake as she liked, realizing very quickly that ferry ticket stations in these small towns were often closed even when the ferry was running. Italy wasn't quite as efficient as what she was used to back in the United States, but there were other charms to make up for it.

The clean, fresh air invigorated her. Rose checked email once a day for work, noting with some surprise that things were running quite well without her, despite the delay with Henry and Mary's project. One payoff from her years of organization and control freak tendencies was that she had good systems in place, even better systems than she thought. With more than a wisp of regret, Rose realized she could have taken a vacation long before now, at least from the standpoint of leaving her business.

Rose stood on the deck of the ferry as it neared the dock in Varenna. She'd enjoyed the last two days mostly on her own, seeing Mateo only once for lunch because he was busy with work. She looked forward to seeing him for dinner tonight. He told her they'd be joined by some of his friends, and Rose wondered how he'd behave around them. She wondered how she'd behave, too.

Being in this place, away from her home and friends and regular life, made this relationship feel foreign, alien. So far, it hadn't impacted her life back home in any way, and he wouldn't have a chance to meet her friends, at least not here. Rose liked the way it was neat and orderly and compartmentalized, and then she remembered that the goal was to move away from that kind of thinking, to get a little bit messy. Wild Rose wouldn't be thinking about keeping Mateo on the side, sharing him with her friends as only a vacation romance story. For a while Rose thought she'd get away with keeping him compartmentalized because they were so far away from her life. But now he was bringing in friends of his own. She sighed, wondering if this bit of real life was going to put a damper on their relationship.

Once the gangway was lowered, Rose walked off with the few other passengers on the boat with her and made the now familiar journey to the restaurant. She wanted a little nap, followed by a shower and a fun evening. When she arrived at the restaurant, she could see Mateo through the window, pacing on the phone. He seemed to be talking intently, and she wondered if it was for business. Then he smiled and laughed, walking further away from the center of the restaurant for privacy.

Rose walked in the door and decided to gently touch him on the shoulder to let him know she was back. The need to feel him when he was near was powerful, even when he was working. As she approached, Rose could hear his end of the conversation. The words were in Spanish, but she understood enough to get the gist of the conversation.

"Carla, I know you're hurting, but I promise it will be better soon." Mateo spoke softly into the phone.

Rose's stomach lurched. Was this *the* Carla, the one who supposedly broke his heart? And if so, why was he talking to her, reassuring her?

Rose began backing up like a deer who'd stumbled on a lion's den. She didn't want Mateo to see her, to know that she'd overheard him. A few steps back and she'd turn toward the door to the flat where she could think this through in private, come up with some kind of explanation.

Rose took a step too far, bumping into a table where two men were having coffee. The table scraped loudly on the floor and their coffee sloshed out of their cups and onto the table. The men scooted back in time to avoid the spill, but the scuffing noise of their chairs alerted Mateo to the scene and he turned around to face her.

Rose apologized to the men, reaching for napkins to help clean the spill. Mateo quickly and quietly finished his call before walking over and interrupting the scene. He acted like nothing had happened.

"Rose, did you enjoy your day of sightseeing? Chef Aldo worried that you didn't take a lunch with you. He sometimes forgets there are other restaurants on Lake Como besides this one." Mateo smiled at her, waiting for a reply.

Rose stood with soggy napkins in her right hand, aware of just how quiet the restaurant had become. Her throat was blocked, choking on the words she wanted to say. The intensity of their connection left no room in her mind or heart for anyone else, and she thought Mateo felt the same way. The phone call was evidence he didn't, and maybe never had. Rose started feeling very foolish, like she'd been played with some smooth talk by an exotic guy, the exact same thing she'd warned Rachel about.

Get it together, Rose. Don't step into the drama until you have more information.

"What's not to love about Lake Como? And no worries for Chef Aldo. I managed to find a perfectly nice pasta for lunch, but I saved plenty of room for dinner tonight." Rose turned to the men at the table. "I'm so sorry for bumping into your table. Please let me buy you another round of coffee."

"There is no need, Rose. These are my two oldest friends and business partners from Madrid, Alejandro and Ruben. Alejandro knows more about wine than any sommelier I've ever met, and Ruben is always on the cutting edge of everything. *Amigos*, this is Rose, who's visiting from America and staying in the upstairs flat. As an honored guest, I've invited her to join us for dinner tonight, so please be on your best behavior."

Rose instantly stiffened at the verbal distance he placed between them. He called her Rose, not Rosa or *cariño*. Worse, he'd called her an honored guest, like she was a visiting aunt and not the woman he'd loved until the sun came up just two days ago.

Why was he hiding their relationship when he'd been so open in front of his employees? Rose wondered if this all had to do with the conversation she just overheard. Or was he embarrassed by her, wanting to keep their attraction a secret? *Don't get dramatic, Rose.* Maybe he just needed a few days of male bonding. Rose kept going back to the worst option: he had a girlfriend in Madrid, and he'd probably had one all along.

"*Encantado, Rose!*" Ruben leapt to his feet and kissed her on each cheek. "I thought I'd have to look at these two ugly *hombres* all night, and now you have saved me. I will arrange for you to be seated across from me so that we don't have to let them spoil our view of each other." Ruben bowed slightly and grinned, an expert at the flirting game. Alejandro rolled his eyes at his friend before turning to Rose and completely ignoring Ruben.

"Welcome to Italy, Rose. Are you enjoying yourself?" Alejandro was more formal in his greeting, yet still warm. He gave her the traditional two cheek kiss of the Spanish. Rose never could remember when it was two kisses or three with all the Spanish and Italians around her. It was like dancing, following the lead of whatever man she was with. She actually preferred the handshake or hug tradition from America, where she didn't have to worry about what to do with her lips—or her heart.

"It's nice to meet you both. I am having a great time in Italy, and what could be better than another delicious meal from Chef Aldo in the company of three charismatic men?" She turned the charm on high, avoiding Mateo's gaze altogether.

"Please let me know if you need anything at all, my dear Rose. Mateo is not nearly the gentleman I am, and he has probably neglected to show you the charms of this beautiful place. I, of course, am happy to rectify this oversight." Ruben again grinned at her as Mateo shook his head.

"That's enough out of you, Ruben. Can you leave our guest alone until dinner at least?" Mateo said. Rose bristled at the comment. *Our guest?* Now he really was treating her like a tenant. That's certainly not how he felt a couple of nights ago when he had her panties in his mouth.

"I will see you this evening, then. I know Chef Aldo will outdo himself tonight if all three owners are here." Rose smiled and turned toward the door, feeling Mateo's eyes on her back as she walked away. Why was it she never thought about walking until she knew someone was watching her? Those fifteen steps to the door felt like an eternity, and as soon as she closed it behind her she fell against it, wondering if all the buildup of the last few days was over.

Was she just some kind of fling to Mateo? That's how it felt, and even though she hadn't given a lot of thought to a forever romance with Mateo, she at least thought it was more than a physical attraction, that there was something else there. Did he feel the same way, or was it all a ploy to get her in bed? She hadn't pegged him as the sort of man who dumps a woman after sex, but the man she just talked to was a different person than the one she thought she knew.

Rose began overthinking again, running through outrageous scenarios in her mind until she was convinced he had a wife and three kids in Madrid, a warrant out for his arrest, or worse. After so much progress on living in the moment and taking him at his word, Rose was slipping back into her old familiar routine, working herself into a frenzy because she couldn't understand the change in Mateo. His actions didn't match up with his words, and because of his two friends she couldn't call him out on it.

Or could she?

CHAPTER TWENTY-FIVE

"NOW, WHERE WERE we?" Mateo tried to get the conversation back on track after Rose walked away, hoping his friends wouldn't ask about her. It was a foolish hope, of course.

"We were watching that beautiful woman walk away. What's her story?" Ruben took a sip of coffee, waiting for an explanation while Alejandro signaled to Lorenzo that they'd take another round of coffee. He knew their conversation was going to take a while, especially now that Ruben had his eye on Rose.

"She's the mother of one of our employees. Well, a former employee. It's a long story, but essentially she came to visit right at the point her daughter decided to take another job in Australia. So she's here for a few weeks on her own." Mateo tried to make it sound very casual, gauging their responses before revealing his own feelings. He'd been alone for five years now, and it would be a surprise to them both to find out he was starting another relationship, especially after the news about Carla's divorce.

Carla. After all this time she decided to call him

back and apologize. In the days of pain and sorrow she was a ghost, but now that he didn't care anymore she wanted to do the 12-step thing and atone for her past sins. The nice guy part of Mateo knew she was hurting and took no pleasure in it. He consoled her and reminded her things would get better; he was proof of that. But a little part of him rejoiced in knowing that people reap what they sow. These past five years had taught him what he really wanted in a relationship, and he was going to take all the right steps with Rose.

After he got through this visit with his friends, of course. They were just too intense, too opinionated, and too nosy for such a delicate stage in a relationship. Mateo and Rose were barely out of the standoff phase when she thought he was after her daughter. No way was Mateo going to risk their progress just because Alejandro and Ruben decided to drop in for a visit.

"Are you still with us, Mateo?" Ruben snapped his fingers, bringing Mateo back into the moment.

"Nice of you to invite her to join us for dinner, Mateo. Anything we should know about that?" Alejandro zeroed in on the real situation faster than Ruben, probably because he wasn't thinking of his own libido. Alejandro was happily married and loved his family life, a fact Ruben found boring and Mateo found charming.

"Rose is here alone, and she's a smart and funny woman. I thought you'd enjoy meeting her and I hope

I'm not wrong about her meeting you, Ruben." With a short laugh, Mateo tried to switch subjects. "So let's get back to business. You've seen the statements from the accountant and know how well we did this season. The restaurant can pay us ten percent more this year than last, even though I recommend we bank it for the future." Mateo closed his folder on the table and leaned back in his chair. "We can dive deeper into the details if you want, but I can tell you guys came with your own agenda. What do you want to discuss?"

"This is why you were the perfect one to run the restaurant, Mateo. Everyone back home told us we were foolish to go into the food business, especially in another country, but you've made it work for us. Good job, *amigo*." Alejandro's words sounded scripted, and Mateo wondered if this meeting had been practiced just like Alejandro's big court arguments. If so, that probably wasn't a good thing.

"Why do I feel like I'm about to get fired or promoted?" Mateo said. They all stopped talking for a moment as Lorenzo arrived with a fresh round of coffee. When he left, Ruben resumed talking.

"Because you're getting both, Mateo." Ruben opened his sugar packet and poured the entire thing into his small cup. "It's time for us all to move on," he said as he stirred. Alejandro frowned at Ruben's abrupt entry into his perfectly planned speech.

"What Ruben is trying to say is that we're ready to sell this investment while it is still performing well. We should go out while we're on top and invest our money in more stable ventures. I have a family now, and Ruben wants to put more of his money into technology. And we both think you need to get back to Spain and stop licking your wounds here in Italy." Alejandro reached out and squeezed Mateo's shoulder, hoping he understood their reasoning.

"So you get fired from the job but promoted because you'll get a nice payout to come back to Madrid and be an architect again." Ruben smiled at him as he picked up his cup. "Someone with your talent shouldn't be hiding out in Italy making coffee for tourists when he could be building and creating in Spain. The recession is lifting, *amigo*. We need you back home." Ruben sipped and waited for Mateo to agree. Mateo knew he worked with techies and engineers all day. Ruben was used to spilling out the logical argument and having everyone either agree or propose an even better solution. Emotional arguments rarely came up. Ruben's world was black and white, no room for gray.

Mateo looked back and forth between his two friends, feeling a little ambushed. Even though he was thinking of moving on with his life and getting out of Varenna some day, he wanted it to be on his own terms. Besides, there was no way they would sell this place at the end of the season.

"You guys know how long it will take to find a buyer? This place had been on the market for two years when we bought it." Mateo wondered if they had even thought this far ahead.

"We already have a buyer, Mateo. He approached us, but we wanted to talk to you first and see if you wanted to give Lorenzo a crack at it. Either way we want to sell it, but we know you've been grooming him for a while." Ruben was so matter-of-fact about it, and it bothered Mateo that they'd had these conversations without him.

"How long have you been thinking about this? And why are you just now including me? We're equal partners, or at least we're supposed to be." Mateo tried not to get angry, but he was the one who'd spent five years making the restaurant into a success, and it bothered him that Alejandro and Ruben would start these discussions without him.

"It's been in the back of our minds for a while, but we didn't have any formal discussions until two weeks ago when the buyer reached out to us. My firm is the attorney of record for the restaurant, so the buyer naturally contacted me first. And once we had a cash offer, it just made sense to move forward. We weren't keeping anything from you, *amigo*. This just happened, but you have to admit it makes sense. It's time to get out of the restaurant game while we still have a profit." Alejandro put his attorney face on, working to create an agreement among the parties at the table.

Mateo knew deep down they were right, but he wasn't ready to admit it. And deeper than that was the issue of going back to Madrid. Could he have a life there again? Did he even want that anymore? He'd kept up his architecture license and association memberships during his time in Varenna. And he knew he wouldn't have trouble finding a job if he needed one. He designed an apartment building in the trendy Chueca neighborhood of Madrid before leaving, and he knew it had already become a landmark in its few short years of existence. That building was a gold star on his resume, a foot in the door to any firm in the city unless he decided to work for himself. But even with that security, was he ready to return to Madrid?

"Well, if you both are committed to this plan, there's nothing else I can do but agree to it. I don't have enough money to buy you out, and even if I did, I don't know that I'd want to own this place without you. We're still the Three Amigos, you know." Mateo sighed. "Let me run this by Lorenzo on my own and see where he stands, and then we'll decide a way to move forward." Mateo signaled across the room to Lorenzo. "Flip the sign to closed for a while, Lorenzo. And bring a bottle of grappa and two glasses. We need to talk."

# # #

"Don't get me wrong—I want the restaurant. I just wasn't expecting to take it over so soon, and I don't have as much money saved as I'd like just yet. To tell you the truth, I was not going to negotiate buying this place after a stellar season like we just had. I was hoping for a little downturn to get a better price." Lorenzo shrugged his shoulders, giving Mateo his honest appraisal of the situation.

"Lorenzo, this is a pretty quick decision for us, too. Believe me, I wasn't even thinking about this a week ago, but I can't deny it's a good time to bow out for the three of us." Mateo chose his next words carefully, not wanting to talk his friend into buying a restaurant he wasn't ready for. It was a profitable one, no doubt, but without some cash reserves it would be hard to maintain, especially starting ownership in the off-season. "It's a lot to take on by yourself. Do you have anyone who could partner with you?"

"I've been thinking of asking Chef Aldo to go in with me, and I'm considering asking Signor Irving for a financial investment. He spends a couple of months here every year renting the apartment, and I know he's a smart investor." Mateo was pleasantly surprised to see how much thought Lorenzo had already put into this. "Of course I'd like to own it outright, but there is safety in numbers, and if I can find a solution that gives me silent partners or at least a fair split of duties like with Chef Aldo, then I think I can swing this." Lorenzo paused for a moment, transitioning from a business tone to a more personal one. "I really appreciate you offering this to me first, Mateo. It means a lot that you would consider me ready for this kind of responsibility." He curled up one side of his mouth into a smirk before adding, "Besides, the restaurant will finally be back in the hands of an Italian and I won't have to worry about a Spaniard messing up the menu or service." Both men laughed at that, and Mateo patted Lorenzo on the back.

"You'll do a great job, Lorenzo, I know it. And you won't have to worry that I snuck some chorizo into the sauce when you weren't looking." This was a long-standing joke between the two of them, that Mateo was looking for any excuse to put his beloved sausage in every dish. Mateo always answered with the fact that Lorenzo just didn't know good chorizo because he was Italian. It was the kind of good-natured ribbing he was going to miss.

Even so, Mateo was relieved they were selling to Lorenzo instead of an unknown buyer who might only be thinking of profit. Varenna was the least touristy stop on Lake Como, and he wanted to keep it that way. He didn't want large tour groups descending on his beautiful little restaurant and pushing out the local patrons and quirky solo travelers who found their way here. And he knew Chef Aldo would quit before turning the restaurant into an Americanized Italian restaurant with bread and olive oil on the table before the meal and cans of fake shredded cheese to shake onto the pasta. He cringed at the thought, recalling the first of many times he was asked for bread before the meal, or for extra cheese on a dish. He wondered what other inaccuracies there were outside of Italy about Italian food, especially in America. He made a mental note to ask Rose about this.

Oh, Rose. This whole idea about selling the restaurant just might freak her out. Here he was saying he was ready to move forward with his life, and then a few days later he's selling his restaurant. Would she think he was moving too fast, that he was going to follow her back to America like a puppy dog? Mateo wasn't sure how this was going to play out with Rose in the long term, but he didn't want to stop the progress they'd made so far. He had to come up with a plan fast, before Rose knew about the sale of the restaurant and before Alejandro and Ruben found out his true feelings for Rose. Mateo just didn't need that complication yet. He loved his friends, but they could be just as bad as his family at trying to run his life. Sometimes he thought his mother used Alejandro as her own personal messenger of guilt over his life choices, though it was easier to distract Alejandro from the topic than it was his mother.

"Hey, boss. You there?" Lorenzo snapped his fingers in front of Mateo's face. He realized with a start that he'd drifted off into fantasy land. "I was hoping you could speak to Chef Aldo for a few minutes tonight. I know he will have some questions, and I'd like him to get the answers straight from you so he feels comfortable investing in the restaurant. Would you mind doing that without Ruben and Alejandro? Chef Aldo is old school, and he doesn't know them as well. He thinks of you as the owner, and I know a conversation with you would ease his mind about a few things."

"Sorry, Lorenzo. Of course I'll talk to Chef Aldo. Just come get me at the table tonight after he's got the courses going and pretend there's a small issue in the kitchen. I'll excuse myself to go talk to him." He briefly thought of Rose again, wondering what she'd wear tonight. Then he wondered what she'd wear underneath. It was going to be very hard for him to contain his feelings for her in front of Alejandro and Ruben. He'd tell her later why he was holding back, but he didn't worry about the dinner tonight because he knew Ruben would flirt like crazy and all attention would be on him. Ruben's normal date was Rachel's age, not Rose's, but he was never able to stay quiet around any beautiful woman.

Mateo brought himself back into the present and said, "I'm glad this is working out, really I am. You are the best owner for this restaurant, and I wish you many years of prosperity and happiness here."

Lorenzo would preserve the ambiance of the place, and Mateo felt good about the change. Now if he could just figure out his personal life, he'd be in good shape.

CHAPTER TWENTY-SIX

WHEN ROSE BEGAN primping for dinner it reminded her of all those weekends in high school with Violet, Ivy, Daisy, and Lily. They'd have the latest issue of *Seventeen* magazine's beauty treatments, and they'd take turns painting each other's nails, giving each other VO5 hot oil treatments, and putting oatmeal on their faces to draw out the oil. There was plenty of talk then about all the boys they liked, both at the high school and in the movies. Rose thought of those Saturday nights now and how there were no actual boys in their lives then, but she was now primping herself for dinner with three handsome Spaniards in Italy. The high school Rose could have never imagined this in her future.

But the Rose of this morning would have never guessed Mateo was still in contact with his ex-fiancée Carla, either. Or that she might not even be his ex. So dinner with three handsome men still meant she was going to bed alone tonight.

Rose knew she was attractive enough that men wanted to sleep with her. Most women were. But she wanted something more, and Mateo's reaction this afternoon in front of his friends made her feel just as insecure as she did back in high school. What game was he playing? She couldn't figure out how they'd gone from such a hot connection just two days before to the cold shoulder, and she was pissed that his actions plunged her into this zone of insecurity.

After the shower she dried her hair and then put some Moroccan oil on it. This was a new beauty tip from Violet, whose dark hair always shone, and it made Rose's auburn hair sparkle in the light. Rose loved being this age, old enough to have a real sense of herself, to appreciate her features and simply be aware of her shortfalls. What else could she do? The Rose of old would have obsessed over her imperfections, but time had taught Rose there was no happiness in that path, and she was glad she'd learned it. *Focus on the hair, don't worry about the little tummy bulge.* By the time she finished her hair, it was a wavy, vibrant crown and she felt like a goddess. She went light on her makeup with a dewy tinted moisturizer and just a coating of mascara. She saved the focus for her ruby red lips.

Rose did a quick review of her options and decided on the garnet red dress. This was a vintage dress she picked up years ago and had never worn. She was shopping with Ivy on one of her visits back to the United States and tried it on, vamping at the full-length mirror at the store while Ivy and the clerk looked on in stunned silence. Rose didn't remember

Ivy's exact words when she finally spoke, but she'd never forget the look on Ivy's face. The clerk rushed around the store looking for the perfect shoes and placed them at her feet like an offering. Rose slipped her feet into the nude peekaboo heels, which made her legs look a mile long. What started out as a joke ended up costing her a small fortune because Ivy wouldn't let her leave the store without the dress, shoes, and a purse. For weeks afterward Ivy sent her emails listing all the places and faces she would wow with that dress. Funnily enough, one of the places was Lake Como (on a double date with Ivy and George Clooney, of course). None had come to pass until now.

The dress hugged her waist, taming that little tummy jiggle, and was cinched with a thin red belt. The bodice had an angular neckline and cap sleeves with a little bit of ruching at the bust, playing up her assets. The skirt flowed out and down to her knees, a nice little umbrella effect over her long legs and those sexy peekaboo shoes. Underneath it all she wore a red pushup bra and matching panties. After the weird vibe from Mateo that afternoon she knew no one else would see them, but she felt a little bit sexier just wearing them. Tonight she needed all the power she could get.

By the time she finished dressing and twirled in the mirror she decided the man most likely to fall in love with her that night was Chef Aldo. She was Wild Rose, 1950s Pinup Starlet and Breaker of Spanish Hearts.

Tonight she was guarding the Fortress of Rose with a ferocious kind of beauty, and damn the man who thought he could conquer her.

Rose put her necklace on, checked the time to make sure she was fashionably late, and headed for the door. Just before she walked downstairs she decided to capture the moment, taking a photo of herself in the full-length mirror and texting it to her friends: *3 dates for dinner tonight. #LateBloomerRevenge*

Rose threw her phone down on the bed, grabbed her scarf, and headed downstairs to find out just what game Mateo was playing.

# # #

Ruben jumped up from the table when he saw Rose come through the door. *"Qué hermosa!"* Alejandro and Mateo turned their heads and stood up. Ruben walked over and took her arm, guiding her to the corner table where they were seated. "You look beautiful tonight, my dear Rose. We are not worthy to dine with you, but we are lucky bastards because there is no competition for your favors in our almost empty restaurant." Ruben laid on the charm, and Rose was grateful for his showmanship because it meant she didn't have to look at Mateo right away. Ruben kissed her cheeks before pulling out a chair for her.

Alejandro said simply, "You look lovely tonight, Rose," before sitting back down. Mateo just stared, momentarily losing himself. Alejandro snapped his fingers in his face. "*Hola*, Mateo. You still with us?"

"Rose, you look beautiful. I'm so happy you could join us." Mateo smiled and sat down, never taking his eyes off her.

"Good evening, gentlemen. It's not often I have dinner with three handsome men at once, so I dressed for the occasion. Thankfully the belt on this dress has a few extra notches so I can still enjoy the food without restraint. I may look like a real lady now, but I promise you I will enjoy this food with gusto." Rose parted her ruby red lips in a giant smile, remembering her conversation with Mateo about the sensuality of eating together. Well, tonight he was going to eat his heart out before she was done with him.

Lorenzo walked over to ask if they were ready to begin their meal, clearing the empty glasses of Aperol spritz the men had been enjoying as an *aperitif*. His tone was stiff and a bit nervous, far different from the warm interactions she'd had with him previously. Mateo nodded, and Lorenzo turned and walked away. Lorenzo seemed preoccupied, or even a little bit worried. She wondered what it could be and why the men at the table couldn't see it. Or maybe they did and just chose to ignore it. Rose was beginning to think she knew absolutely nothing about men, but it was still more than they knew about women.

Ruben took the lead in conversation as they enjoyed their wine and *antipasti*, sharing stories about their childhood exploits. It sounded as if they'd always been this way, with Alejandro as the serious one, Ruben as the flirt, and Mateo as the smooth talker. In every story, Alejandro tried to warn them of trouble, Ruben talked them into the trouble, and Mateo quietly tried to get them out of trouble, or at least to soften the blow of the punishment. Mateo's angelic face often prevented him from being blamed, so it was agreed amongst them he would always admit fault if there was no clean way out. It was a pretty smart plan for three adventurous boys.

Judging from the stories, these three had been a handful as children, and Rose was secretly thankful she had just one child. She couldn't imagine a trio of Rachels to manage. She laughed at Ruben's stories, imagining them to be only half true, and enjoyed the distraction from her hurt over Mateo. Rose wondered if she'd fallen for his angelic face and if he was looking for a way out of the trouble with her. Mateo had already negotiated himself into her pants and heart, but she wasn't going to be so forgiving if this was all a game he was ready to quit now that he'd had some fun.

When the pasta course arrived, Lorenzo leaned in low to speak to Mateo, who excused himself from the table to check on something in the kitchen. Ruben poured more wine and asked Rose about her childhood and whether she got into as many scrapes as they did. She told Alejandro and Ruben about her unusual upbringing with the Late Bloomers and how her friends were more like sisters, even to this day.

Alejandro and Ruben didn't know who John Elway was, but they roared with laughter when she told them about Ivy's rumor in high school that Rose was this famous football player's distant cousin just so she could snag a date to prom with her crush Sammy Tice.

"I think we might need to meet this woman, Ivy. Maybe the next time I'm in London you can make an introduction?" Ruben never let his foot off the gas when it came to meeting, flirting, and seducing women.

"I'm not sure if it's a good idea to put you two together, Ruben. There might be an international treaty that prevents that kind of thing." She winked at him. "It was my group of friends who convinced me to come to Italy, you know. I haven't yet decided if they are getting me into trouble or out of it or something in between." Rose took a sip of wine and looked over at Mateo talking with Lorenzo at the bar. *What was going on with him?* She decided to take advantage of his absence to do some reconnaissance with his friends. "Speaking of trouble, how is it that you three bought this place together but Mateo is the one who runs it? Did he lose a bet to get exiled to Italy?"

"Oh, he came here to lick his wounds. We bought this place right after his fiancée Carla broke up with him, so he volunteered to stay and get it going. It was a rough time for him, but we honestly never imagined he'd stay here so long. She really did him wrong." Alejandro shook his head as he plunged his fork into his pasta, rolling it up against his spoon like a pro.

"Yeah, but she's back on the market now and he won't be here much longer. Life changes. Who knows what will happen?" Ruben smiled at Rose before taking a big sip of wine. "But why are we talking about him? He's not nearly as interesting as me."

Rose laughed to keep the mood light, but she could feel her stomach knot. No wonder he'd cooled toward her. His friends arrived with news that his one true love was single again and he was making plans to go back to Madrid for her. Rose remembered his words to Carla on the phone: *I promise it will be better soon.*

All those words about being ready to move on with his life might have been true—Rose just wasn't the one Mateo wanted to move forward with.

After the heat of their night together, the romantic meals and secrets shared, how could he drop her so fast for a woman who broke his heart five years ago? Rose thought of the chemistry between them, the heat and intensity. If he was ready to leave her for Carla, the two of them must burn hotter than the sun. Rose had never had such a connection with anyone, ever, and she thought Mateo felt the same way. Now she was realizing that maybe it was only special for her. She imagined Carla as a Penelope Cruz lookalike, one whose passion and fiery nature made Rose look like a mouse in comparison.

"So which one of you runs the restaurant after Mateo leaves? And please tell me you're keeping Chef Aldo. This pasta is the best thing I've ever eaten." She dug into her plate, eyes down to hide her emotions, and let Alejandro and Ruben start fighting over which one of them would be the best manager if they had to do it.

"You would try to date all our female customers! There is no way you could ever run a restaurant, Ruben," Alejandro stated.

"If it were up to you, we'd turn this into a family-friendly pizza joint and there would be children running everywhere!" Ruben countered. He leaned over to Rose and loudly whispered, "Children are bad for my digestion."

"What he means to say is that a restaurant full of children likely means no single women, and Ruben couldn't stand that." The three of them laughed, and at that point Lorenzo walked up to tell them about their next course, an osso buco served over risotto. He also introduced their next wine, an Amarone of some distinction.

"Whoa, are you trying to deplete the stock of the expensive stuff before the official handover or what?" Ruben joked, reaching out to squeeze Lorenzo's arm.

"Hey, you surprised me today. I've got to start thinking like a boss, and one way to do that is to move more product, right?" Lorenzo smiled at both Alejandro and Ruben. "Besides, I know how much you like to impress beautiful women." Lorenzo gave a small bow to Rose. "Mateo will be back in time for the osso buco, and your server will be over with your wine in a moment. Enjoy." Lorenzo turned and left.

Rose realized the strain between Lorenzo and the other men before was that they were dumping the management of the restaurant on him so Mateo could go back to Madrid and be with Carla. Obviously Alejandro and Ruben thought it was a good idea for Mateo to be with Carla or they wouldn't encourage him to go.

Rose was glad she didn't jump to conclusions earlier, but now it was all laid out in front of her. Mateo was going back to Madrid with the full support of his business partners. He was in contact with Carla, telling her it would all be better soon. And, most importantly, he was pushing Rose away while at the same time keeping all this information from her.

He was a liar and a player, just like she first suspected when Rachel emailed the picture of him. Why hadn't she trusted her gut back then? The target might have changed, but the arrow was still sharp enough to break a heart.

Mateo rejoined the table, nodding at Alejandro and Ruben that he'd taken care of things. Rose wondered what he meant, but she decided not to engage with him unless she had to. The wine gave her a warm glow, and combined with the heat of her pain from being privately dumped in public she knew her mouth was probably too loose for its own good. She was glad to see the server returning with their dinners, and shortly afterward with the Amarone.

They toasted to good food, looking each person in the eye as was the Spanish custom. As she looked at

Mateo, Ruben repeated the old wives' tale that not looking into each other's eyes would lead to seven years of bad sex. *Bad sex? How about no sex with him ever again?* Rose thought.

What was she thinking, coming to Italy and having an affair with a man she hardly knew, one she thought was initially after her daughter anyway! She felt foolish, and then even madder for being made to feel foolish. Rose was an accomplished, attractive, and smart woman, and she didn't like being played. And that was exactly how she felt at the moment.

Through the rest of the evening she shamelessly flirted with Ruben, knowing he was the most harmless one at the table. At least he put all his cards on the table, not faking his interest in the shadows while hiding them in the light in front of others. He didn't call her *cariño* or talk about new beginnings. He simply flirted, one attractive person to another, with no strings. She wished Mateo had been so honest. Now everything he'd ever said to her was suspect, whispers in the dark that wouldn't hold up in the light of day. Rose was glad to be seeing this now before her heart got too involved. Rachel was gone, and it was time for her to leave, too.

One thing she liked about being forty was the lack of need to play along with this kind of drama. She was done, ready to chalk this experience up as a failure and move on to the next one. In her twenties and thirties she might have tried to make it work, banking on the chemistry to carry her through, but at this point she knew the futility of that kind of plan. With age came wisdom, and Rose wasn't going to overlook hers.

"So how much longer will you be staying in Italy, Rose? I'm here for a few days and would love to take you out to dinner without these bozos. It is bad for my digestion to share a beautiful woman's attention with unworthy men." Ruben was laying it on thick, and Rose enjoyed the fact that he said these outrageous things as much for his own enjoyment as hers. He was a true showman.

"I'm leaving for Milan tomorrow and then off to London." As soon as she said it, Mateo's eyes went wide. *He must think I'm stupid enough to stick around for another go before he runs back to Carla*, she thought. That made her even madder than before, that he would try to play her and then think she was too dumb to know it when the evidence was right in front of her. She might have misjudged his character before, but now that the blinds were removed, she was seeing all of his flaws. Thank god she didn't get any deeper into this.

The Late Bloomers were going to have fun analyzing this situation later. She couldn't wait to hear the names Ivy made up for Mateo. This was a special skill of hers, to create politically incorrect nicknames for the men who didn't work out.

"I thought you were staying for a few weeks?" Mateo asked casually. Rose noted that he didn't ask her to stay longer or say anything to note that she was more important than a tenant. The evidence kept piling up.

"Oh, there's really no reason for me to stay now, is there? Rachel's gone to Australia and I don't want to spend the rest of my holiday alone. I think I'll go see my friend Ivy in London and possibly head up to Scotland for a bit. I hear the men wear kilts up there." Rose smiled and winked at Ruben as she said it.

"Rose, you are killing me! Why would you want to see a Scotsman in a kilt when you could see a Spaniard in a well-cut suit!" Ruben was mock offended she would consider any other nationality in her romantic pursuits. He stood and rotated slowly, brushing imaginary lint from his shoulder, allowing her take in his stylish outfit.

"Oh, Ruben. You know there is no future with us. You are too much a lover of women to stay with one, and this is something I knew about you in the first five minutes. I like a man who's honest about who he is. There aren't enough of them in this world." She raised her glass to him, "A toast to you, Ruben. Don't ever change."

"Ah, a woman who can appreciate my talents. Not every woman is so attuned to my charms. Thank you, Rose." Ruben smiled back her.

"Well, it's easier to appreciate your charms when I'm not entangled in them, Ruben." Rose enjoyed the verbal jousting with him, especially when it prevented her from engaging with Mateo. If she played her cards right, she thought she might make it upstairs to her apartment without having to talk to him at all, and then tomorrow she would make a fast getaway.

"Well, on that note I will depart to the street to smoke my evening cigarette. Alejandro, do you want to join me? We can console each other over the fact that Rose is leaving us so soon after we met." Ruben put on a hound dog face, pouting a little for dramatic effect, as Alejandro rolled his eyes at him. Obviously he'd seen this act before. The two men excused themselves from the table and Rose froze, realizing she'd just lost her shield because Mateo didn't smoke. She picked up her napkin from her lap and dabbed at her lips, hoping Mateo would leave first. He waited until his friends were out the door before turning to her.

"When did you decide to leave?" His voice was tightly controlled, only saying what was necessary.

"Today. This afternoon, actually. It has become crystal clear to me that staying is not in my best interest." Rose looked directly at him as she said those last words, challenging him to contradict her.

"We haven't had a chance to talk since Alejandro and Ruben got here, and I have a lot to tell you. I'm not sure what's happened to make you want to leave," Mateo pleaded with her.

"I'm sure you do have a lot you want to tell me, but I'm not listening anymore. I appreciate the use of the flat, and if you want me to pay for my time here I'll happily do it. But I'm leaving tomorrow and I'm not coming back. You get on with your life, and I'll get on with mine." Rose stood up, giving him a full view of what he was missing, and added, "I hope this next phase of your life brings you happiness, Mateo."

"Rose, I think there's been a misunderstanding." Mateo sounded hurt.

"No, the only misunderstanding was mine, and it happened before today. Have a good night, Mateo," she said.

Rose held her head high and walked back toward the door, taking a last minute detour behind the bar and through the kitchen. She wanted to see Chef Aldo, thank him for his attention over the last week, and wish him well. And honestly she wanted to leave on a high note, not with her tail tucked between her legs.

"An early night, my dear?" Chef Aldo asked.

"A wonderful night, Chef. Thank you for a delicious meal. I've never had better." Rose was going to miss this funny and talented man.

"I thought your table would be talking deep into the night, the way you've been going. Is everything okay?" Chef Aldo pushed gently.

"Everything is fine, Chef. I just realized I've been spending way too much energy in Varenna. Rachel is gone now, and it's time I moved on, too. Thank you for sharing a little bit of your world with me." Rose held her head high, shared the three kiss greeting, and then walked back into the restaurant to find it empty. Outside the window she could see Mateo talking with Ruben and Alejandro in the street, gesturing wildly with his arms. She didn't know if he was just telling them a big story or if they were getting in trouble for letting the cat out of the bag about Carla and Madrid, but she didn't care anymore. The only fond memory of a man she'd have from this trip was Chef Aldo.

Rose closed the door behind her and leaned against it, finally able to drop the tough girl persona and indulge in a good cry. She wasn't expecting Mateo to be the love of her life.

Scratch that.

She actually was starting to think he was the love of her life. How else could Rose explain their connection, the way he made her feel? And to know it was all a game to him, a way to pass the time until he moved back to Madrid and his jetsetter life with a Penelope Cruz lookalike who made him feel even more than the passion they shared just two nights ago.

How could a gardener from America compete with that?

The whole situation made Rose feel small and inconsequential, a response she couldn't shake off. She was a smart and accomplished woman, and she wasn't going to stick around and watch her self-esteem die a slow death. Time to get out and save herself.

From now on, she was going back to her old ways, back to keeping men at arm's length and seeking out fun but meaningless relationships like the one she had with her politician friend Steve. She'd rather be known as "Dear Concerned Citizen" than a fool.

CHAPTER TWENTY-SEVEN

"HOPE YOU DON'T have any hot dates planned for the rest of this week because I'm coming to crash on your guest couch. You know I'm a light sleeper, and that kind of sexy adventure just keeps me up all night." Rose gave Ivy a wan smile through the screen on her laptop, trying to be lighthearted and feeling anything but.

"Darling, all my dates take place in expensive hotel rooms or swank resorts. You don't think I'd let men come back to my place, do you?" Ivy joked back, and that's why Rose loved her so much. Ivy wouldn't get serious until Rose was ready.

"Mateo turned out to be a dud, and now that Rachel's gone there's really no reason to stay in Italy. Mind if I come for a visit?" Rose knew she wouldn't mind, but she didn't want to show up unannounced.

"Of course I don't mind. *Mi casa es su casa*. Whoops. You probably don't want to hear any Spanish right now, do you? Tell me what's up with your Spaniard, unless it is that he is a horrible lover, and if that's the case then just make something up for me.

Life is too hopeless if even the exotic lovers are terrible." Ivy gave Rose plenty of room to tell the story the way she needed to in the moment, and Rose was grateful.

"Well, just as it seemed like he was the most perfect man on earth and I happened to meet him at the moment he was ready to get back into the dating game, reality came crashing down. His two business partners turned up and let me know they were changing management at the restaurant right away and Mateo's big breakup from the past was now single again—the one I overheard him talking to on the phone. Coincidence? I think not. What an asshole. And of course I had to hear about all this from two guys I just met, after Mateo cold-shouldered me in front of them." She took a deep breath. "I felt like such an ass, Ivy. I mean, a complete fool. I should have trusted my first impression of him as a total lecherous playboy, only he was after me and not my daughter."

"Oh, Rosie Girl. Come on over to London and we'll get you all fixed up from this little fiasco. The good news is that he wasn't after Rachel and you saw through him early on. But I have to know: did you sleep with him? Because we need to have some in-depth info if I'm to come up with a good nickname. An artist can't produce her best work without inspiration." Ivy winked at her and waited for the laugh she knew was coming.

"Ivy, you are the best. Yes, he definitely deserves an awful nickname. The sex was incredible, at least I thought so, but if you can pack up and leave just two days after mind-blowing sex to hook up with your old love, then I guess it wasn't as good as I thought. It was honestly the best sex of my life, and I'm embarrassed and hurt that it obviously wasn't the same for him." Rose wondered if she was a terrible lover and just didn't know it until now.

"You're not at the end of your life, Rosie Girl. You have plenty of opportunities to keep discovering the best sex of your life. Believe me, there are levels I never knew existed just a few years ago," Ivy said.

"I'll trust you on that one, Ivy." Rose sighed. "Mateo's acting confused right now, like he doesn't understand why I'm leaving. I'm not planning on spelling it out for him just so he can gloat over my heartbreak. I know he wants to have sex again, but that's not going to happen." She flashed a wicked grin. "But I did wear the famous red dress you picked out to dinner with him and his two business partners, so he's feeling the ache of our missed connection a lot more than I am right now."

"Good girl! If you're scheming like that, I know you're going to be just fine." Ivy was proud of Rose for not wallowing in despair and leaving on a powerful note.

"He is one sexy man, and the chemistry between us was hot. It's been a long time since I've had that with a man, and I have to admit I was afraid it would never happen again. So this was either my last-ditch attempt at hot sexy love or the evidence that it can still happen for me. Let's go with the positive, shall we?" Rose ran her fingers through her hair and then removed her earrings.

"One thing I know for sure, Rosie Girl. It's a numbers game. Gotta play to win." As ever, Ivy was practical about her chances at love.

"You had more luck in love over here than I did, Ivy." Rose grinned, knowing she had her attention. "Mateo's business partner Ruben is some bigwig in the tech business in Madrid. He shamelessly flirted with me all night, but when I told him the story about you and John Elway in high school and said that you lived in London, his ears perked up. In fact, he stopped flirting with me just to ask about you. I was your wingman and you weren't even here to appreciate it!" Rose laughed, knowing Ivy would get a kick out of it, too.

"Well then, this trip wasn't for nothing, was it? Just because you didn't find Mr. Right doesn't mean it can't work out for me," Ivy said, resuming the light banter she knew Rose needed.

"I'm checking flights now and will email you details later. I'm going to Milan on the train first thing tomorrow and will fly from there. Thanks a million, Ivy. You are the best." Rose was grateful for friends she could rely on completely.

"Of course I'm the best. I'm just glad you still remember that after all this time. I'll see you soon, Rose. And don't forget to lock your door. I have a feeling Romeo is going to make a Hail Mary move to win you back. At least that's what he'd do if he was smart. See you soon, love."

Rose logged off and undressed, folding up her beautiful dress and putting it in her suitcase. She was fairly well packed after the afternoon news, so it wouldn't take her long to be ready in the morning. It was time to get the hell out of here.

CHAPTER TWENTY-EIGHT

"TSK-TSK. THIS is not good, Mateo." Chef Aldo shook his head. "When a woman is crazy mad and a raving lunatic, you have a chance at making up. When she's stony like a statue, you haven't got a chance. I'm sorry, my friend."

"I don't know what in the hell just happened. I came in here to talk to you, then she announced she was leaving, and Mateo and Alejandro said they didn't talk about me at all. How in the hell can I fix this when I don't know what just happened?" Mateo pounded the butcher block counter with his fist.

"You have to give her some space, and hopefully by daylight you'll figure out what happened. I'd put my money on that little Ruben causing the problem. His mouth never stops."

Mateo walked out to the restaurant but it was dark, everyone already gone. He could go back to the flat and ask Ruben and Alejandro what had happened, but that would alert them to his personal life. If at all possible, he wanted to protect this relationship from the outside world just a little bit longer. Mateo's concerns about his friends were coming true, even without telling them. Imagine how much worse it would be if he had!

No, he couldn't wait until the morning. One way or another, this was getting resolved tonight.

# # #

There was a knock at the door just as Rose finished washing her face before bed.

"Rosa, please let me in. We need to talk. I don't know what's going on, but I don't want to lose you like this." Mateo was pleading softly at the door.

Lose me "like this?" Rose supposed he preferred to lose her after a few more rolls in the hay to get him all primed up for Carla in Madrid. She thought he was a complete asshole, only strengthening her resolve to leave.

"Let's just appreciate the memories and get on with real life, shall we?" Rose knew from her years of owning a business that the longer these negotiations went on, the worse it was for her. She aimed to be decisive from the start, only agreeing to negotiate when she knew there was a chance she'd change her mind. And in this instance, there was no chance. Rose wasn't letting him step a foot in the door, either physically or emotionally.

"I can't be the only one who thought we had something going, Rose. And you checking out like this without explanation makes me doubt everything you said before. I know you felt the same things I did." Mateo was pulling out all the stops. Ivy was right, this was a Hail Mary.

"Mateo, I can assure you that I was not feeling the same things as you. My motives were completely different than yours, and now that we know this about ourselves, it's time to say goodbye. So goodbye, Mateo. And goodnight." Rose said it with as much finality as she could muster, knowing she had to stop this conversation now.

She heard a loud bang as he slapped the door with his hand and she jumped back, expecting the door to break. Rose could hear him retreating down the steps and realized it was a final outburst, the last word in their final conversation. The sound of their breakup was a crack hard enough to break her heart, but not hard enough to break the two-hundred-year-old door that stood between them.

# # #

Just before daybreak, Rose was awake and packed. The restaurant didn't open until 8 a.m., so she was sure she'd beat the arrival of the staff—and Mateo—by leaving now. She'd already checked the train timetables and knew she could catch one coming from Tirano at 6:35 a.m., getting her to Milan Centrale station in plenty of time to get to the airport and fly to London today. She'd be at Ivy's flat before afternoon tea, though the way she was feeling she might as well go to a pub and drown her sorrows in a pint of beer until Ivy finished with work.

The city was quiet in the early morning, with only the bakers at work. The smell wafted out onto the street as Rose walked with her trolley bag, the noise of the wheels hitting the cobblestones as loud as gunshots. She tried lifting her bag to cut down on the noise, but it was too heavy. *Oh hell,* she thought. Varenna was the scene of her heartbreak, so she stopped caring how it felt. Rose wanted out as fast as possible, and if her departure woke a few people, she didn't care anymore.

Rose arrived at the train station just in time to board. She pushed her bag in the luggage compartment and sat down, looking out the window just in time to see Mateo leaning against the post on the platform. He looked terrible, as if he hadn't slept all night. Her heart leapt for a moment, picturing some kind of movie reconciliation, but then she remembered this was real life and he was leaving to be with Carla. Any kind of make up would be solely physical, and her heart was too tied up in this to keep that perspective. Mateo was a far cry from her casual relationship with men like Steve, and she knew it.

Mateo leaned against the post with his arms crossed, looking directly at her. If the train weren't there, she could reach him in just a few steps. But he stood like a statue, motionless, and she stared back at him. Why had he come? And how did he know she'd leave so early?

The train whistle sounded and the final few passengers boarded. Rose knew this was goodbye, and she turned back in her seat and looked down at the book she had in her hands. Her eyes watered as she tried to focus on the page, and she blinked back her tears. No matter what, she wasn't going to look back at Mateo. This little adventure was over, and it was high time she realized it.

CHAPTER TWENTY-NINE

"WHAT IN THE hell did you say to Rose about me last night?" Mateo was at the bar, drinking his fourth cup of coffee of the morning. He didn't sleep a wink the night before, and it was going to be a challenge to get through the day. Mateo's hand throbbed where he'd hit it against the door, and he vaguely wondered if he'd broken a bone.

He'd just watched Rose leave on the train, standing like a fool on the platform because he didn't know what to say or do. He couldn't imagine her getting so upset about the restaurant, if that's what it was, or that he hadn't told her about it yet. The only thing he was sure of was that Alejandro and Ruben had a hand in this.

Alejandro and Ruben held up their hands and stepped back, surprised at the harsh vibe from Mateo so early in the morning.

"Do you think we could have our coffee before you get all *telenovela* on us?" Alejandro raised his hands in mock surrender.

Mateo loudly banged out the grounds and started

making their coffee, Ruben and Alejandro exchanging confused glances while his back was turned. Mateo could see them in the mirror, his anger softening a bit as they seemed just as confused as he was.

Mateo put their coffee on the bar and leaned forward on his elbows. "Okay, guys, talk. What did you say to Rose when I wasn't there?"

Ruben shrugged. "We didn't really talk about you. I mean, I remember her asking why you were running this place instead of one of us, and I quickly moved the subject back to me. Why would I talk you up to a beautiful woman, *amigo*?" Ruben smiled, trying to lighten the mood, but Mateo was having none of it.

"What did she ask about me, and how quickly did you move on from the question? I'm not kidding, man. I need to know exactly what you said." Mateo was trying hard to keep it together.

"I told her you came here to lick your wounds after breaking up with Carla." Mateo could see the realization dawning on his face. "I'm sorry, *amigo*. I didn't know you guys had a thing going. You should have told us and we'd have been more careful. I thought we were just making conversation."

Alejandro's forehead crinkled in concern, and Mateo knew it would kill him to think he'd had a part in a breakup. For a boring lawyer type, Alejandro was surprisingly romantic.

"Oh hell, man. I told her Carla was back on the market. And I also said you were heading back to Madrid soon. I didn't mean the two things were related, though I wondered if you and Carla would hook up again. I'm so sorry, Mateo. I think I gave her the idea that you were going back to Carla." Ruben might have been a player, but he didn't intentionally try to hurt people, least of all his oldest friend.

"Let's talk to her when she comes down. Don't worry, Mateo. We can straighten this out for you. Once she knows we're selling the restaurant this will all start to make sense. Hell, we'll probably be laughing about it over lunch." Alejandro reached out and patted his friend on the forearm.

"Too late, guys. Rose left on the train this morning at 6:30. I watched her go, and until now I couldn't figure out why she changed so fast." He was pissed at his friends, but he knew they didn't do it on purpose. And he had to share some of the blame for keeping everyone in the dark. "You're right that part of this is my fault, too. I should have told you about her and not tried to hide it."

"When you introduced her we had no idea you had any feelings. You were pretty formal. Hell, man, I wouldn't have flirted so hard if I thought you were interested in Rose. And if I thought you weren't interested, then she probably got that vibe, too." Ruben paused for a moment. "I don't know a lot about women, *amigo*, but I do know they don't like to be dissed. And you definitely dissed her if you treated her like a customer instead of your woman."

Mateo knew he was right, and the three of them sat there talking about how all those little missteps turned into the ugly situation in front of them. Just like when they were kids, though, they stopped focusing on how they got into trouble and put all their combined energy into getting out of it. Only this time they couldn't depend on Mateo's angelic face.

# # #

The best thing about Italy is the close proximity to London, Rose thought. She was glad to be away from the country she'd always associate with Rachel leaving home for good and for breaking her heart. She vowed never to eat pasta again in retaliation. What else could she add to the list? Parmesan cheese, Italian wine, gelato, pizza. Maybe all of those except pizza.

Rose pulled her suitcase from the conveyor belt at baggage claim like a pro this time, her anger making her stronger than before. Then she wheeled her way through the airport, expecting to find a cab to take her to Ivy's flat. When Rose finally made it through to the arrivals gate, she was surprised to see Ivy waiting for her, wearing a limousine driver's cap and holding a poster board sign that read, *Chancy Chorizo*. Rose immediately started laughing, forgetting the heartbreak for a few moments. She ran up and hugged Ivy, laughing so hard she started crying.

"I had a burst of creativity while waiting for you to get here, Rosie Girl. Mateo's new nickname is Chancy Chorizo, the Spaniard who looks delicious but gives you heartburn. It's a good fit, don't you think?" Ivy was grinning from ear to hear, happy that she made Rose smile.

"You have no idea how happy I am to see you, Ivy. You are the only medicine I need." Rose lay her head on Ivy's shoulder, squeezing her in a side hug as they walked toward the exit.

"Well, I don't know about that. I've also stocked up on gin, tonic, and lemons, and I've already put an order in for a curry to pick up in one hour, so we'd best be on our way. Oh, and I also rented all three Bourne movies for you to watch if you can't sleep tonight. I know how you like the spy flicks to get your mind off the real-world trouble. One way or another, we're going to get you through this thing." Ivy smiled over at Rose and said, "Besides, how embarrassing would it be for you to stay hung up on a guy named Chancy Chorizo?"

They both laughed as they walked through the sliding doors and out into the drizzly London weather.

CHAPTER THIRTY

IVY AND ROSE took the Underground from Heathrow to the Piccadilly Circus station, then changed lines to go one stop up to Marylebone to finally reach Ivy's flat. They saw more people during this hour-long commute than lived in Rose's small town of Hobart. She was pretty sure she wouldn't see this many people in an entire month back home. Rose thought of her simple life in Arizona and her peaceful and scenic twenty minute drive to work every day. She knew Ivy didn't have a car and depended on the Underground and taxis to get around in London. After seeing the traffic and lack of parking, Rose could see why Ivy chose not to have a car. Besides, she lived in the same neighborhood as the US Embassy, so she could walk to work every day.

Rose loved Ivy's flat. It was a small but modern one-bedroom in a posh building with a doorman, and she even had access to a communal garden out back. Like Ivy, it was stylish but quirky. She had a beautiful crystal chandelier in her tiny dining area, but it was offset by a purple velveteen fake deer head with antlers as a coat rack in the foyer. The flat was full of surprises like that, contrasts that gave a clue to Ivy's unusual personality.

Rose's favorite was a folksy painting Ivy commissioned after befriending a local artist at a farmer's market a few years ago. Five women stood like paper dolls holding hands, but instead of hair, each one had flowers growing from their head. The artist did a pretty spot-on impression of each of the Late Bloomers. Rose loved the roses surrounding her head and falling to her shoulders, and the painting made her smile.

While Rose heaved her suitcase to the side of the door, Ivy went into the kitchen and made two gin and tonics before spooning their takeout curries on proper plates. She set the food and drink down on the coffee table, lit a few candles, and switched on some reggae music.

"Let's get comfy for the night, shall we?"

It didn't take long for them both to change into their yoga pants and curl up on the big red couch to eat.

"Do you think anyone uses yoga pants for actual yoga?" Rose asked.

"Yoga pants are the socially acceptable version of sweat pants." Ivy was an expert on such matters, so Rose believed her even though she would have worn them no matter what.

"This is delicious. It's like the Indian version of the Mexican food we grew up eating and far spicier than anything I had in Italy. I didn't realize how much I missed the heat until now." Rose was glad she had on stretchy pants, because she had an order of the fluffy naan bread still left to eat, and she wasn't going to let it go to waste.

"So nothing spicy on your tongue in Italy, eh? Not even a little chorizo to whet your appetite?" Ivy winked, waiting for Rose to start spilling the story about Mateo.

"Oh, Ivy. I really thought there was something there. There was flirting, and deep sharing, and a blistering hot connection. And the sex. Oh my god, Ivy. The sex was out of this world, or at least it was to me. And I can't for the life of me figure out how I could have misread him. If I hadn't overheard him on the phone with Carla myself I wouldn't have believed it." Rose pulled apart her naan, feeling zero guilt about the bloat she was going to get from this meal. It's not like she'd be taking her clothes off for anyone anytime soon.

"One thing I know for sure, Rosie Girl, is that you are a smart woman. You have a pretty good read on people. He either worked damn hard to fool you, which seems like a lot of planning for a little bit of sex, or there's something missing here. What were the last words you said to each other?" Ivy was in business mode, going into the facts and looking for a resolution to the problem.

"He knocked on my door after our call, but I didn't let him in. He said he didn't want to lose me like this.

I don't know what the hell *like this* means, but in the heat of the moment I took it to mean that he didn't like me finding out what kind of guy he really was. One thing that does make me feel better in this whole scenario is bowing out before the final humiliation. As if that's any real consolation." Rose sighed and stuffed another piece of naan into her mouth. Why did chewy bread pair so well with sadness?

"So let's run down the facts here. You had a serious "I'm ready to give this a go" conversation, followed shortly thereafter by mind-blowing sex that almost set the world on fire. Then his friends come to town and Mateo introduces you as merely a tenant on holiday. But he did invite you to dinner with them. You overhear a conversation on the phone with his ex that sounds like she might not be an ex. And then you find out from those friends when he's not there that his old girlfriend is single again and he's going back to Madrid." Ivy counted off these facts on her fingers, then held up her hands as she continued. "Everything right so far?"

Rose nodded her head, worried as usual about Ivy's intense focus on her personal life. She knew this was going to end with some kind of elaborate plan, one that Rose may or may not be allowed to disagree with.

"Okay, so who's going to run the restaurant if Mateo's leaving? These guys wouldn't leave their investment to a stranger when they're so far away. Restaurants rely too heavily on cash, and the inventory is easy to eat and drink up with freebies to friends. I just don't see these guys patting Mateo on the back and leaving the investment unguarded just so he can get back together with his ex-girlfriend." As usual, Ivy was focused on the facts, not the assumptions.

"Well, it looks like the manager is going to take over. His name is Lorenzo, and he's a local guy that seems pretty responsible." Rose was trying to be objective about this, but it was hard for her to think about the restaurant when she didn't think it had anything to do with the problem.

"So is he as handsome and charismatic as Mateo? Or is he a low-key, get-it-done type of guy? Because I'm telling you, if these guys are smart—and you tell me they are—they know they need a handsome, outgoing guy running the joint in a tourist destination. Those places thrive on online reviews, and if the manager is a dud, even an effective one, it will impact their business." Ivy started looking up the reviews for the restaurant on her phone. "Look at these, Rose. Mateo gets mentioned all the time. He is the heart and soul of the restaurant. No way those guys would let him walk out so easy. They all have money tied up in this, remember?"

"Well, it doesn't matter what they're thinking, does it? He's leaving, which they even admitted to and seemed okay with, and he's going back to Madrid. Which is where Carla lives, where he had most of his business success, and where his friends and family are. I don't think I need to know more than that because I can't compete with all that." Rose went to the kitchen to make them another round of gin and tonics, which seemed like the official cocktail of the UK, judging from the rows of gin she saw at the duty-free shops at the airport. Rose still thought of Mateo every time she saw wine and couldn't bear to have a glass without him. Though she did think that maybe she could safely indulge in her favorite boxed wine when she got home. Maybe she'd even start drinking it out of plastic juice glasses to completely break the spell.

"I dunno. I think we're missing something here, Rose. Maybe you should have given him a few minutes to explain himself before walking out—at least so I could have some closure from this affair." Ivy grinned at Rose, who rolled her eyes before handing over the tumbler of gin and tonic.

They spent the rest of the night talking about Ivy's life, the various casual boyfriends, her chance of a promotion within the US Embassy, and when she was coming back to Arizona to visit again. It felt good to be sitting cross-legged on Ivy's couch with her hair in a ponytail just talking about life. With Rachel grown and gone, she needed more time with her friends, and this was a great start.

When Ivy started yawning, Rose told her to go to bed. Before leaving, Ivy pointed out the ottoman that held the pillows and linens for the couch and then hugged her tight.

"You're gonna be okay, Rosie. You just have to give that Chancy Chorizo a day or two to work through your system. That's all."

CHAPTER THIRTY-ONE

"HEY, RACHEL. HOW'S it going?" Mateo heard shouting and yelling in the background and wondered what Rachel could be doing at that moment.

"Hey, Mateo. It's good to hear from you! I'm on the tour bus in Sydney, taking our group to dinner. What's going on?" Rachel sounded as if she were at the bottom of a well, especially when she put her hand over the phone to talk to someone else. "If you need me to translate a menu or something this is not a good time."

"Listen, I was wondering if you could give me Ivy's phone number. Your mom left something here and I want to arrange to get it back to her before she flies home." He didn't want to go into too many details with Rachel, and he hoped she would think the request was no big deal. Mateo didn't even know if Rachel was aware her mom left.

"Mom's not too attached to stuff, so I wouldn't get too paranoid about it. But sure, I'll text you her phone number so you can coordinate it." Rachel was already looking up Ivy's phone number and sending it to him.

"Okay, you should have it now. Anything else? We're almost at our stop."

"No, that's great, Rachel. Thanks so much. Hope you're having fun at the new job. You know we miss you around here." Mateo meant it, even if it sounded tacked on.

"I miss you guys, too, Mateo. Give Lorenzo and Chef Aldo a hug for me." She paused for a moment. "On second thought, punch the chef on the shoulder for me. I gained five pounds while I worked there and it's all his fault." Rachel laughed as she said goodbye, returning to her job as cat herder for a busload of rule averse Italians.

# # #

"Before we go any further, I have to ask a serious question, *amigo*." Alejandro was in attorney mode, making sure everybody at the table appreciated the seriousness of this proposal. "How much do you want to be with Rose? Because you can't step back from this after you start. You are a total jerk if you go after her, win her back, and then decide you don't really like her that much after all." Mateo started to protest, but Alejandro held up his hand and continued. "I just want you to be sure that she's really the one, or at least probably the one, before you go down this path. You'll find yourself in an even worse situation if you discover the morning after you've won her back that you don't want her. If she's not the one, then it's best to let it stay ended, even if it is messy. *Entiendes?"*

Ruben nodded his head, agreeing with Alejandro. "You know we're behind you, Mateo, no matter what you decide. But Alejandro's right. It's your first serious relationship after Carla; are you ready to make it The One? Especially right after you find out Carla's single again? You know how I feel about this; there are plenty of fish in the sea. I think you and Alejandro are crazy for wanting to settle down, but I love you anyway, you crazy bastards." Ruben left it with a light touch, his usual style, but Mateo knew he wouldn't have taken a stand on this if he didn't agree with Alejandro that he needed to take a serious look at his feelings before moving ahead.

Mateo was angry at their fear that his feelings might not be true, but he knew they were just looking out for him. His blood was running hot, and he tried to cool down and look at the situation dispassionately. But how could he be dispassionate about Rose? From the very moment he saw her, he was hooked. As he got to know her, he fell deeper. And then when they had sex, Mateo felt the deepest connection he'd ever had with another person. How could he be dispassionate about that?

But the guys had a point. What would their relationship look like going forward? He was leaving Varenna, and she had a business back in the States. They couldn't stay in this cocoon, and they'd never even talked about what a future looked like. He wondered if he was making a mistake, chasing after a woman he might love but who had a life of her own 6000 miles away. Mateo thought of the logistics of their relationship for only a moment before deciding they could work it out, one way or another. He didn't want to count out a relationship because it wasn't perfectly plotted out. He had that once before with Carla, a woman in his own hometown, who spoke his language, who knew his circle of friends. Their relationship perfectly matched on paper, and it still didn't work out. Mateo wasn't going to make the mistake again of trying to connect all the dots for happily ever after.

"I get it, guys. I know how it looks. Poor Mateo has been hiding out in Varenna for five years, and the first time he has more than one date with a woman he falls in love. It's not like that. And it's definitely not related to Carla. I can't explain it to you, or even really to myself. I just know she's the one I want, the one I need, and I think she feels the same way. She's just protecting herself because she thinks I'm going back to Carla." Mateo ran his fingers through his hair, frustration over his own stupidity building. "I should have trusted her with the information about the restaurant, and I should have trusted you guys with our relationship."

Alejandro nodded his head once, a signal that the issue was settled. He intertwined his fingers and stretched out his arms, then cracked his knuckles. A quick roll of the shoulders, and he was ready.

"What the hell was that, man?" Ruben was

laughing at Alejandro's warm-up.

"You ever go into a strategy session for a problem that combines logic and emotion? This is what I do for a living, *hombre*. You don't want to go into this kind of workout without a proper warm-up. Skinny guy like you, you'll probably sprain something." Alejandro patted his friend on the shoulder as they both looked over at Mateo and smiled. They were ready to get down to business.

"Okay, what we know is that she's in London with her friend Ivy, but we don't know for how long. And since she's got her own business to run, the odds are that she'll fly home after this. So we can't waste any time reuniting the lovebirds." Ruben tried to match Alejandro's lawyer style, but he had his own twist. "Rose still likes me. I mean, how could she not? So I'm thinking that I open the door for you, *amigo*."

"You, the man who's never had a serious relationship in his life, want to take the lead on winning back the love of mine? I don't think so." Mateo shook his head. "Rose needs to hear this from me."

"Of course! But, Mateo, if she can't stand the sight of your face right now it doesn't matter what you have to say. Rose needs a friendly reintroduction to you, someone to pave the way." Ruben squeezed Mateo's shoulders in a mock massage. "Don't worry; I'm not going to pass messages for you like a kid in school. I'm just going to reacquaint her to the charms of a Spanish man, get her all warmed up for you, *amigo*.

Then she's all yours."

Mateo saw the logic in this, but his heart was still wrapped up in doing it all by himself, to fly to London and make things right. But he realized he didn't even know where she was.

"The first hurdle is figuring out where she is. London is a big place. How do we find her?" Mateo regretted not making a final plea at the train station, at least finding out where exactly she was going.

"We have Ivy's phone number, right? I think I should call. If Rose's friends are as loyal as yours are, she won't talk to you. Besides, you all know how much women love me." Ruben grinned.

"This woman is not like your normal twenty-something club babes, Ruben. You're going to have to step it up to impress her. And this is far more important than your usual conquest, *amigo*. I need you to get me a meeting with Rose." Mateo felt the need to impress the seriousness of the situation on him.

"I promise to get you a meeting. And if I don't, I will personally fly to the United States and find Rose and plead your case. But it won't come to that. We will get you a meeting, Mateo, but after that, it's up to you." Ruben tapped the table with his hand, setting the plan in motion.

They agreed that Alejandro would stay behind and start the paperwork on the sale of the restaurant before heading back to Madrid. There was also the small chance that Rose would come back here, maybe plotting the same kind of plan they had. Even though it was a long shot, Mateo felt better that someone remained behind just in case. He wanted to cover every possibility. There was no way he was going to lose her again.

"Do you think we should call now and let Ivy know we're coming? I don't want Rose to think I'm just letting her go without a fight." Mateo paced the floor of the restaurant, trying to think of something to do other than wait for the next train to Milan.

"If you call her right now you might scare her off. Remember, man. She thinks you lied to her and dumped her for another woman. It won't hurt for her to have a couple of days to cool down. I can tell that woman's blood runs just as hot as yours does. Give her a chance to get back to normal before you guys meet. If you rush it, you'll lose her forever," Ruben said.

Chef Aldo walked out of the kitchen, wiping his hands on his towel. Normally he wouldn't interrupt his three bosses, but since he was soon to be a part owner of the restaurant, he felt entitled. Besides, none of these jackasses had a bit of sense when it came to women or else they wouldn't be in this predicament. Leave it to the Spaniards to mess up something as simple as love.

"*Perdonami*. You are talking about the beautiful Rose, are you not?" Chef Aldo looked at all three men, then settled his eyes on Mateo. "The only way to win her back is to be honest and walk with her through her anger. Don't fight it or downplay it; flow with it until it is only an ember. Every Italian man already knows this, but I'm letting you in on the secret because I can tell how much you love her." With that, he flipped his towel over his shoulder and walked back into the kitchen.

Ruben and Alejandro looked at each other and burst out laughing, wondering what this chubby bald man could teach them about women. Chef Aldo peeked his head back out the door.

"You can laugh as much as you want after you've been with the same woman for forty years and kept her satisfied the whole time. Until then, shut the hell up and learn from your elders." The kitchen doors swung shut again as Chef Aldo departed.

Mateo shrugged his shoulders at his friends. "They don't call his wife the happiest woman in the village for nothing."

CHAPTER THIRTY-TWO

THE AIRPORT WAS bustling, and Ruben was in his element. Just a few days in Varenna and he was already missing the vibe of a big city, and if he couldn't be in his beloved Madrid he might as well be in London. Mateo was less enamored of the city, especially with the drizzling rain falling.

"C'mon, Mateo. Let's take the train into town and give Ivy a call. But first, we should eat. I googled and found a Spanish restaurant called Ibérica in Marylebone. It's the same neighborhood as the US Embassy where Ivy works, so we'll be close if she agrees to meet up with me to talk about you and Rose. Plus, we get to finally eat some civilized food." Ruben's stomach grumbled at the thought of proper *tapas* and jamon, glad they were in sophisticated London and not some pub-filled fish n' chips village. Ruben hated English food.

Just over an hour later they were seated at the bar at Ibérica, talking in Spanish to the waiter and generally feeling at home. It was early lunchtime, and Ruben sat at the end of the bar watching people enter while Mateo kept his head down nursing his wine and picking at his *tapas*.

"Do you know what you're going to say when you see her?" Ruben munched on some olives while he watched a group of three attractive women enter the restaurant. "*Dios mio*, the cuisine in this country is shit, but the women are hot."

Mateo looked over to see the three women he had his eye on. "Remember why we're here, Ruben. It's my love life you're worried about right now, not yours. Give me at least twenty-four hours of focus, okay?"

"Sure, sure. No problem. But we haven't called Ivy yet, so there's no harm in meeting some of the local citizenry, right? I mean, come on. Look at them!" Ruben couldn't take his eyes off the table, especially the redhead at the center holding court. He loved a woman who could banter and captivate an audience just like him, though he rarely met what he considered his match. Had he given it a moment's thought, he'd realize it was because he was dating women who were barely adults, still finding their way in the world. The women who shared his level of confidence and experience were, not surprisingly, the same age as him.

Full of himself, Ruben walked over to their table, devising his strategy along the way. If these women were eating at a Spanish restaurant, he'd play up his Spanish charm.

"*Buenos dias, senoritas.*" He gave a slight bow and flashed his best smile.

"Oh, can you just give us a few more minutes, please? We haven't had time to look at the menu yet." The redhead exaggerated a couple of blinks, staring him down. She was American or Canadian, definitely not English. And she had attitude. Ruben was instantly hooked.

The blonde on her left side whispered, "I don't think he's a waiter."

"Of course he's not a waiter. He was sitting at the bar there when we walked in and he thought this was some kind of pickup bar instead of three professional women having lunch together. Maybe he even thought we'd giggle and flirt with him for giving us a moment of his attention." The woman looked at him with challenging eyes, waiting for him to respond.

"You wound me, dear lady. I am here with a heartbroken friend, one who is here to win back the love of his life. I only came to ask for your advice before we go to meet her. She is a smart, beautiful woman like yourselves, so of course it seemed logical to get your input." Ruben hoped the truth would help him in this situation, though he hadn't always been so honest in courting women in the past.

"You picked the wrong day, buddy. My best friend just had her heart broken by a jerk, so I'm not feeling very moved to help men right now. If you ask me, this mystery woman is probably much better off single. I know I am." She flashed a big, insincere smile at Ruben. "Now if you don't mind, we want to get back to our lunch." With that, she looked down at her menu, dismissing him.

Ruben slunk back to the bar, ego stinging from her rejection but still wildly attracted to her.

"She saw that coming, didn't she?" Mateo couldn't help but be amused, especially after all the years he'd watched Ruben try his lines on women at restaurants, clubs, and beaches. He and Alejandro knew that's why Ruben stuck with women twenty-five and under, because once they got past that age they were pretty wise to his moves.

"A small setback, meaningless. Not a reflection of my mojo at all, *amigo*. I think the cold weather in London dampens my heat a little. I'll just have to work a little harder next time." Ruben sat down and resumed eating his lunch. "Okay, back to the main subject. Do you know what you're going to say to Rose?"

"I'm just going to be honest, tell her why I didn't introduce her as my girlfriend to you two, and then give her the truth about the restaurant, about Carla, and about how I feel about her. I'm going to follow Chef Aldo's advice and just hold steady through the blast. Honesty is my plan." Mateo was nervous, even more so because they still hadn't called Ivy and didn't even know if Rose was still in London.

"All right, let's get this party started, then." Ruben signaled to the waiter for their bill and stood, putting on his raincoat. As he laid his cash on the table, Mateo put on his coat and turned to face the front door. "One more chance with the redhead, okay?"

Ruben whispered. Mateo groaned but knew he'd probably get the brushoff quickly. As they walked by the table he got a good look at all three women, office workers on a lunch break judging by their professional clothes. At the moment he looked their way, the redhead in the center gasped and stood up from her chair. He thought she was going to say something rude to Ruben, but instead she pointed directly at him.

"Mateo?"

He looked around, wondering how this woman knew him. And Ruben looked at him quizzically, wondering the same thing.

"Ah, do we know each other?" Mateo was a little embarrassed, as people from other tables were starting to stare at the tall woman pointing the accusing finger at him.

"I can't believe you're here. I thought you were going to Madrid, into the waiting arms of your one true love." She looked at him, still standing, but now with her hands on her hips. "Did your plane get rerouted?" Her voice was full of snark.

How does this woman know about me? Mateo's mind was buzzing. He saw a lot of tourists at his restaurant, but he felt sure he would have remembered such an attractive woman, especially one he'd apparently pissed off. *Oh shit,* he thought. *American. Could this be Ivy? There's no way this could be Ivy.* Followed quickly by: *Oh my god, I think this is Ivy.*

Ruben's mind was doing the same search, and he came to the same conclusion a moment later.

"You're Ivy?" Ruben smile was slow and wide. He shook his head. "Rose wasn't kidding. You are a live wire." His voice was dripping with admiration.

"I'm sorry I can't say that Rose's description of you two was very flattering. I guess now we can add stalker to the list. What in the hell are you doing in London in my neighborhood?" Ivy was in lioness mode, and she didn't care how many people were watching. Her coworkers shrunk down a little, sending live updates of their embarrassment to friends on their phones.

"There's been a huge misunderstanding, and I want to straighten it out. If Rose still wants nothing to do with me after that, then fine. But she at least deserves to know the truth before she makes her final decision. Will you tell her I'm here?" Mateo stood his ground, not caring who heard his plea or what they thought of him. All he wanted was a tiny bit of Ivy's compassion.

"Did your friends let the cat out of the bag too soon? Were you hoping for a few more shags before you returned to Madrid? Come on, Mateo. You can't be a good player and get so attached to your conquests. That's douchebag 101." Ivy threw her napkin down on the table. "Rose is too smart for a man like you. You were lucky to get what little you did." Ivy reached down for her purse and turned to her dining companions, "I'll see you back at the office. I've suddenly lost my appetite." She picked up her jacket and looked disdainfully at both men, "Gentlemen, let's not cross paths again. I don't think it would go well for you." And then she walked out the door.

Mateo turned to Ruben and said, "Oh my god."

"I was thinking the same thing, *hombre*. She's perfect." Ruben kept staring at the door, wondering when he'd see Ivy next.

"Not her, you idiot. Now we have no way of reaching Rose, and I'll never be able to tell her the truth. I can't believe of all the damn restaurants in London we'd run into Ivy here." Mateo sat down at the fourth chair of Ivy's table, oblivious to the stares of her coworkers or the rest of the patrons in the restaurant who were still watching the show. "I can't lose her, Ruben. I just can't."

Ruben put his hand on Mateo's shoulder. "Don't worry, *amigo*. You'll win her back."

CHAPTER THIRTY-THREE

"WHAT'S GOING ON, Rosie Girl?" Ivy didn't even wait until she got back to the office to call.

"I'm leaving soon to go shopping at a market I found online. I was thinking of making some enchiladas and homemade salsa for dinner. How does that sound? You're getting too far from your roots eating all this sushi and curry and whatnot." Rose was scribbling out a grocery list as they talked, knowing she could find any ethnic ingredient she wanted in this city, including the ingredients for a good enchilada sauce and fresh corn tortillas.

"That sounds delicious. Listen, before you go to all that trouble, there's something you should know." Ivy wasn't sure how to tell her about Mateo and wondered if she should wait until tonight to do it in person.

"What, don't tell me you aren't eating carbs anymore. I saw you mow through that naan bread last night." Rose laughed, totally unaware of the seriousness of the situation.

"I don't know how to say this, so I'm just going to

say it, Ivy style. Just promise me you'll wait until I get home to do anything, okay?" Ivy wasn't too far from her flat, and she regretted not going there directly to deliver the news. But it was too late to follow that plan now.

"Ivy, you're starting to freak me out. What's going on?" Rose's voice became serious.

"I just saw Mateo here in London." She paused, letting the words sink in.

"You have to be mistaken, Ivy. Mateo is either still in Varenna or on his way to Madrid. I don't even think he knows anyone here. As smart as you are, there is no way you picked him out of a crowd based on a few pictures. You're good, but you're not that good." Rose's voice lost some of the stress, convinced Ivy was overreacting.

"No, Rose. I talked to him. And to the guy with him, who I can only assume is Ruben. They were at a popular Spanish restaurant near my office called Ibérica, and I was with my coworkers. Ruben actually came over to our table to flirt, and I dismissed him like all unworthy suitors. But then when he got ready to leave I saw his friend get up from the bar and immediately knew who they were. And when I called his name Mateo knew who I was, too." Ivy was breathless delivering the news, still feeling the adrenaline rush through her body from the encounter.

"I don't understand. Why are they in London? Are you sure it was them? My Mateo?" The desperation and confusion in her voice tugged at Ivy's heartstrings.

Was she right to bring this kind of drama into her friend's life? Maybe she should have kept quiet. Ivy stopped at the crosswalk, realizing it was not up to her to shield her friend from reality. Rose would hate being kept in the dark, unable to make informed decisions.

"He's here to win you back. He says there has been a huge misunderstanding, and he wants you to hear the truth before you decide to call it quits." Ivy paused, waiting for Rose's reaction. "Rose, are you still there?"

"Yes, I'm still here. I just don't know what kind of misunderstanding it could be. Why would he come all this way to talk to me if he was planning on getting back together with Carla?" Rose was confused, and so was Ivy. There was only one way to clear it up, and that was to hear the other side of the story.

"Do you want to hear him out? I can set up a meeting in a neutral place where it's easy to walk away. Hell, I'll even come with you since I know he'll probably bring that sleazy Ruben with him. Or we can totally ignore him and let him slink back to Madrid or the sewer or wherever it is guys like that go. You just tell me what you want, Rosie Girl, and I'll make it happen." Ivy was still in protector mode, trying to save her friend from hurt but knowing it was inevitable either way. You can't love with guarantees.

"I'm going to meet him. I know I'll regret it if I don't at least hear what he has to say, and I'm tired of living in a constant state of defense. I'm already hurt, so there's nothing else he can say to make it worse. Mateo wouldn't come all the way to London to hurt me on purpose, I know that much about him. I'm not sure what he could say to make it better, but I'm willing to hear it." Rose sighed. "No matter what happens, I'm leaving this relationship clear-headed and with no regrets."

"Okay, Rosie Girl. But let me suggest that you do it in public. If you're in private, he'll use the chemistry you have between you to cloud the issue. And I saw him today—holy hell that is an attractive man. You have to meet in public so he has to depend on his words and not his body." Ivy was back in business mode, thinking of all the outside factors that could affect a negotiation.

"I'm not going to jump into bed with him the moment I see him, Ivy. Give me a little credit!" Rose protested a little too much for Ivy's taste.

"Like I said, I saw the sexy bastard. I hate him for what he's done to you and even I got a little flutter when he looked at me. Though that could have also been his friend Ruben. You know how much I like a guy who needs to be tamed." Ivy licked her lips like an animal considering its prey.

"Ivy, you really are the worst, you know that?" Rose laughed at her friend, grateful again that she had such strong and vibrant women in her life.

"You have no idea the depths of my depravity, Rosie Girl. You'll have to wait for the celebrity tell-all book I write in my old age for the juicy details." Ivy grinned. "But enough about me. Let's figure out the best place to break his heart. I mean, uh, listen to his sob story. How about Millennium Bridge? It's a pedestrian bridge that crosses the River Thames, so if he gets out of hand you can just push him over and keep walking."

"I am still amazed that you have a job at the embassy, Ivy. Really, is there no screening process at all in our government?" Rose asked.

Ivy didn't miss a beat. "Okay, so how about Millennium Bridge at 9 a.m. tomorrow at the halfway point? You can walk and talk, and then when you break his heart you can point him to Shakespeare's Globe Theater on the other side of the river. Chancy Chorizo can take his drama to the stage where it belongs."

"That sounds perfect, Ivy. But how will we get in touch with him? Did he tell you where they were staying?" Rose asked.

"I don't think you have to worry about that. My phone has rung three times in a row while we've been on this call, so some little birdie must have given Mateo my number. Think he called in a favor from Rachel?" Ivy frowned. "Don't worry, Rose. If you want to meet him I'll set it up for you. Best that you don't talk to him until you're face-to-face. These kinds of conversations are never productive over the phone." She took a deep breath. "I'll call him right now and arrange for you to meet him tomorrow morning on the bridge and let you take it from there. But tonight?

Tonight is all about enchiladas, so get to shopping. I'm going to be starving when I get home from work tonight. Remember, I just walked out on my lunch!"

# # #

"I knew you couldn't resist me, American Woman." Ruben was in peak form, ready to continue the banter that began in the restaurant.

"I wondered who had been been blowing up my phone with all the desperate calls. I should have known it would have been you, Señor." Ivy's voice was dripping with condescension. She might have thought Ruben was attractive, but she also knew he was trouble. After twenty years of dating men from around the world, her radar was well-tuned. Still, she had a job to do for Rose, so she'd better get to it.

"You can call me Ruben, if you like. I know I'd very much like it," Ruben teased.

"You seem like the type who loves hearing his own name. And you'd like hearing me say it, especially when you learn that I speak fluent Spanish and can trill the "r" so well it would break your heart. But it's not gonna happen, Señor. We've got business to take care of here, and it doesn't involve the two of us." Ivy knew a man like this required a very short leash or he'd cause her serious trouble.

"I like a woman who treasures good friendships. We have that in common, you know. Probably one of many things. We should talk about it over dinner, in

Spanish." Ruben was relentless.

"I don't think so, Señor. You can put that chorizo back in your pants because it's getting no play here. *Entiendes?*" Ivy couldn't help but show off her Spanish a bit. She wanted to punish Ruben a little for being so confident and attractive. Or at least for being confident and attractive enough to distract her from her mission. Ivy didn't like losing the upper hand.

"Then let's get down to business, American Woman. Where shall the lovebirds reunite? Mateo would like to take Rose to lunch or dinner so they can talk this out. Anywhere you suggest," Ruben offered.

"I'm sure he'd love a romantic setting to plead his case, but that's not going to happen. He can state the facts on the Millennium Bridge and hope Rose doesn't throw him in the River Thames when he's done. Tomorrow morning, 9 a.m. He should probably wear something waterproof." Ivy enjoyed the verbal sparring with Ruben and was already regretting the coming end of their association. He was a worthy opponent, and she could imagine many scenarios—too many, in fact—where she could show him a thing or two about her superior negotiating skills.

"Should we meet nearby in case it does go bad? I can dive into the Thames to rescue Mateo and you can quickly escort Rose away from the scene of the crime before the cops come. I was thinking a nice little cafe?" Ruben was trying to find a way to stay in touch with Ivy, no matter what happened with Rose and Mateo, but she chose not to make it easy for him. A guy like Ruben didn't stick around for easy.

"You can dive in and rescue him if you like, but my Rose doesn't need to be rescued. She'll be just fine on her own. Besides, I'll be at work, dealing with bigger bad guys than you two." Yes, Ivy was definitely going to miss this man who didn't back down from a challenge.

"Then I will wait to see you at Mateo and Rose's engagement party. I, for one, think they will make up tomorrow. And before you know it, we'll all be very good friends laughing about this over dinner," Ruben said. "You should probably go ahead and tell me your favorite restaurant so I can make reservations for us all." Ruben started singing the lyrics to "American Woman," and Ivy couldn't help but admit his sexy Spanish lilt made the song even better. Well, she'd admit it to herself, at least.

"I'll tell you what, Señor. If they get back together, I'll take you to my favorite Moroccan restaurant, but you're still paying. And if they don't get back together, Rose and I will go there ourselves and celebrate the end of this affair. How does that sound?" Ivy felt her control slipping, the door opening just wide enough to let him in.

"That's the best offer I've had all day. I'll tell Mateo to meet Rose halfway across the Millennium Bridge tomorrow at 9 a.m., and then I'll expect your call later in the day to arrange our dinner date." Ruben hummed a little bit more of "American Woman" before ending the call.

He turned to Mateo and said simply, "It's on."

"Well, I'm glad you were able to fit my love life into your agenda, Ruben. I really appreciate that." Mateo punched him on the shoulder a little harder than necessary.

"Hey, you were always top of mind, *amigo*. I take my job as wingman seriously, and if I have to flirt with Ivy to win back your woman, I will do it without complaint."

CHAPTER THIRTY-FOUR

ROSE CINCHED THE purple raincoat at the waist. She borrowed it from Ivy, thankful for once that Ivy's flamboyance actually flattered her skin tone. Paired with her darkest jeans, knee-high black boots, and her gray cashmere sweater, she looked the part of a fashionable Londoner out for a morning stroll. She wrapped her neck in a big gray and white scarf and looped the strap of her messenger bag around her neck. Rose thought she looked good, but she wished Ivy was still at home to give her the final once-over. She grabbed the big black umbrella from the stand by the door and walked out into the mist, wondering if this day was going to change her life or be one big letdown. Either way, she would at least have answers very soon.

Rose entered the Underground at Marylebone, glad to have Ivy's Oyster card so she didn't have to figure out the price of her trip at the kiosk against the wall. She knew millions of people used them every single day, but she was still a little intimidated by the rush of busy people who all seemed to know what they were doing. Rose might look like a Londoner today, but she was still a small town girl from Arizona. Rose kept referring to the map on her phone, changing trains once at Oxford Circus, right after the British voice on the speaker told her to "mind the gap" when leaving the train.

Rose thought of all the strange differences between American and British English, how they expressed the exact same thing in totally different phrases. If she hadn't heard the phrase before, she wouldn't immediately know that "mind the gap" meant "watch your step." Or that a mobile was a cell phone, or trainers were sneakers, or the boot was the trunk of the car. The funniest mix-up she'd ever heard about was from Ivy, shortly after she arrived in London. She said something about a fanny pack to a coworker, who immediately spit soda from his nose. That was how she learned the word "fanny" meant something a little more private in England than it did in America.

Without a translator, there could be a lot of confusion, and the more Rose thought about differences in language and phrasing, the more she thought she might have jumped to conclusions with Mateo. Maybe what she saw and heard was through her own filter, her own view of the world, and not the way he saw it. That was the only way she could reconcile the man she knew so intimately at his flat and the stiff stranger she had the final dinner with in Varenna. Something did happen, no doubt, but maybe it wasn't what she thought.

Mind the gap. That's exactly what she planned to do today, to close the gap in understanding between them and move forward with her life, either with or without him.

Rose got off the Tube at St. Paul's and walked outside. She checked her watch: it was 8:45 a.m. She only needed five minutes to meet up with Mateo at the center of the 1000-foot bridge, so she took a moment to admire St. Paul's Cathedral. When she was in grade school, Prince Charles and Lady Diana Spencer were married at St. Paul's, which was the first she'd learned of it. Ivy, Violet, Lily, and Daisy stayed over at her house and they went to sleep at 6 o'clock, right after dinner, so they could wake up at 2 o'clock in the morning and watch the coverage leading up to the big wedding. The five of them were obsessed with the idea of kings and queens and princesses. Their hippie mamas were not very happy about their royal obsession, but like most things with kids, it was just a phase. Still, Rose remembered that night, their sleeping bags laid out on the floor in front of the television and buckets of popcorn to munch while they watched Diana's twenty-five-foot long train follow her up the stairs to enter the church.

Here Rose was now, looking at the church in person, and going to meet her own Prince Charming. Or at least that's what he used to be. She hoped there was still enough of that left for a fairytale ending. *Don't get your hopes up*, she thought.

She checked her watch again: 8:52 a.m. It was time

to start walking, to find out once and for all if they had a future together. She vowed to herself that she'd be okay no matter what. Just as she took the first step away from the church she felt her phone buzz. A quick look showed a message from Violet, no doubt staying up late back in Arizona to find out what happened. *Don't forget, you're a Wild Rose. xoxo*

No matter what happened here today, she knew her friends would see her through. Rose sent a message back to Violet. *Armed with your necklace and your love. xoxo*

And then she walked to the middle of the bridge to meet the man who'd broken her heart.

# # #

Rose's heart caught in her throat when she saw him. Mateo stood toward the side of the bridge, looking out over the Thames with his hands in his pockets. Dozens of Londoners walked by him, too busy with their own problems to notice. He was wearing a gray fitted jacket that fell to his mid-thigh over dark pants. His favorite monk strap shoes were glistening in the rain, probably getting ruined. Around his neck was a tan cashmere scarf. He braved the weather without a hat or umbrella, droplets collecting in his wavy hair. He should have looked terrible in his despair, but he was still the same handsome man. Rose didn't know why she expected him to look different after just a couple of days. She felt a huge change in her own life, and she wanted to see the same reflected in him.

Rose walked up to him and he smiled, reaching his arms out to hug her. Rose stepped back, shaking her head. Ivy was right; physical touch was just going to complicate the conversation. Rose wanted to hear it straight, as basic as court testimony, so she could judge the situation accurately.

"You look beautiful, Rosa. But you always do." She could hear the longing in his voice, and it stirred her heart.

"You look good, too, Mateo. But I never expected to see you in rainy London. Why did you follow me?" Rose knew it was up to her to keep this conversation on track, the emotions safely tucked away until the facts were out in the open.

"Rosa, you left under a cloud of doubt, one that I helped create, and I want you to know the truth before you make your final decision," Mateo said.

"What makes you think I haven't made my final decision?" Rose bristled at the idea that she ran off without thinking it through, that she could be regretting her actions—even if it was true.

"Because you agreed to see me, to hear me out. There's more to this than you think you know, and every bit of it includes you. You are the center, Rosa, not anyone else. I'm a fool for trying to keep our relationship quiet in front of my friends, and I'm a fool for not telling you about such a big change in my life with the restaurant. But I won't be the fool who loses you, not after I've spent my life looking for you."

Mateo's passion attracted a few pedestrians on the bridge who stood off to the side to watch. Rose inwardly cursed herself for picking such a public place. Then she remembered she didn't pick it and silently cursed Ivy. Rose wanted nothing more than to go to him, put her arms around him, and never let go. But she kept her feet planted in place, one hand in her coat pocket and the other on her umbrella.

"Then tell me the facts. Tell me that the woman who broke your heart five years ago isn't single again. Tell me that you're not in touch with her, soothing her hurts over the phone and telling her things will be better soon. And tell me how you didn't dump the restaurant in Lorenzo's lap so you could run back to Madrid to be with her. Tell me how you didn't hide our romantic relationship completely from your closest friends, or how you didn't tell me you were going back to Madrid when you made love to me. I want to hear your version of the facts, because the ones I know don't have me at the center of anything except a big joke." Rose's temper flared as she recounted the story out loud, remembering every ounce of hurt from the past few days.

"Rosa, I'm sorry I didn't tell Alejandro and Ruben about you. They came to town on business, and I wanted to clear all that up before I told them about you. You can see how Ruben inserted himself into my life before he knew I had a girlfriend. Can you imagine what it would have been like otherwise? Of course you can; you heard about our accidental lunch with Ivy." Mateo ran his fingers through his damp hair in frustration. "Rosa, they just consume me sometimes, and I wanted to keep our relationship to ourselves, to let us enjoy it without outside intervention for a little while longer. It was a selfish move, and I can see in hindsight just how stupid it was. I was worried they'd say or do something to scare you away or break the spell, and instead I made it even easier for that to happen. I'm so sorry, Rosa."

"Of course they wouldn't care if you saw more than one woman at a time. I've met Ruben and know how he operates. But even if I did believe you on this point, it doesn't change the fact that you're moving to Madrid and talking to Carla and you never said one word to me about either one. That's pretty strong evidence that you're a sonofabitch in my book, especially after all the words you said about us." Rose was boiling from the inside out, which combined with the rain, put her in a steam bath. She knew her hair had started to curl in tendrils against her face.

"Rosa, once you get to know Ruben and Alejandro better, you are going to see exactly why I didn't tell them about us right away, especially after they came to tell me they had a buyer for the restaurant and wanted to sell. It was their idea, Rosa, not mine, but I'm not against it." Mateo's eyes pleaded with her to give him a chance.

"You're selling the restaurant? I thought you were just leaving it to Lorenzo to run?" Rose was confused, not understanding this turn of events.

"Alejandro and Ruben came to me with a buyer for the restaurant. Alejandro is our lawyer, so the offer went to him. I don't know how much you know about the restaurant business, but we've been fairly successful, but even so it's hard to sell a restaurant when you want. The kind of people who can buy a place like ours don't come along every day. I expected it to take at least two years to find a good buyer, but we have one who came directly to us for a cash sale. It's hard to say no to that, especially when Ruben and Alejandro are ready to get out of the business and I can't afford to buy them out. I'm not even sure I'd want to own it by myself even if I had that kind of money." Mateo grabbed the railing on his right, almost as if he were bracing himself for her reaction. "We decided to offer the restaurant to Lorenzo first before taking the deal we were offered since he's been with me so long, and I think he's going to buy it."

"What does Carla have to do with all of this?" Rose wasn't going to back down until she had the entire story.

"Carla has nothing to do with this!" Mateo yelled, attracting the attention of about twenty people walking by. "That's just the thing: her breakup was just idle gossip Ruben and Alejandro brought back from Madrid. Carla cheated on me five years ago, and now her husband cheated on her. People say she deserves it and maybe she does, but it's not for me to judge. She was calling me to apologize, finally knowing what it's like to be on the other side. It was nothing more than that." Mateo ran his fingers through his hair, the waves turning into wet curls. "I don't care about Carla anymore. Our relationship ended five years ago, and it will never restart whether you stay with me after today or not. My heart belongs to you, Rosa. You are the only woman I want."

Rose's head started spinning. She pieced together what she knew and how she knew it, and she realized how it all got so turned around. *Mind the gap.* If Mateo had only been honest with her from the start this wouldn't have happened, but she had to be honest with herself. Would she have trusted the financial information and status of her business with a new relationship? Would she introduce the Late Bloomers to Mateo in the early stages of their romance? They were pretty intense, and she could see why a smart person would keep a fragile new relationship under wraps for a while before exposing it to lifelong, outspoken friends.

Still, she was pissed that Mateo wasn't honest with her from the start, and she was mad at herself for not believing in him when his behavior up to that point gave her no reason to believe he was a jerk. If they were going to have a fighting chance, they'd both have to learn to open up and stop relying on their old defenses.

"Kiss, kiss, kiss!" They turned to see a small group of tourists on the bridge who'd been watching their conversation. These people were smiling and chanting, waiting for Mateo and Rose to seal the deal so they could move on with their sightseeing.

"This might be the first time in my life when I'm happy to have someone tell me what to do." Rose stepped forward and put her hands on Mateo's waist while he embraced her. Just before he leaned down to kiss her she put her index finger on his lips. "I can assure you it won't become a habit."

"Oh, *cariño*, I had no doubt." Then he leaned in and kissed her, the small crowd clapping and cheering.

CHAPTER THIRTY-FIVE

"I HAVE TO tell Ivy and Violet first. They'll be worried that I did throw you into the Thames if they don't hear from me soon." Rose playfully punched Mateo's shoulder and picked up her phone.

"Fine, then I'll call for room service. They make this dreadful concoction called an English fry-up that is basically what it says. Eggs, bacon, sausage, beans, mushrooms, tomato—all served on a platter. They even fry the tomato, I think. But it is full of protein and I think we're going to need it." Mateo wagged his eyebrows like Charlie Chaplin and Rose smiled.

"That sounds good. I actually like a proper English fry-up. They are a lot like the American ones, minus the blood sausage, of course." She wrinkled her nose at the memory of the time Ivy brought some to the US for them to try. Never again. "Do you need to call Ruben?" she asked.

"No, he stopped for coffee at a cafe with big glass windows nearby. He told me he'd wait there for me to come by, good or bad. We passed him fifteen minutes ago, so he knows things are okay. He'll probably stay away from the hotel today to give us some privacy." Mateo paused for a moment before adding, "He's probably disappointed Ivy isn't with you. I think he was counting on seeing her again."

Rose sat down on the chair in Mateo's hotel room and looked up at him. "I don't know if the world can handle Ivy and Ruben together for more than about five minutes. It's probably good to keep them apart for now. She's still a little protective of me." Rose loved having such a fierce ally, but she knew it would take Ivy longer to change her feelings about Mateo than it did Rose. Ivy had only seen the heartache, not the joy.

"As well she should be. I know I have to convince your friends I'm a stand-up guy, and I'm okay with that. They are important to you, and I know in time they will be important to me, too. I can't dislike anyone who has your best interests at heart," Mateo said. Rose was glad he realized it wouldn't be an instant lovefest with the Late Bloomers, but she knew over time it would be okay.

Rose pulled out her phone to text Ivy and Violet, but she didn't know what to type. How to tell them that she'd done a complete reversal on her feelings about Mateo? *Well, it's not like it's the first time I've done a 180 this week*, she thought. She sighed, thinking about how to tell them in a way that didn't make her look stupid or worry them that she hadn't thought it through. And then she realized she was overthinking it again. She just needed to tell them, let them know she was okay, and get on with her life.

Rose had to start living in the real world outside of her own head and composed a message: *411: No ex. Restaurant being sold by partners. He only wants me. All is well. Will call you later with details. xoxo*

She pushed send and turned her phone off, not wanting to be disturbed for the next few hours.

"Room service will be here in forty-five minutes. What shall we do while we wait?" Mateo sat on the bed as he said it, slowly unbuttoning his shirt.

"Oh, I think we can figure something out," Rose said as she slipped off her shirt.

Touching him again, especially chest to chest, heartbeat to heartbeat, centered her. Less than twenty-four hours before, she thought he was out of her life for good. The pain of their almost breakup brought tears to her eyes. Mateo brushed them away with his thumbs as he brought his forehead down to touch hers.

"We were made for each other, Rosa. I will never be so foolish and risk losing you again." He leaned in to kiss her, gently at first, and then with a deepening passion. This man followed her across Europe to win her back, and she'd never doubt his loyalty or assume the worst of him again.

"I can't wait to make love to you under the desert sky on my terrace. You're going to love Arizona." Rose started pulling his shirt down from his shoulders. She thought of her neighbors the coyotes and how she'd give them a run for their money in the howling department.

"You want to visit Arizona? I thought we'd just stay in this hotel room forever." Mateo nuzzled her neck and laid her back on the bed.

Rose immediately pulled back, breasts on full display.

"Oh my god. You think I'm going to Madrid, don't you?" Rose put her hand up to her mouth, the realization of their situation finally dawning on her. She'd been so caught up in the drama and reconciliation that she forgot to think about the logistics. Rose lived in Arizona. Mateo lived in Varenna for now, with no reason not to return to Madrid and resume his architecture work. What future did they really have, once they stopped playing at this affair and returned to real life?

"Well, of course you'd go to Madrid. You speak Spanish. And your daughter has now left home and my restaurant in Italy is sold. Why wouldn't we go to Madrid?" It seemed clear to Mateo, but she knew it was because he didn't understand what she put into building her landscape design business in Arizona.

"Mateo, I have a successful business in Arizona, a house I built, and a life. I haven't been hiding out somewhere else. I don't need to start over or start again. I already have a life there, and I worked too hard to leave it all behind for a man I didn't even trust just twenty-four hours ago. Can't you see that?" Rose sat back on the bed in defeat.

"But Rachel is gone, your friends have moved away, and you told me the Wild Rose in you wanted something new. I thought that meant a life with me?" Mateo put his hands on her shoulders, drawing her back into him. "I can't believe we went through all this drama just to discover we have nowhere to live together. This is unacceptable to me." Mateo stated it as if saying it out loud would change their reality.

"What would you have us do? You aren't willing to give up your life and professional connections to come to Arizona with me, and I'm not willing to do that to come to Madrid for you. So where does that leave us?" They'd never talked about this before. The relationship had gone from cold to hot very fast, and then the idea of losing each other made them both act dramatically. Now that they were past that, could the simple logistics of everyday life tear them apart? Rose felt like they'd lit the fuse on a giant firework and a small sneeze snuffed it out.

"Rosa, we can work this out. We will work this out. Where I live is not nearly as important as who I live with. And I want to be with you." Mateo said the words and meant them, but even he wondered if the feeling would last if either one of them was taken away to a place they didn't want to be.

Their sadness brought them together again, and this time their lovemaking was slow and gentle, almost as if they were afraid of further cracking the fragile shell holding their relationship together. When room service arrived, they sat in their white fluffy robes and ate, each quietly thinking about what they would give to stay in this relationship...and what they wouldn't.

CHAPTER THIRTY-SIX

ROSE WALKED THROUGH the door that afternoon and laid her key in the tray on the hall table, pausing as she looked around Ivy's flat. Her home was a perfect reflection of her personality, and it was set up to cater to her life. The kitchen was small because Ivy didn't cook. The money was spent on the details, the quirks that made the place unique. Even though Ivy was American, she fit perfectly in London, perfectly at her job. Rose thought about what Ivy had sacrificed in the name of love and realized it wasn't much. But that was the kicker: she didn't seem fazed by it. In fact, she seemed pretty damn happy. Rose couldn't imagine Ivy giving up this beautiful flat, or her great job, for a relationship. Ivy knew what worked for her, and she kept looking for a love that included what she already knew she wanted in her life.

Rose thought about her own home in Arizona. She loved it, no doubt. The home wasn't totally built with her own hands, but she did design it and pay for it. And she lived there for many happy years with Rachel as she built her business from scratch. Violet lived there, too, but now she was leaving for New York. Rose knew Rachel wasn't coming back, and she tried to determine if she lived in Arizona because she loved it or because that's all she'd ever known. Was she just being stubborn to want to return there, or would she resent Mateo forever if she moved to Madrid? Her head was spinning with the consequences of each decision, and she was depressed that her hot love affair was unraveling over location.

Rose thought about her business, the one she hadn't even checked on in the last few days with all the drama in her personal life. Was she really dedicated to it, or to what it stood for in her life? Rose knew she was overthinking things again, so she decided to cut off that train of thought and do some actual work. She pulled out her laptop and turned it on while she poured herself a glass of water. She'd answer a few emails, check on things, and then shower and get ready for dinner with Ivy. Rose told Mateo she wanted to be with Ivy tonight, and they had plans to meet up tomorrow for breakfast to start working through the logistical problems in their relationship. Rose thought she'd come up with a magical solution between now and then, one that would make the decision easy for both of them. She knew she was fooling herself.

The first email she saw was from her client Henry.

Dear Rose,
I'm writing with some terrible news. Mary had her

first hip surgery, and while the doctors were inside they found cancer. It started in her kidneys and spread to her hip bone, which is why she's had so much trouble walking. We thought we were in for a year of surgery and recovery for her hip replacements, and now it looks like Mary won't be leaving the hospital.

Rose felt the tears building. Henry and Mary were such nice people, and they'd worked hard all their lives to have a retirement home in Arizona where all their grandkids could visit. She was heartbroken for them.

We won't be returning to the house in Arizona except to sell it, and that won't happen until it's just me. I won't be leaving Mary's side until this is all over. I don't know the logistics of this or if you're even interested, but I'd like to use the deposit we sent you to make a basic garden and pool area for the house, something that will help it sell. I don't even care what you do at this point. I've already contacted our real estate agent and she'll work with you to figure out the best improvements to make to sell the house if you decide to take the job.

Rose was full on crying at that point, thinking about the stupidity of her arguments about logistics with Mateo while also realizing her business was effectively at a standstill. Then she felt like an ass for thinking of herself when Henry and Mary were in such a terrible situation.

Thank you for helping us realize our vision of a desert retirement. Our timing wasn't so good in making it come true, I guess, but that's not something we have any control over.

Best wishes, Henry

Rose sat staring at the screen and felt compelled to call Rachel. The time difference was ten hours, so she'd likely be asleep.

"Mom, it's 3 a.m. Is everything okay?" Rachel's voice was sleepy.

"Yes, honey. Everything is fine. I'm sorry to wake you, but I had to hear your voice. You know how much I love you, right?" Rose tried to keep her voice strong. She didn't want to worry Rachel.

"Of course I do, Mom. And I love you, too. What's going on?" Rachel was starting to wake up.

"I just want you to know that I'm proud of you for chasing for dreams, no matter what. Life is short, you know? And any time spent waiting is taking a risk that you'll never do it. I'm proud of you for doing it, and I'm sorry for ever doubting your decision." As Rose said the words to Rachel, she began to feel the vibration in herself. She wasn't just telling Rachel it was okay to buck convention, take the less known route, or risk failure. She was telling herself the same thing.

"Thanks, Mom. Though you could have waited to tell me that. I'm young, but I still need my beauty sleep, you know." Rachel laughed, and Rose joined her.

"You follow your heart, and that's what makes you beautiful. I'm sorry I woke you, Baby Girl. Go back to sleep and we'll talk again soon, okay? I love you." Rose remembered rocking her to sleep as a child, never taking more than two minutes. Rachel had a gift and would likely be asleep again before she had time to put the phone on the nightstand.

"Nighty night, Mom. I love you, too." Rachel's voice was so drowsy Rose wondered if she'd even remember their call in the morning.

Rose's heart felt like it had been blown wide open. She still didn't have any answers about her relationship with Mateo, but she did know that she wouldn't let something as simple as logistics stand in the way. She and Mateo could live anywhere as long as they were together, and they would figure this out.

CHAPTER THIRTY-SEVEN

IVY TOOK ROSE to her favorite restaurant in London, a Moroccan hideaway in Marylebone with the best lamb tagine in town. They were seated in a cozy, cave-like room with an arched ceiling and the traditional lamps with cut metal shades. The light played in shapes across the ceiling and walls, giving the room an exotic feel.

Rose and Ivy took their seats on richly cushioned benches backed with pillows, all the fabrics in rich golds and reds. The table was overlaid in hammered copper with rows of giant nail heads holding it in place on the sides. The votive candles on the table reflected the copper, and the total effect of this opulent room made both women feel like royalty.

"This is how we should live all the time, don't you think?" Rose said.

Ivy nodded in agreement as she scanned the menu, looking for her favorite dishes. A server in traditional North African dress came to their table to tell them about the specials, including Ivy's favorite lamb tagine as well as a vegetarian pastilla. Rose asked for the details of the pastilla and learned it was a traditional Moroccan pastry filled with squash, eggplant, carrots and mushrooms, then sprinkled over the top with powdered sugar and cinnamon. She could feel her mouth water.

"Once you've had the food here you'll never think of men the same way again. Really, how can they compete with the overall experience of this?" Ivy smiled, ordering them two glasses of the Argentinian Malbec from the robed waiter. It was her favorite wine with Moroccan food, and she knew Rose would like it.

"Did you ever think we'd be eating such exotic food back when we were kids? Sometimes I can't believe the lives we've lived...you especially." Rose admired her friend's choices and knew she worked hard to live the life she wanted.

"Well, I always knew, Rosie Girl. This is the life I've always wanted. Though I have to admit I did take a trip to Morocco and didn't like it at all. Adventure doesn't always turn out the way you plan. Give me Morocco via London any day." She smiled as the waiter returned with their drinks. They placed their orders and then got down to the subject they'd been avoiding ever since Ivy walked in the door from work.

"So, now that you're all sexed up, are you thinking clearly?" Ivy wasn't dumb, and she knew if the meeting went well how it would end. "I really hope you didn't do it at my place. I don't even bring my own dates back there, you know. It's an estrogen-only zone by design."

"We went back to his hotel, so don't worry. But even though we cleared the air on Carla and why he's leaving Varenna, it left us to deal with the elephant in the room, the one that could be our undoing." Rose took a drink of wine and then looked up as the waiter returned with their appetizers: butternut hummus, grilled eggplant, and falafel. Despite the giant breakfast with Mateo, she could feel her stomach grumbling.

"Ah, so you've come across the obvious problem, which probably wasn't so obvious when you were busy putting tab A into slot B." Ivy, as usual, was blunt. "How will you be together when your life is in the US and his is...well, wherever his is."

"Why didn't you point this out to me before, Ivy? I can't believe I didn't think of it until now." Rose dipped into the creamy hummus, making a little moan as she ate.

"Before I thought it was just a shagfest, a way to break you out of the routine you'd sunk into and get back into life again. I didn't know you were going to fall in love with your Romeo." Ivy dismissed the thought with a wave, as if she couldn't be expected to think of everything.

"Love? I don't know. I guess it is, though we haven't said it to each other yet. But I do want to be with him, Ivy. I do. I know I do, no matter what. But I can't just walk away from my entire life, and I know he can't either. Tell me, my diplomatic friend, what's the middle way?" Rose popped a falafel in her mouth.

"The middle way sucks, my friend. It means neither of you gets what you want, but if the main goal is to be together, then I guess that's what's important. If you ask me, though—and you are—my recommendation is that you pick a third place. Equal sacrifice, equal difficulty, and you get to create a brand-new life together." Ivy sipped her wine and watched Rose gorging on the mezze platter. "Don't sprint the marathon, Rosie Girl. We still have our main dishes coming, followed by dessert and mint tea." She smiled at Rose's obvious enjoyment of the food, a quirk she'd had since they were kids. How could someone so attuned to the pleasures and consumption of food be so terrible at accepting the pleasures of life and love?

"A third way? That's something I never considered." Rose thought for a moment what the third way could be and then realized it wasn't really up to her. It was a conversation she should have with Mateo.

"That's why they pay me the big bucks here in London Town." Ivy smiled and took another drink.

CHAPTER THIRTY-EIGHT

"DID YOU ORDER dessert, *señoritas*?" Ruben appeared at their table, a tray filled with flaky baklava, vanilla ice cream, and pistachio pudding on his hand. Rose couldn't help but laugh, but Ivy was furious.

"What in the hell are you doing here?" Ivy fumed.

"American Woman, you promised me dinner at your favorite restaurant, and I see that you've brought another date. I can't blame you, though. I find Rose quite charming myself. But I do think you could at least do me the honor of sharing dessert." Ruben was relentless in his pursuit of Ivy, holding her to the bargain they'd set the day before.

"Our agreement was not for a particular date and time, Señor." Ivy put an emphasis on the last syllable, throwing her napkin down on the table and standing up as she did so.

"Wait, you had an agreement to go out with Ruben? What am I missing here?" Rose was amused at the situation, mainly because she rarely saw Ivy flustered. And she was definitely flustered.

"Oh, she didn't tell you? Well, this American

Woman and I made a little wager. She said you would rather throw Mateo in the River Thames than take him back, and I told her I thought love would prevail. A dinner was wagered at her favorite restaurant, and it looks like she forgot to invite me. Are you a sore loser, Ivy? Or were you planning to come back tomorrow with me and make it extra romantic?" Ruben's charm was like a knife, and while it wasn't Rose's style, she knew Ivy took it as a challenge. The two of them were reeking pheromones, and she just wanted to get out of the way of the street fight or sexfest that was to follow.

"Well, I'm glad our romantic troubles were beneficial to you both. I think I'll leave you two to figure this one out. I'm going home, Ivy. I, um, think I'll see you later." Rose picked up her purse and jacket and stood. "Ruben, it was good to see you again. As always, I'm glad I'm not the one in your radar. Good luck. I think you're going to need it." And with that, Rose walked out of the restaurant and into the night. She was surprised to find Mateo waiting outside.

"Can I walk you home, *cariño*? I know you wanted the evening to think, but I had a feeling your dining companion would be otherwise occupied." Mateo offered his arm.

"I'd like that, Mateo." She paused for a moment before accepting his arm. "I've been thinking about our problem, the idea that we can't decide who should give in on where to live." Rose waited to hear what he'd say.

"Ah, so have I. And I think I have a solution."

Mateo's eyes glittered under the streetlights.

"Really? That's funny, because so do I." Rose wondered what he had to say.

"I think we shouldn't live in Arizona or Spain. There's too much for each person to overcome in either scenario." Mateo stopped and put his hands on her shoulders.

"Mateo, I was going to say the same thing! We don't have to pick one of the two. We can come up with a third way!" Rose was overwhelmed, thinking she'd have to sell him on this idea. "I don't know why we didn't see it before. We can build a life together anywhere.

"Well, I have to admit to getting some outside counsel on this." Mateo smiled at her.

"You're not the only one. I consulted my best friend the diplomat this afternoon. Who did you talk to?" Rose was curious who in his life would tell him to leave Madrid, because she knew it wasn't Ruben or Alejandro.

"I talked to Rachel. I told her of our situation, the problem with figuring out a path, and asked her what she thought. And she said we should come to Australia. Now, I know she's not the most reliable— she'll probably leave for Timbuktu as soon as we land —but I did start thinking about throwing a wide net to see where we'd want to live and who would allow us to work. You're a landscape designer and I'm an architect. There has to be a need for that somewhere, right?" Mateo was so earnest, like a schoolboy wanting a pat on the head for the right answer.

"You'd really move anywhere and start all over with me?" Rose was awed by his commitment to a life with her, especially when he didn't know where it would be.

"Rosa, I love you. I want to be with you for the rest of my life, whether that is in Madrid, Arizona, Australia, or the South Pole. I am yours all over this world, and I will do anything to make our life together successful." Mateo put his hand on her chin and looked at her. "Do you want me the same way? Because it only works if we're both in this 100 percent."

Rose flashed back to the start of this adventure, when Mateo was only a picture in an email from Rachel. She instantly reacted to this handsome man, a visceral pulse that warned of a coming change in her life. How could she have known then where this would lead? And would she still have come to Italy if she'd known how much her life would change?

Rose reached up toward her neck to clutch her necklace, the reminder of what she said she wanted. Vi's mom Miriam flashed into her mind, along with the sunflower painting from her studio on the day she died—a slash of blue paint across a field of yellow. Miriam always went after what she wanted in life, and even at the end she took the sky with her. Rose wanted that kind of life, the kind filled with laughter, joy, and indulgence, a life with no more regret, no more stepping back, and no more waiting in the wings. And now she was on the cusp of having it.

This was Wild Rose's chance to fully flower, sinking her roots into the soil of a new adventure with a man who fed her heart and soul.

"Mateo, if I've built one business, I can build another. The same goes with the house. But I can't find another man like you, and I don't even want to try. I love you, and I want to be with you, no matter what we have to do to make it happen. Yes, yes, and yes. Let's do this." Rose reached her hands up and grabbed his wavy hair in her fists, pulling him down to her for a kiss worthy of a movie ending. They stood underneath the lamplight on a busy street in London as people bustled around them, damp from the drizzle, imagining their future together in Oz.

Thank you for reading *Wild Rose*'s story. Would you please leave a review wherever you purchased this print edition? Indie authors like me depend on reviews from readers like you to help other people find our books. Your review also influences the algorithm at sites like Amazon, which means you can help *Wild Rose* get shown to more potential buyers with just a few sentences.

Thanks so much for helping indie authors like me carve out a place for our stories.

Keep reading for a preview of Book Two, English Ivy!

Book Extras

Thank you for reading about Rose's adventure in love and travel! I've created a set of free bonuses to go along with the book, and you can check them all out here.

>>>Go to http://betsytalbot.com/wild-rose-reader-goodies/ to get your book extras

Did you like this book? Please tell your friends! The best way to support indie authors like me is to leave a review at Amazon, Goodreads, or on your own blog. I like Facebook and Twitter recommendations, too!

Want to stay in touch? Check out cover art for the series, short stories, virtual launch party info, and insider information on The Late Bloomers at BetsyTalbot.com. While you are there sign up for email alerts and get a romantic Italian dinner recipe from Wild Rose's very own Chef Aldo.

Thank you for your support of indie publishing.

About The Late Bloomers Series

After a lifetime of friendship bordering on sisterhood, five 40-something women from Arizona each embark on their own adventures in love, travel, and discovery around the globe. Knowing themselves far better than they did in their 20s and 30s, these seasoned women are ready to take on the world. If 40 is the new 20, these women are just getting started.

Book 1: *Wild Rose* (March 2015)

Successful landscape designer and single mother Rose Quinn races to Italy to save her 19-year-old daughter Rachel from making a huge mistake with an older man – the same mistake Rose did at the age of 20. When secrets are revealed on the shores of Lake Como, Rose faces her own lifelong misconceptions about love and the illusion of control with handsome Mateo, relying on her lifelong best friends the Late Bloomers to see her through this transformation.

Book 2: *English Ivy* (August 2015)

Ivy Cross, an American living in London for the past 15 years, is used to being in charge at work and at play. When she clashes with Spanish tech superstar Ruben Serrano, Ivy wonders if she's finally met her match. Will he bend to her will, or will she break him? Ivy can't see it any other way, but her best friends The Late Bloomers work together to show her a third option.

Book 3: *Tiger Lily* (February 2016)

Lily Lang works as an emergency doctor in devastated parts of the world. As good as she is at healing people who desperately need her help, she can't seem to mend her own broken heart. That is, until she meets the artist Cundo, who challenges her assumption that hard work means no time for love. Her lifelong best friends the Late Bloomers support Lily from afar as she explores Cuba – and her heart – with this free-spirited man.

Book 4: *Violet Sky* (July 2016)

Violet Stack is a jewelry designer with a successful line sold in top department stores. After a big contract and a move to New York at the age of 42, Vi wonders if she can create a love life as successful as her business with the reclusive sculptor Jack Allan. Can her lifelong friends The Late Bloomers help Violet see the bigger design?

Book 5: *Whoopsie Daisy* (January 2017)

Free-spirited Daisy Foster is a food writer in Portland who has a knack for getting people to follow her lead. When she lands a gig as a judge on a television cooking show set in France, her charms don't seem to work on line producer Pascal Blondel, who doesn't think she has the right credentials. As they battle their way through the season, they discover more cooking on this show than just the food. But can they put their egos aside to enjoy it? Daisy depends on her good friends The Late Bloomers to decipher this complicated recipe of love.

How This Book (and Series) Came to Be

In 2010, my husband Warren and I sold everything we owned to travel the world. The decision was not a light one; we both had good jobs, a nice house, and good life. But after my younger brother and a good friend both had brushes with death at the age of 35, I began to look at life in a different way. After two years of planning, we set off on our adventure, never realizing how completely it would change our lives. (You can read more about that at my website at BetsyTalbot.com.)

The inspiration for this book came during a hike back in 2012. I'd been thinking of inviting my mother to come join us on an adventure instead of making a trek back to the US to visit. My mother is not a travel lover, preferring usually to be with her garden, her home, and her friends.

As it usually is with a long hike, I had plenty of time to imagine what a visit from my mother would be like. She is a sweet soul, always caring for other people, and I imagined what it would be like if she had no one else to look after but herself. What would that look like? It wasn't long before I imagined a set of circumstances where she would be left in a new place without me – perhaps a storm or a severe travel delay – and how she'd bloom in place.

This little germ of an idea was typed into an Evernote file and tucked away, one of many "someday" ideas.

Then in January 2013 we were in Morocco for a month with another couple who writes and works mostly online like we do. After cooking a tasty tagine, pouring cocktails, and turning on some music, we sat on cozy couches and talked about what we wanted to accomplish in the future.

I talked about romance books, how writers I knew were having huge success with these stories but none of them had characters I could relate to. The main characters were in their 20s or 30s, a stage I've already passed and don't long to return to. The future is ahead, and I want to imagine more of what that will look like.

The four of us agreed that the market is big enough for all kinds of books, so we dared each other to write one quirky romance that didn't fall into the norm and to publish it within a year. The ideas were pretty wild, let me tell you. (Well, actually I won't tell you, just in case they ever write them.)

I thought back to the germ of an idea, the story of a young mother with a grown daughter who goes off on her first solo adventure. That idea spread to include other scenarios with different characters, and before long I had a five-book series plotted out.

I guess you could say this series technically started out as a dare, but the idea for this story has been germinating for a few years. And now that it's been fleshed out, I can't wait to tell you about the four other amazing women in this series.

Much of what I write is drawn from the bits and pieces of real women I know, real places I've been, and real experiences I've had or been told about first-hand. It all meshes together to create brand-new characters who are going to entertain us all for years to come.

Thank you for reading the story that's been rolling around in my head for so long. And if you want to know more about the writing process for a romance (at least mine), you can check out the "How I Became a Romance Writer" series on my website at BetsyTalbot.com.

Next up is *English Ivy*, a fiery redhead from America who lives and works in London. I hope you'll come back to read her story (and the inspiration behind it!).

Happy reading,

Betsy Talbot

Lubrin, Spain

February 12, 2015

Acknowledgements

No book is a solo endeavor, least of all mine. I'm fortunate to know some pretty incredible people through my work and travel, and they generously contributed their expertise, opinions, and flavor to this book.

Alison Cornford-Matheson, Andrew Matheson, and Warren Talbot were with me in Morocco in January of 2014 and we challenged each other to write a love story by year's end. It is due to their encouragement (and copious amounts of wine) that this book came to be.

Bestselling romance author Melissa Foster gave me advice on the story, cover, sex scene, and general marketing of a romance book. She also sent a few beta readers my way. When people told me the romance genre was perhaps the most collaborative and generous in the book world, I didn't believe them. Now I do.

Paula Russell, art historian and Italy expert, helped me pick the destination for Rose's adventure as well as gave me advice on the logistics of Varenna and Lake Como.

Simona Quatela, my Italian neighbor in Spain, helped me with some of Chef Aldo's phrases and habits.

Akiyo Kano, my creative coach, read the first draft (as she does all my books). We sat on the floor of my office afterward while she gently told me that my sex scenes and storyline needed work. It's due to her coaching that the steam factor and emotional connection are so strong in this book.

Javier Luengo Olmos coached me on romantic Spanish music. While I couldn't use all the information he gave me in the story, it did make it into the playlist for *Wild Rose*.

Dave Fox advised me on the training schedule for a new tour guide.

This book was sent out for two rounds of beta reader feedback. This was crucial in locking down a compelling storyline, and these people did not fail me in my request for honest, critical feedback. I can't create in a vacuum, and these Late Bloomer Betas helped me polish this book in a way I never could have on my own:

Alison Cornford-Matheson, Andrea Aguilar, Carol Byrnes, Carrie Karnes-Fannin, Carol Carver, Carole Dillard, Cathi Bouton, Phyllis Vannostrand, Cheryl Moran, Gale Cushenbery, Debbie Whitlock, Dixie Dixon, Erin Ollenberger, Georgie Brander, Alice Rienzo, Jaime Shafer, Grace Rodrigues, Idara Bassey, Lori Osterberg, Jan Wenzel, Janet Grappin, Juli Gover, Joe Benik, Kirsten Stafne, Karen Silsby, Laurette Goss, Laurie McClary, Linda Lapichak, Lori Wostl, Luc Jacobs, Mary Gebhart, Michelle Goerdel, Margaret Shaw, Mary Bright, Mickey Kampsen, Margaret Walton, Sandra Pisarski, Renee Iverson, Joan Kerr, Roxane Baxter, Ruth Vahle, Sallie Holgate, Sandra Levy, Shawn Tuttle, Kate Sommers, Summer Blackwell, Trena Johnson, Trisha Rogers, Patricia Lewis, Evy Heath, Veronica Pacini, Carrie Voorhis, Pamela Olson, Maria Nash, Kristen LaJeunesse, Pat Fordyce, Mindy Haber, Laura Frost, Jan Iams, Linda Chilson, Cinta Garcia de la Rosa,

Denise Mickalonis, Tracy Egbert, Andrea Mihelich, Sue Jochens, Lynn Mullan, and May O'Connor.

My editor, Angela Barton, gave me feedback on the book after the Late Bloomer Betas finished reading and then polished it up line by line before publishing. She is a joy to work with.

Danijela Mijailovic provided me with beautiful covers for the entire Late Bloomers Series. Her creativity has put a great face on my stories.

Connie Gray, who didn't provide one bit of criticism because she is my mother. She supports everything I do, and it's why I'm confident enough to try most things. That is the best gift I've ever been given.

Last but certainly not least, I thank my business, life, and crime partner, Warren Talbot. You did everything from making coffee to brainstorming ideas to managing the cover design and more. You are the Mateo to my Rose, the partner who encourages my crazy ideas and soothes my neurotic tendencies. This book would not have happened without you. Thank you.

Preview of English Ivy
(Book 2 in The Late Bloomers Series)

CHAPTER ONE

Ivy mentally ran through the plan one more time as the Secretary of State gave the speech. First, she'd fake an upset stomach to her colleague Ben, touching her abdomen and nodding gravely before slipping quietly out the door. Then a firm nod to the Secret Service agents situated outside, secure in her clearance badge as a senior US Embassy employee to move freely about the building.

The carpet would muffle the sound of her high heels as she quickly walked down the empty hallway, and then she'd slip into her office and close the door. The press conference was mandatory for all staff, so Ivy would have the entire building to herself. But all she'd need was in her office. A few quick strokes to enter her password on her laptop, and then she would open the draft of the email she'd been perfecting for weeks. One click to send.

Ivy would take one last look around the office she'd occupied for the last five years, half her total stay in London— the functional, government-issued desk covered with manila folders; the dark blue carpet whose only selling point was the ability to hide stains; and the stand by the door, home to the umbrella she carried to work most days.

She'd shrug on her trench coat, wrap her Hermès scarf movie-star style around her long red hair, and take the elevator down to the lobby. At the top of the steps outside, she would pause, taking in this view for one last time—Grosvenor Square ahead with Dwight D. Eisenhower's statue greeting visitors, a giant gold eagle above her head proclaiming demurely that the Embassy belonged to the United States.

One final goodbye to Sal and Chester, the guards at the gate, and Ivy would be free. Walking away from Hyde Park, she'd look up into the uncommonly sunny sky, cover her sparkling green eyes with oversized sunglasses, and head for the Piccadilly Circus tube station. An hour later she'd emerge at Heathrow Airport.

Once on board, Ivy would settle into first class, order a glass of champagne from the flight attendant, and look out the window into the fading daylight sky as the plane taxied down the runway full speed ahead to her exciting new life. She wouldn't even bring a suitcase, leaving all the baggage of her current life behind. Everything from that point forward would be new—new job, new clothes, new country. Maybe even a new man, one who didn't even own a suit. Her mouth curled into a slow smile, feeling the rush of takeoff. She gripped the arms of her chair just as she would on a real plane.

"You can't be that excited about trade agreements," Ben whispered, elbowing her in the side.

Ivy snapped out of her fantasy, instantly transported from champagne in first class to bottled water in the conference room. The Secretary of State stood at the podium up front, outlining the latest link in the ongoing chain of economic cooperation between the United States and Great Britain. Reporters from the *Financial Times*, BBC, and Sky News were there, raising their hands to ask questions and scribbling furiously in their notebooks like actors in a political drama.

Ivy sighed, feeling the weight of her nine millionth press conference, the Groundhog Day cycle of repetitive, microscopic advances at work that were undone and then redone by whoever won the last election.

Ivy looked over at Ben and shrugged. "I was compiling my grocery list."

"The curry takeout queen of London? I doubt that." Ben grinned, waiting for Ivy to pounce back as usual.

"I'm slipping out. Cover for me if Sylvia comes by?" Ivy patted his arm and then stood up, not waiting for an answer. She was glad she'd taken the seat at the end of the row.

Outside the door, she took a deep breath and replayed the first part of her fantasy, all the way into her office. Instead of sending the resignation email that she'd typed up weeks ago, she sat in her chair and surveyed her surroundings. The walls were closing in daily, and if she didn't leave soon, she'd be crushed inside her shrinking life.

The one bright spot in her office was the silver frame, a photo of Ivy with her best friends together in New York. She remembered the wine, the food and the laughter around the table that night. Since then her friends had all made big life changes. Rose was moving to Australia with the man of her dreams, Daisy was heading to France soon to be a judge on a cooking show, Violet's jewelry line was being sold at Barney's, and Lily was bouncing back from her divorce. Only Ivy was the same now as she was when she posed for that photo.

She touched each face on the photo, full of love for these women who were her closest friends. Ivy wasn't jealous. Who wouldn't want their friends to find success and happiness? But she wanted the same for herself. Surely that didn't make her a bad person.

Ivy put the frame down and took a drink from her water bottle, glancing at the forlorn plant on the edge of her desk. She doused it with the remaining water in her bottle.

"Little ivy, we need to find a place where we can grow. This place is killing us." She pulled the crunchy brown edges off the leaves and dropped them into the pot to decompose.

Her friends in the US thought her life was glamorous, and a few years ago it was. But now, ten years into her life in London and five years in the same position at the Embassy, she had to face the truth. Ivy was in a rut, stuck in her job and with a non-existent love life. She was about as wild on the weekends as her elderly neighbor Mrs. Bingham.

The formerly adventurous Ivy Cross, breaker of rules and hearts, had crossed the threshold of middle age and lost her spark.

She was on a mission to get it back.

#

"For a guy starting a new life, you sure are bringing a lot of your old life with you." Ruben grunted as he carried the last heavy box into the living room of Mateo's nearly empty flat. He looked around, wondering why Alejandro wasn't helping them.

"It's more like a new version than a total reboot. I need to keep the basic operating system." Mateo wiped his forehead with the back of his hand as he smiled.

"I appreciate you speaking my language," Ruben countered. "Is it time for *cerveza* yet?"

They were packing up the last of Mateo's belongings before his move. Never again would Ruben crash on Mateo's couch after a late night out. Never again would the three of them watch *fútbol* together in this place. And all those fun weekends on Lake Como were over now that they'd sold their restaurant.

Known as the Three Amigos, they were inseparable since childhood. Now Alejandro had kids and a busy law practice in Madrid, and Mateo was marrying Rose and moving to Australia. Only Ruben still lived the same life he'd had since just after university, something that had never bothered him until now.

Alejandro came into the room, holding three bottles of Mahou. "While you guys sweated in here, I cleaned out the refrigerator. This is all that's left." He gave each man a bottle of beer.

"Always taking the toughest jobs, aren't you? We appreciate your sacrifice," Ruben said with a grin as he grabbed his bottle.

"My strongest muscle is up here," Alejandro said as he tapped his head with his finger. "You should try working your brain as much as you do your biceps." Alejandro avoided the gym like the plague, and it showed.

Ruben's energy had always been high, and if it weren't for the gym and his sadist of a trainer, he'd explode. Those relentless hours of punishing workouts not only kept him hard and lean, they alleviated the pressure continually building in his body. Without an intense workout every day, he couldn't function. Alejandro, on the other hand, was happily growing soft with middle age. He'd always been the thinker of the three, a good trait for a lawyer.

"We only need one set of brains for this team," Ruben joked, even though all three of them earned the highest marks at university. But only Alejandro was known for it. Throughout their lives, Ruben usually suggested the ideas that got them into trouble. Alejandro was the planner who tried to reason with him to find safer alternatives. And angel-faced Mateo was always the one who begged forgiveness if they got caught. Ruben thought it was an effective strategy, and he wondered how he'd fare now that he had to do most of it by himself.

Ruben raised his beer in mock seriousness. "To Mateo, a good man who was tragically taken from us far too soon."

"May he rest in peace—every night after shagging the brains out of the beautiful Rose," Alejandro chimed in.

The three men laughed as they clinked bottles and drank, the icy cold beer a welcome reward for their work.

"I still can't believe you're getting on a plane tonight. Even when you lived in Italy, you were just a couple of hours away. Now I'll have to plan a holiday just to hang out with you." Ruben couldn't help but mourn the loss of his good friend, even though he was happy for him. He pointed his thumb toward Alejandro. "And this one is always too busy with work and the kids to hang out with me."

"Ruben, I'm a happily married man. I'm not going clubbing with you. You know you're always welcome to hang out at my house." Alejandro trotted out the familiar lines, used to Ruben's complaints about his tame lifestyle.

"But the only beautiful woman there is already taken."

"Do you ever get tired of being on the prowl?" Mateo asked with a laugh.

Ruben felt the sting of his words in a way he wouldn't have in the past. "You make it sound like I'm some wild animal. And no, it doesn't get old," Ruben said, lying through his teeth.

"Wild animal? More like a house cat chasing its tail," Alejandro said with a laugh, clinking bottles with Mateo.

"You guys are just jealous. You're stuck with the same woman forever, and I still have variety." Ruben smirked.

Mateo shook his head and set his empty bottle down on top

of a box. "I'll tell you what a wise old man said to me: 'It's easy to be a good lover for one night. The real challenge is to keep it hot with the same person for years.'"

"That is the best closing argument I've heard in years. You guys ready for some food?" Alejandro gathered their empty bottles and put them in the recycling bin, Mateo following behind to get the last bag of trash. Ruben watched them, two men comfortable in their relationships and decisions. They were so calm and contented, something he'd never been able to feel with one person. Ruben always felt like a shark, in constant motion just to keep breathing.

Maybe the monogamous life was right for them, but he couldn't see it for himself. He was still a man of conquests, and he didn't think he'd ever find a woman to change his mind. Ruben was wired this way, and no amount of convincing from his friends would change him.

"You can ask your sweet Rose what kind of lover I am after I blow her friend Ivy's mind," Ruben said, cocky swagger back in place.

"Ivy Cross? She'll never go out with you," Mateo said. "Not only is she not into you, she's not into anybody."

"You underestimate my charm," Ruben replied. "Besides, she lost a bet and owes me a date. And I plan to collect later this week in London."

"It's been nice knowing you, Ruben." Mateo embraced him in a big bear hug. "I'm on the plane to Australia tonight, so I won't be able to come back for the funeral."

"Don't worry. We'll make it a good service. I hear they can do a lot with makeup these days to cover up the trauma." Alejandro joined in on the ribbing.

"I wonder if all his ex-girlfriends will show up?" Mateo asked, pretending Ruben wasn't even in the room.

"Just send one invitation to the twelve-step group they all join when he dumps them," Alejandro said.

"Joke all you want, my friends. But there is no woman who can withstand my charms. Not even the prickly Ivy Cross."

Alejandro looked at Mateo. "I've never met her, but after the stories I've heard after the fiasco with you and Rose, I think Ruben should buy dinner tonight. He won't be around to pay his credit card bill next month, and I'm in the mood for some expensive wine." The three men laughed as they locked the door and headed out for their last night in Madrid as the Three Amigos.

# # #

Purchase your copy of *English Ivy* at betsytalbot.com/english-ivy/ to continue reading Ivy's adventure now!

What one reviewer had to say:

"I absolutely loved Ivy...She makes bold moves that other women could only WISH to make, making her a character who a reader can enjoy living vicariously through."

~ A Well Read Woman, 5 stars

CPSIA information can be obtained
at www.ICGtesting.com
Printed in the USA
LVHW091538051120
670840LV00020B/358